# 20 DAYS 天 New TOEIC

## 文法高分特訓

### High-Score Trainning

附贈全書例句
外師親錄MP3

**92**分鐘

在新ＴＯＥＩＣ測驗中，總共分為兩個部分；第一部分為「聽力測驗」，第二部分即為許多考生畏懼的「閱讀測驗」；而在「閱讀測驗」中，總共有三個單元，分別為Ｐａｒｔ５的「單句填空試題」、Ｐａｒｔ６的「短文填空試題」以及Ｐａｒｔ７的「文章理解」。而Ｐａｒｔ５和Ｐａｒｔ６在解題時需要具備閱讀理解能力加上文法、語法的知識。這兩部份的試題佔全部題目２００題中的５２題，所以準備ＴＯＥＩＣ測驗時，絕對不可以忽略文法在測驗中所佔的重要性。

時間管理，也就是時間分配，是閱讀測驗拿高分的關鍵。為了將時間留給英文份量較多的Ｐａｒｔ７，請盡可能縮短Ｐａｒｔ５、Ｐａｒｔ６的解題時間。本書中的每一天練習題目中，Ｐａｒｔ５的格式設定為每次２０題（實際考試題目數量約一半）時間限制為７分鐘。練習在短時間內解題，請務必在實際考試中有效分配解題時間。

那麼，ＴＯＥＩＣ測驗中究竟需要什麼樣的文法、語法知識呢？ＴＯＥＩＣ測驗官方機構，針對ＴＯＥＩＣ考試最高水準Ａ級（８６０分以上）的英語能力描述如下，「英文能力已十分近似英語母語人士，能夠流暢有條理地表達意見，在自己的經驗範圍內，對於專業以外的話題，也能充分了解，以及能使用合適的表現方式。英語能力距離母語人士僅一步之隔，除了可以正確掌握語彙、文法與句子結構外，並且具備流暢使用的能力。」也就是說，在ＴＯＥＩＣ測驗中，如測驗名稱代表的意義，必須具備能夠「使用英語的國際溝通能力」所必需的必要文法、語法知識。

在ＴＯＥＩＣ測驗中，不會出現雞蛋裡挑骨頭般的題目，也就是說，你不需要具備連母語人士解題時都覺得困難的文法、語法知

識。只需要從中學開始到高中所學習的基礎文法知識，加上日常生活與商務情境中使用的英語，就足夠應付ＴＯＥＩＣ測驗；但即使如此，在ＴＯＥＩＣ測驗中必備的文法觀念，例如：不定詞、分詞、分詞構句、假設法等等，對這些文法觀念感到棘手的人，可能就無法在ＴＯＥＩＣ測驗中得到高分。

因此，本書整理文法、語法項目後，重新編輯提供符合ＴＯＥＩＣ測驗出題方向的文法、語法總複習課程。過去對文法、語法感到棘手的人、自大學入學考試之後就遠離文法學習的人，以及平常自學英語但對文法觀念仍是沒有自信的人，或是參加多次測驗仍然無法有效提高分數的人，請利用本書解決你的問題。

本書另一個最大的特色是，在文法觀念說明中的所有例句，都是使用日常會話與商務會話時經常使用到的口語表達。學習者可以放心地使用本書的例句於日常生活的繪畫中，而且藉由實際運用，可以讓自己記住文法、語法的知識。因此，請讀者們多加利用本書附贈的外師親錄ＭＰ３。

除了Ｐａｒｔ 5與Ｐａｒｔ 6需要文法、語法知識之外，Ｐａｒｔ 7的文章理解以及第一部分的聽力測驗也都必須具備文法、語法知識。此外，ＴＯＥＩＣ測驗中出現的文法、語法項目都是實際使用英文溝通時必備的知識，所以本書不僅可以提高你的ＴＯＥＩＣ測驗分數，也能提高讀者的英語能力。

**白野伊津夫**

本書安排的課程於２０天內完成。頁面側標的數字表示第１天、第２天……的課程天數。此外，本書中的例句全部收錄在附贈的ＭＰ３中。請注意，書中所收錄之用來比較錯誤之例句並未收錄在ＭＰ３中，ＭＰ３中只收錄正確句子。

# 關於TOEIC測驗

TOEIC是 Test of English for International Communication（用來測量使用英語國際溝通能力的測驗系統）的簡寫，TOEIC測驗並非如一般英語測驗，是為測量考生具備多少英語知識所設，而是為了測量考生可以使用英語來達到何種溝通程度，也就是測驗考生的「英語的運用能力」。所以，TOEIC測驗是一種將考生在學校教育中學到的英語知識，以實際運用能力為評量基準所進行的國際通用測驗；也就是說，這是一種將英語的「知識＋運用能力」當作溝通能力來進行評量的測驗。

TOEIC測驗是由ETS（Educational Testing Service）開發製作的測驗系統，ETS設計過的測驗系統，包括申請美國與加拿大大學時所需的TOEFL測驗（Test of English as a Foreign Language）、美國高中生為了申請大學所需的全美大學入學共同測驗（SAT）、研究所入學共同測驗（GRE）、管理研究所入學測驗（GMAT）、法律研究所入學測驗（LSAT）以及其它美國大部份的公家測驗。

由於這是能力測量考試，所以評價標準必須固定。如果標準不能固定，將會缺乏做為測驗的可信度（validity）。在ETS利用龐大的資料與精密的統計處理，將測驗標準化（equating），成功把誤差降至最低（滿分990分±25分）。

除了公開測之外，也有團體測驗用的考試（IP test），近年來，隨著企業國際化，利用這項考試的企業暴增。

在台灣，每個月都會在北中南各地舉行TOEIC測驗，報名的方式分為通訊報名或網路報名，請於報名期間內完成報名手續（郵戳為憑），並確認各項資料（如：測驗日期、考區基本資料等）是否正確，報名費用是1540元新台幣，其他詳細的考試資訊請參考多益測驗台灣官方網站（http://www.toeic.com.tw/index.htm）。

# TOEIC分數可以用來做什麼？

ＴＯＥＩＣ雖然是英語能力測驗的一種，但是與英文檢定（實用英語技能檢定）之類的考試不同，不僅沒有分級也沒有及格、不及格的分別。成績單只會顯示聽力測驗成績（４９５分為滿分）與閱讀測驗成績（４９５分為滿分）以及總分（９９０分為滿分）。不過，與一般入學測驗等分數不同，ＴＯＥＩＣ的分數如前所述，誤差值很少，所以可以安心使用ＴＯＥＩＣ分數作為客觀測量英語能力的標準。近年來，有許多企業利用ＴＯＥＩＣ當作英語能力測驗，這也是因為ＴＯＥＩＣ分數較為客觀的關係。

ＴＯＥＩＣ分數可檢視自我英語能力，或是評定集團成員的英文程度。例如，同一個人每隔一段時間接受考試時，因為評量標準不變，所以可以知道使用英語溝通的能力進步多少（或是退步多少）。因此，想自我檢視英語能力時，可以先參加一次考試，再依考試結果設定學習目標，這是提升英語能力最好的方法（關於評價標準請參考下一頁的說明）。

此外，學校及企業可以透過ＴＯＥＩＣ測驗推斷出各自的平均分數，除了可以比較團體間的溝通能力，也可以了解同一個團體在不同時間點的學習成果。例如，若得知Ａ公司的新進員工平均分數是３９０分，Ｂ公司的平均分數是４５０分，則可比較兩個公司的分數；此外，若得知Ｃ公司去年新 進員工的平均分數是３８５分，但是今年平均分數超過４００分，則可藉此比較公司內部的前後平均分數，作為評量教育訓練的基準及成果。

## Proficiency Scale
## TOEIC分數與溝通能力水準相關表

| 水準 | TOEIC分數 | 評價（說明） |
|---|---|---|
| A | 860以上 | **英文能力近似英語母語人士，能夠流暢、有條理地表達意見。**<br>在自己的經驗範圍內，對於專業以外的話題也能充分了解及使用合適的表現方式。除了可以正確掌握語彙、文法與句型結構外，並且具備流暢的使用能力。 |
| B | 730以上 | **具備在任何情境下都能適當溝通的能力。**<br>可以完全理解日常會話，且能立即回答；即使話題屬於特殊領域，也具備對應的能力。在業務執行上沒有什麼大障礙。正確性與流暢性因個人而異，有時候在文法、句型結構上可能出錯，不過仍可以正確地傳達想表達的意思。 |
| C | 470以上 | **滿足日常生活所需，在限定的範圍內，具備業務上的溝通能力。**<br>能夠理解日常會話重點，回答時也沒有障礙。但面對複雜情況或需要準確的應對與傳達意思時，就會看出優劣之差。已經學會基本的文法、句型結構，即使表現能力不足，但至少具備自我表達時應有的語彙及能力。 |
| D | 220以上 | **具備日常會話最基本的溝通能力。**<br>如果對方的說話速度比較慢，或對方能複述、換一種講法，便能理解簡單的會話。可以回答與自己相關的切身話題。在語彙、文法、句型結構上仍有許多不足的地方，如果對方可以考量說話者為非母語人士，可以大概推測出說話者想表達的意思。 |

| E | 220以下 | **無法以英文溝通。**<br>即使面對速度較慢的簡單會話，也只能了解部分內容。只能片斷地排列單字，對實質的意思傳達沒有幫助。 |
|---|---|---|

# 新 TOEIC 測驗的題型

| Listening<br>Section<br>聽力測驗<br>（45分鐘） | Part 1 照片描述（Photographs） | 10題 |
|---|---|---|
| | Part 2 應答問題（Question-Response） | 30題 |
| | Part 3 簡短對話（Short Conversations） | 30題 |
| | Part 4 簡短獨白（Short Talks） | 30題 |
| Reading<br>Section<br>閱讀測驗<br>（75分鐘） | Part 5 單句填空問題（Incomplete Sentences） | 40題 |
| | Part 6 短文填空問題（Text Completion） | 12題 |
| | Part7 文章理解（Reading Comprehension） | |
| | ‧單篇文章理解（Single passage） | 28題 |
| | ‧雙篇文章理解（Double passage） | 20題 |

＊台灣地區於2008年3月開始實施新制的ＴＯＥＩＣ測驗。

# 目錄

## 1st Day　五大句型

## 2nd Day　名詞

## 3rd Day　冠詞

# CONTENTS

# CONTENTS

# CONTENTS

**Grammar**

# 1st Day 五大句型

MP3 001

The conference started at one o'clock. ———— 「第一句型」
（會議從一點鐘開始。）

The work is hard. ———————————— 「第二句型」
（那件工作相當困難。）

I took a chance. ——————————————— 「第三句型」
（我已嘗試過了。）

He gave me some advice. ——————— 「第四句型」
（他給了我一些建議。）

He called me a coward. ———————— 「第五句型」
（他叫我懦夫。）

從句子的**要素**來看，英文可以分類為以下**五種句型**：

### （1）第一句型：主詞（S）＋動詞（V）

MP3 002

**只要有主詞（S）與動詞（V）就能組成一個意思完整的句子**。這個句型的動詞是完全不及物動詞。通常連接修飾語後會變成較長且較完整的句子。接續在動詞之後的修飾語，則依照**方向、狀態、場所、時間**的順序排列。

The **parcel arrived**.
    S        V
（包裹已經送達。）

The **elevator stopped** suddenly.
    S        V      狀態
（電梯突然停止。）

Mr. **Johnson left** for Chicago by plane this morning.

    S      V      方向      狀態      時間

The **accident happened** at the intersection early in the morning.

    S         V            場所          時間

## （2）第二句型：主詞（S）＋動詞（V）＋補語（C）

Japanese **workers are diligent**.

               S      V      C

（日本的勞工是勤勞的。）

**Jack is** an **architect**.

  S   V        C

（傑克是建築師。）

在這個句型中的動詞如果沒有補語，那麼句子的意思就不完整，所以被稱為**不完全及物動詞**。不完全及物動詞之中有①表示「是～、～狀態」的 be, continue, hold, keep, remain, stand、②表示「變成～」的 become, come, get, go, grow, run, prove、③表示「感覺～、覺得～、好像～」的 appear, feel, look, seem, smell, sound, taste、④其它，如 die, marry 等等。

The contract still **holds** good.

（契約仍然有效。）

The rumor **proved** true.

（這謠傳結果是真的。）

That **sounds** interesting.

（那似乎很有趣。）

Cathy **married** young.

（凱西很早就結婚了。）

### （3）第三句型：主詞（S）+動詞（V）+受詞（O）

在「主詞+動詞」後加上**受詞（O）**的句型。被用在這個句型上的動詞稱為**完全及物動詞**。

**I canceled** my **appointment**.
S     V          O

（我取消預約了。）

**We must expand** our **business** overseas.
S       V            O

（我們必須將業務擴展至海外。）

### （4）第四句型：主詞（S）+動詞（V）+ 間接受詞（IO）+直接受詞（DO）

在「主詞+動詞」後加上**間接受詞（IO）**與**直接受詞（DO）**的句型。間接受詞大多是「人」，直接受詞大多是「物」。這個句型的動詞稱為**授與動詞**。

**I will send you** a **facsimile**.
S     V      IO        DO

（我會傳真給你。）

這個句型雖然可以改寫為「**主詞+動詞+直接受詞+介系詞+間接受詞**」的句子，不過這是屬於第三句型。

### （a）「to+間接受詞」的例句

Mr. Brown **handed her** a note.
Mr. Brown **handed** a note **to her**.

（布朗先生親手把備忘字條交給她。）

He **offered me** a job.
He **offered** a job **to me**.

（他給了我一份工作。）

They **gave their teacher** a big bouquet of flowers for her birthday.

They **gave** a big bouquet of flowers **to their teacher** for her birthday.

（他們在老師生日時送了一大束花給她。）

屬於這一類型的動詞還有 deny, give, lend, promise, refuse, send, tell, teach, pass, pay 等等。

### （b）「for＋間接受詞」的例句

Will you **get me** a taxi?

Will you **get** a taxi **for me**?

（可以幫我叫計程車嗎？）

He **ordered me** a new dress.

He **ordered** a new dress **for me**.

（他訂做了一件新衣服給我。）

Will you **choose me** a good painting?

Will you **choose** a good painting **for me**?

（可以幫我挑一幅好畫嗎？）

屬於這一類型的動詞還有 buy, cook, find, make 等等。

### （c）「of＋間接受詞」的例句

May I **ask you** a question?

May I **ask** a question **of you**?

（我可以問你一個問題嗎？）

【注意】 直接受詞是代名詞時使用第三句型。

I'll sell you it. 〔錯誤〕

I'll sell it to you. 〔正確〕（我會賣給你。）

**（5）第五句型：主詞（S）+動詞（V）+**
**　　　受詞（O）+補語（C）**

這個句型是在「主詞+動詞」之後加上**受詞（O）**以及用來補充說明受詞的**補語（C）**。這時，「**受詞＝補語**」的關係成立。屬於這個句型的動詞稱為**不完全及物動詞**，除了感覺動詞及使役動詞之外，還有 believe, call, elect, find（把 O 稱為 C ）、keep（保有～）、leave（使處於某種狀態）、think 等等。

**They named** the **child Mark** after his grandfather.
　S　　V　　　　　O　　　C

（他們以他的祖父之名，將小孩命名為馬克。）

**You can't call** the **show successful**.

（這場演出並不算成功。）

**I left** the **light on**.

（我一直讓電燈亮著。）

**（6）基本的構句與五大句型**

There **is** a **policeman** at the corner.〔第一句型〕
　　　V　　　S

（轉角有警察。）

Here **is** your **passport**.〔第一句型〕
　　　V　　　S

（你的護照在這裡。）

**I want you to work** overtime.〔第五句型〕
S　V　O　　C

（我希望你加班。）

**He asked me to type** the letter.〔第五句型〕
S　V　O　　C

（他請我幫他打那一封信。）

**I told him to make** the report.　〔第五句型〕
S　V　O　　C

（我叫他寫一份報告書。）

**I saw him leave** his office.　〔第五句型〕
S　V　O　　C

（我看到他離開他的辦公室。）

**It is impossible** for me to take a long vacation.　〔第二句型〕
S　V　　C

（我不可能可以請長假。）

〔**參考1**〕句型根據句子的**要素**，也就是**主詞、述語動詞、受詞、補語**的組合不同，而衍生出不同的句型。可以當作**主詞**的有**名詞、代名詞、不定詞、「疑問詞＋to不定詞」**（how to do 等等）、**動名詞、名詞子句**等等。除了動詞可以當作**述語動詞**外，在包含助動詞的句子中，「**助動詞＋動詞**」（will go 等等）這個部份也是當作述語動詞。可以當作**受詞**的有**名詞、代名詞、不定詞、「疑問詞＋to 不定詞」、動名詞、名詞子句**等等。**補語**是指「補充說明述語動詞意思」的詞。可以當作**補語**的有**名詞、代名詞、形容詞、to 不定詞**（He seems to be happy. 等等）、**原形不定詞**（I saw him steal the money. 等等）、**過去分詞**（I heard my name called. 等等）、當作**形容詞子句**的「**介系詞＋名詞〔代名詞〕**」（This is of no use. 等等）、**名詞子句**等等。

〔**參考2**〕為了加以說明句子的要素 —— 主詞的意思，而加上各種詞（句），這個詞（句）稱為修飾語。**修飾語**可以分類為修飾主詞、受詞、補語的**形容詞性修飾語**，與修飾述語動詞及補語的**副詞性修飾語**。**形容詞性的修飾語**包括形容詞、冠詞、名詞、不定詞、動名詞、現在分詞、過去分詞、形容詞子句等等。**副詞性的修飾語**包括副詞、不定詞、分詞

（Having a cold, I can't attend the meeting. 等等）、當作**副詞子句**的「**介系詞＋名詞〔代名詞〕**」（He went to Miami by car. 等等）、**副詞子句**等等。

## 練習題

時間限制 **7**分鐘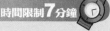

請在以下各題目的(A),(B),(C),(D)之中選出最適合的答案填入空格之中。

1. People in this town are very _____.
    (A) companion          (B) warming
    (C) friendly           (D) amiably

2. Our company _____ a new branch office in New York last year.
    (A) open               (B) opened
    (C) opening            (D) to open

3. I'll meet _____ at the airport.
    (A) them               (B) they
    (C) their              (D) with they

4. We kept _____ throughout the show.
    (A) standing           (B) to stand
    (C) stance             (D) stood

5. It seems _____ he has forgotten his appointment.
    (A) so                 (B) as
    (C) to                 (D) that

6. The factory stood _____ during that period.
    (A) tall               (B) behind
    (C) halt               (D) idle

7. He taught the trick _____ me.
  (A) for
  (B) on
  (C) to
  (D) over

8. The mother denied nothing _____ her child.
  (A) to
  (B) of
  (C) for
  (D) beneath

9. I asked her _____ 20 copies of the report.
  (A) to be made
  (B) to make
  (C) make
  (D) have made

10. I believe his proposal to be very _____.
  (A) practice
  (B) practiced
  (C) practical
  (D) practically

11. Excuse me, but would it be possible _____ change my flight to an earlier one?
  (A) of
  (B) at
  (C) to
  (D) in

12. The great actor died _____ at the peak of his career.
  (A) small
  (B) young
  (C) youth
  (D) child

13. He promised _____ that he would achieve his sales goal.
  (A) me
  (B) to me
  (C) of me
  (D) on me

14. We will immediately send _____ an e-mail with further information about the product.
  (A) you
  (B) to you
  (C) at you
  (D) with you

15. He put the blame _____ the dispatcher for the delay in shipment.

    (A) in              (B) with

    (C) at              (D) on

16. The three automakers remain _____ domestically and internationally.

    (A) compete         (B) to compete

    (C) competitive      (D) competition

17. The gentleman said to the waitress, "May I ask a favor _____ you?"

    (A) of              (B) to

    (C) from           (D) by

18. Ignoring John's strong desire to become a garage mechanic, his father made _____ become a doctor.

    (A) he             (B) his

    (C) him            (D) of his

19. To my surprise, the director called the plan _____.

    (A) succeed         (B) successfully

    (C) succeeding     (D) a success

20. The New York City subways are old and they look _____.

    (A) for it         (B) it

    (C) at it          (D) into it

# 正確解答

1

1-(C) friendly 是形容詞，意思是「親切的、友好的」。

2-(B) opened a new branch office 的意思是「成立分公司」。

3-(A) meet 是「迎接」。受詞使用受格。

4-(A) kept standing 是「一直站著」→第二句型。

5-(D) It seems that... 是「似乎……」。that 之後接續名詞子句當作補語→第二句型。

6-(D) stood idle 是「停止、不動」→第二句型。

7-(C) trick 是「秘訣」。He taught me the trick. 與 He taught the trick to me. 兩種講法都可以。

8-(A) The mother denied nothing to her child 的意思是「母親對於自己的小孩言聽計從」。也可以說 The mother denied her child nothing.

9-(B) I asked her to... 的意思是「我請他去做……」→第五句型。

10-(C) believe 的意思是「認為……」。practical 的意思是「現實的」→第五句型。

11-(C) it 是形式主詞，後面接不定詞子句（to change...）→第二句型。

12-(B) 這個時候的 die 是不完全不及物動詞，die young 的意思是「夭折」→第二句型。

13-(A) 採用 promise＋間接受詞（me）＋直接受詞（that...）的句型，不可以用 promised to / of / on me that...→第四句型。

14-(A) I will send you an e-mail 的語序是主詞＋動詞＋間接受詞＋直接受詞。間接受詞（you）之前不可以有介系詞→第四句型。

15-(D) put the blame on... 的意思是「把責任歸咎於……」。

**1**

16-(C) remain的意思是「保持……」屬於不完全不及物動詞,所以選擇形容詞(competitive)接續其後是正確答案。

17-(A) 接續在 ask 之後的 a favor 是直接受詞,所以在間接受詞(you)之前必須有介系詞→第三句型。

18-(C) his father made him become a doctor. 的意思是「他的父親令他成為一名醫生。」及物動詞的 make 之後必須接「受格」,所以正確答案是 him。him=doctor,所以這是第五句型。

19-(D) 這個句子的 call 是及物動詞,意思是「把~稱為~」,補語的部份必須是(冠語+)名詞或是形容詞→第五句型。

20-(B) they look...的部份,從上下文意來看可以知道意思為「看起來像那樣」,所以選擇 it 是正確答案。本句的 look 是不完全不及物動詞,意思是「看起來(像)~」。look it 與 look so 的意思一樣→第二句型。

# 練習題的中文翻譯

1. 這個城鎮的人非常親切。
2. 我們公司去年在紐約設立分公司。
3. 我在機場迎接他。
4. 我們一直站著看秀。
5. 他似乎忘了約定。
6. 在那段期間那間工廠停工。
7. 他教我那個秘訣。
8. 母親對自己的小孩言聽計從。
9. 我請她幫忙影印二十份報告書。
10. 我認為他的提案很實際。
11. 不好意思，我可以將班機時間提早嗎？
12. 那位偉大的演員，在生涯最顛峰時英年早逝。
13. 他承諾我達成銷售目標。
14. 有關商品詳細資料我們會馬上以電子郵件寄給你。
15. 他將出貨延遲的原因歸罪於運輸公司。
16. 三大汽車製造商不管是在國內還是國外仍然維持競爭力。
17. 那位紳士對女侍者說：「可以請您協助嗎？」
18. 無視於約翰想成為汽車修理技師的強烈願望，他的父親希望他成為一名醫生。
19. 令我非常驚訝的是，導演說這個計畫很成功。
20. 紐約市的地下鐵很老舊，實際看起來也的確如此。

## 2nd Day 名詞

He bought a brand-new car. ——————「普通名詞」
（他買了一台全新的車。）

How is your family? ——————「集合名詞」
（你家人好嗎？）

Milk is made into butter. ——————「物質名詞」
（牛奶可製成奶油。）

They fought for freedom. ——————「抽象名詞」
（他們為自由而奮戰。）

Jack flew to London. ——————「專有名詞」
（傑克飛往倫敦了。）

We manufacture calculators. ——————「可數名詞」
（我們大量生產計算機。）

Would you like some coffee? ——————「不可數名詞」
（你要不要喝點咖啡？）

### （1）依意思區分的名詞種類

依照名詞本身的意思可以分成五個類型，分別是**普通名詞**、**集合名詞**、**物質名詞**、**抽象名詞**、**專有名詞**。

### （a）普通名詞

同種類的人或物的共通名稱，例如 car, desk, school, secretary, student, telephone 等等。大部份的名詞都屬於普通名詞。

The **secretary** forgot to put a **stamp** on the **envelope**.

（秘書忘了在信封上貼郵票。）

### （b）集合名詞

表示同種類的人或物的集合體的名詞，例如 family, class, team, nation, committee, audience, crowd 等等。

Mr. Scott sits on the steering **committee**.

（史考特先生是營運委員會的成員。）

### （c）物質名詞

表示無法分割成為個體的物質的名詞，例如 air, water, milk, butter, coal, gold 等等。

Will you spread **butter** on the **bread**?

（可以幫我把奶油塗在麵包上嗎？）

### （d）抽象名詞

表示只有抽象觀念而沒有具體形象的名詞，例如 love, peace, freedom, justice, happiness, kindness, health 等等。

**Love** and **reason** do not go together.

（愛沒有道理可言。）

### （e）專有名詞

表示特定的人或場所等名稱的名詞，例如 John, Jefferson, New York, London, Italy 等等。

**Paul** was transferred to **Los Angeles.**

（保羅調職到洛杉磯。）

## （2）依形態區分的名詞種類

將名詞依形態區分，可分成「**可數名詞**」與「**不可數名詞**」兩種。

### （a）可數名詞

普通名詞與集合名詞大部份都是可數名詞，可數名詞的特徵是加上不定冠詞 a 或 an，或者是變成複數形。

This **case** can hold 50 floppy **disks**.

（這個盒子可以裝入５０片軟碟。）

Thirty **teams** participated in the soccer **tournament**.

（３０支球隊參加這場足球聯賽。）

### （b）不可數名詞

不可數名詞可分為抽象名詞、專有名詞、物質名詞，不可數名詞的特徵是不加上 a 或 an，也沒有複數形。

Do you put **sugar** in your **coffee**?

（你的咖啡要加糖嗎？）

You must think of your **health**.

（你必須考慮自己的健康。）

## （3）普通名詞應該注意的用法

### （a）用「a／an＋單數名詞」、「the＋單數名詞」、「無冠詞的複數名詞」來表示種類全體。

**A cat** has nine lives.

（貓有九條命。）〔引申：命大、倖免於難。〕

**The cat** has a keen sense of smell.

（貓的嗅覺非常敏銳。）

**Cats** are wonderful pets.

（貓咪是很好的寵物。）

### （b）使用「the＋單數普通名詞」形式，變成抽象名詞。

**The pen** is mightier than **the sword**.

（筆墨勝過刀劍。）

名詞

## （4）集合名詞應該注意的用法

### （a）可以當作單數、也能當作複數的集合名詞

將集合體當作一個單位時則為單數用法，當作各別組成成員時，即使是單數形，也能當作複數使用。例如 audience, class, committee, crew, family, team 等等。

My **family is** large.

（我家是大家族。）

My **family are** all well.

（我家人都很好。）

### （b）經常當作複數使用的集合名詞

cattle（牛）、clergy（神職人員）、police 等集合名詞經常被當作複數使用，所以不會加上 a 或 an，也不會變成複數形。

The **police are** investigating the murder case.

（警察正在調查那件殺人案件。）

### （c）經常當作單數使用的集合名詞

不會加上 a 或 an，也不會變成複數形，表示數量多寡時使用 much（許多）、little（少）。表示可數時使用 a piece of 或 an article of。baggage／luggage（行李）、clothing（衣服）、machinery（機械）等等，都是經常被當作單數使用的集合名詞。

We had little **furniture**.

（我們沒什麼傢俱。）

I bought a **piece of furniture**.

（我買了一件傢俱。）

## （5）物質名詞的計量方法

物質名詞的計量方法是使用容器或數量單位。

**a cup of** coffee（一杯咖啡）

**a glass of** beer（一杯啤酒）

**2**

a **bottle of** whiskey （一瓶威士忌）
a **spoonful of** sugar （一匙砂糖）
a **pound of** meat （一磅肉）
**twenty liters of** gasoline （20公升汽油）
a **loaf of** bread （一條麵包）
**two slices of** bread （兩片麵包）
a **piece of** chalk （一隻粉筆）
a **sheet of** paper （一張紙）
a **cake of** soap （一塊肥皂）
**two lumps of** sugar （兩塊方糖）

## （6）抽象名詞的計量方法

抽象名詞中，有些抽象名詞可以使用 a piece of、a bit of 等量詞來計量。

Let me give you **a piece of advice**.

（讓我給你一個建議。）

It is a valuable **piece of information**.

（那是一則重要的資訊。）

## （7）專有名詞應該注意的用法

### （a）加上 the 專有名詞

雖然專有名詞原則上不加冠詞，但是以下專有名詞必須加冠詞 the：
**河川及海洋名稱、半島及運河名稱、交通工具名稱、公共建築物及設施名稱、書報雜誌名稱、複數形的專有名詞（家族、山脈、群島、合眾國等等）、加上形容詞的人名、加上「of＋名詞」的專有名詞。**

the Nile （尼羅河）
the Pacific Ocean （太平洋）
the Malay Peninsula （馬來半島）
the Panama Canal （巴拿馬運河）

the Hikari（光榮號）

the White House（白宮）

the Pentagon（五角大廈）〔美國國防部的別稱〕

the Eiffel Tower（艾菲爾鐵塔）

the Wall Street Journal（華爾街日報）

the Reader's Digest（讀者文摘）

the Bible（聖經）

the Hamiltons（漢米敦家）

the Himalayas（喜瑪拉雅山）

the Philippines（菲律賓群島）

the United States of America（美利堅合眾國）〔美國的全名〕

the late Mr. Grant（已故的格蘭特先生）

the University of Virginia（維吉尼亞大學）

〔注意〕 **公園、車站、橋樑、道路、大學**等名稱通常不加冠詞 the。

Central Park（中央公園）

Victoria Station（維多利亞車站）

London Bridge（倫敦橋）

Fifth Avenue（第五大道）

Harvard University（哈佛大學）

### （b）專有名詞變成普通名詞時

專有名詞加上 a / an 或 the 表示「～的人」、「名為～的人」、「～家的人」、「～的作品」。

He wished to be **an Einstein**.

（他希望變成像愛因斯坦那樣的人。）

**A Mr. Smith** is here to see you.

（有一位名叫史密斯的先生來拜訪你。）

He is **a Kennedy**.

（他是甘迺迪家的人。）

He has a genuine van Gogh.

（他擁有一幅梵谷的真跡。）

## （8）應該注意的名詞複數形

### （a）「子音＋o」結尾的名詞，通常加上 -es。

tomato → tomato**es**          hero → hero**es**

potato → potato**es**

〔例外〕piano → piano**s**          photo → photo**s**

### （b）f 或 fe 結尾的名詞，大多數先變成 v 再加上 -es。

knife → kni**ves**          half → hal**ves**

leaf → lea**ves**          wife → wi**ves**

〔例外〕belief → belief**s**          roof → roof**s**

chief → chief**s**          safe → safe**s**（保險箱）

### （c）不規則的複數形

man → m**e**n          foot → f**ee**t

goose → g**ee**se          ox → ox**en**

woman → wom**e**n          tooth → t**ee**th

mouse → m**i**ce          child → child**ren**

### （d）複合名詞的複數形

mother-in-law → mother**s**-in-law（岳母）

passerby → passer**s**by（行人）

woman writer → wom**e**n writer**s**（女性作家）

go-between → go-between**s**（中間人）

### （e）可以使用複數形的名詞

由二個部分所構成的單字，如器具、衣物、學術領域名、病名、或以-ing、-able結尾的名詞等，皆以複數形表示。

scissors（剪刀）          pants / trousers（褲子）

economics（經濟學）          measles（麻疹）

savings（存款）          earnings（所得）

glasses（眼鏡）　　　　mathematics（數學）
physics（物理學）　　　mumps（腮腺炎）
belongings（財產）　　valuables（貴重物品）

**（f）單／複數意思不同的名詞**

arm（手腕）— arms（武器）
custom（習慣）— customs（關稅）
good（善行）— goods（商品）
manner（方法）— manners（禮貌）

# Note

## 練習題

請在以下各題目的(A),(B),(C),(D)之中選出最適合的答案填入空格之中。

**1. This is an outline of our company's _____.**

    (A) politic         (B) police

    (C) polity         (D) policy

**2. Have I got any _____ today?**

    (A) call         (B) mail

    (C) letter         (D) telegram

**3. This portable TV is a fascinating _____.**

    (A) device         (B) devise

    (C) devising         (D) devisal

**4. I always had the highest _____ for your father.**

    (A) regards         (B) regarding

    (C) regardless         (D) regard

**5. My _____ are not sufficient to support my family.**

    (A) salary         (B) earnings

    (C) income         (D) revenue

**6. The shuttle bus was tied up in heavy _____.**

    (A) traffic         (B) trafficker

    (C) transport         (D) transportation

**7. She left all her _____ on the train.**

    (A) belong         (B) belongs

    (C) belonging         (D) belongings

**8. Since I am the person in _____, I have decided to start this project.**

    (A) authorize         (B) authorization

    (C) authority         (D) authorities

2

9. Security is our top _____ today.
   (A) primary          (B) primarily
   (C) prime            (D) priority

10. When you leave the room, put all your _____ in the safe.
    (A) value           (B) valuable
    (C) valuables       (D) valuation

11. Mr. Jones rented an apartment _____ overlooking Central Park for $3,000 a month.
    (A) on the Fifth Avenue    (B) at the Fifth Avenue
    (C) on Fifth Avenue        (D) in Fifth Avenue

12. Travelers in economy tend to carry on too _____ pieces of luggage.
    (A) lots            (B) a lot of
    (C) much            (D) many

13. This website contains _____ about where to stay, eat, and shop in New York.
    (A) information      不可數    (B) informations
    (C) inform          (D) informative

14. He had to wait 30 minutes for his _____ to arrive, and another 30 minutes to clear customs.
    (A) a luggage       (B) luggages
    (C) luggage         (D) a few luggages

15. The health club in the hotel has squash courts, aerobic classes, workout _____, and a sauna.
    (A) equipment    不可數    (B) an equipment
    (C) equipments      (D) a plenty of equipment

集合名詞

**2**

16. Mr. Hayward graduated last month from Harvard with a degree in _____.
    - (A) economy
    - (B) economic
    - (C) economical
    - (D) economics

17. Fresh _____ and baked goods are displayed and sampled as the mall opens its farmers market.
    - (A) produce
    - (B) produces
    - (C) products
    - (D) producing

18. Because their bus arrived at the factory very late, the group of clients had _____ time to see its new facilities.
    - (A) few
    - (B) a few
    - (C) several
    - (D) little

19. You can make some extra _____ without ever leaving your driveway.
    - (A) currency
    - (B) dollar
    - (C) cash
    - (D) coin

20. The Philadelphia plant's _____ is idle now, and the factory's 200 workers have gone home.
    - (A) machines
    - (B) a machine
    - (C) machinery
    - (D) machineries

# 正確解答

1-(D) policy 是「方針」，polity 是「政治型態」。

2-(B) 請注意題目中有 any。mail（郵件）是不可數名詞。

3-(A) device 是「設備」。

4-(D) regard（尊敬、敬意）是不可數名詞。在書信中使用的 regards，意思是「問候、致意」。

5-(B) earnings 是「所得」，通常使用複數形。

6-(A) heavy traffic 是「繁忙的交通」。

7-(D) belongings 是「隨身攜帶的物品」，通常使用複數形。

8-(C) person in authority 是「負責人、掌權的人」。

9-(D) priority 是「優先考慮的事」。

10-(C) valuables 是「貴重物品」，通常使用複數形。

11-(C) 由於字首使用大寫，所以 Fifth Avenue 是指專有名詞的道路，也就是「第五大道」，因此不加上定冠詞。

12-(D) pieces 是 piece 的複數形，因此修飾可數名詞的 many 是正確解答。much 是用來修飾不可數名詞。沒有 too lots 和 too a lot of 這種說法。

13-(A) 填入空格的單字是 contains 的受詞，所以必須是名詞。information 是名詞。由於是不可數名詞，所以 informations 是錯誤答案。

14-(C) luggage 是集合名詞，沒有複數形。此外，也不會在 luggage 前加上 a。

15-(A) equipment 是集合名詞，沒有複數形。通常使用 plenty of（許多的），而不使用 a plenty of（英、美方言）。

16-(D) degree 的意思是「學位」，所以在 a degree in 之後必須接續學科名稱。Economics 是「經濟學」。

2

17-(A) 請注意在空格之前有 Fresh（新鮮的）。produce 除了有「產品」的意思外，還表示「農產品」。

18-(D) 本句中的 time 是指「時間」，屬於不可數名詞。如果是指「次數」與「～倍」時，則為可數名詞。little 修飾不可數名詞；few / a few / several 全部都是用來修飾可數名詞。

19-(C) 請注意空格前的第二個字 some（一些）。currency / dollar / coin 都是可數名詞，所以填入空格的必須是複數形。cash 是不可數名詞。

20-(C) 動詞是 is，所以主詞應該是單數。plant's（所有格）之後不接續冠詞。

# 練習題的中文翻譯

1. 這是我們公司方針的概要。
2. 今天有我的郵件嗎？
3. 這台手提電視是非常棒的設備。
4. 我一直打從心底地尊敬您的父親。
5. 我的薪水不夠養家。
6. 區間接駁車陷入擁擠的車陣中。
7. 她將全部的隨身行李留在火車上忘了帶走。
8. 既然我是負責人，我決定開始進行這項計劃。
9. 今日，安全管理是我們優先考慮的事項。
10. 離開房間時，請將所有的貴重物品放進保險箱。
11. 鐘斯先生一個月花三千美金在第五大道租了一間可以俯瞰中央公園的公寓。
12. 乘坐經濟艙的旅客，常會攜帶過多行李進入機艙內。
13. 這個網站包含了在紐約的住宿、飲食、購物等相關資訊。
14. 他必須花３０分鐘等待領取行李，另外必須再花３０分鐘通過海關。
15. 這間飯店的健身俱樂部包括壁球室、有氧課程、健身器材以及三溫暖。
16. 海華先生上個月從哈佛大學畢業，取得了經濟學的學位。
17. 購物中心的農產直銷區開幕後，不僅陳列新鮮的農產品及烘焙食品，也提供試吃服務。
18. 由於他們的巴士到達工廠時已經很晚了，所以參訪的客戶團幾乎沒有時間參觀新設備。
19. 你不用出門，就可以賺取額外的收入。
20. 現在費城工廠的機器閒置，並且已經有２００名員工被辭退。

# **3**rd | Day 冠詞

I'd like to send a parcel to England.
（我想寄包裹到英國。）

She is an excellent typist.
（她是個優秀的打字員。）

He didn't go to the concert.
（他沒有去那場音樂會。）

---

### （1）冠詞的種類

冠詞分為**不定冠詞 a / an 與定冠詞 the** 兩種。不定冠詞的語源是數詞 one 的變形（one → an → a），定冠詞則是 that（那個）的變形。

#### （a）不定冠詞

不定冠詞表示不特定的東西，只會接續可數名詞的單數形。a 接續字首為子音發音的單字，an 接續字首為母音發音的單字。

**a** house（家）　　　　　　　**a** university（大學）
　[haʊs]　　　　　　　　　　　[ˌjunəˋvɝsətɪ]

**an** honest person（正直的人）　**an** umbrella（傘）
　[ˋɑnɪst]　　　　　　　　　　[ʌmˋbrɛlə]

#### （b）定冠詞

定冠詞表示特定的東西，接續所有種類的名詞單數形及複數形。在子音之前發音為 [ðə]，在母音之前發音為 [ði]。

**the** horse（馬）　　　　　　**the** union（工會）
[ðəˋhɔrs]　　　　　　　　　[ðəˋjunjən]

**the** honor roll（資優生名冊）    **the** uncle（伯父）
[ði`ɑnɚ]                          [ði `ʌŋk!]

〔注意〕當名詞接續所有格，或是 one, another, some, any, each, either, neither, every, no, this, that 等與冠詞有相同作用的詞時，<u>不需再加上冠詞</u>。

## （2）不定冠詞的用法

### （a）表示不特定的一個東西

I also need **a** stapler.

（我還需要一個訂書機。）

### （b）替代 one，表示「一個」。

I waited for **an** hour.

（我等了一個小時。）

### （c）表示種類全部，意思是「～任一」（any）

**A** dog is a faithful animal.

（狗是忠誠的動物。）

### （d）表示「同一種的」（the same）

Birds of **a** feather flock together.

（物以類聚。）

### （e）表示「某種」（a certain）

In **a** sense, it is blackmail.

（在某種意義上，那是勒索。）

### （f）表示「每～」（per）

How many words can you read **a** minute?

（你每一分鐘可以讀幾個字？）

### （g）表示「一些」（some）

You should look at the picture from **a** distance.

（你應該保持一點距離來看那幅畫。）

### （h）接續專有名詞，表示「像～一樣的人」、「名為～的人」

She wanted to be **a** Florence Nightingale.

（她希望成為像弗羅倫斯‧南丁格爾一樣的人。）

There was a call for you from **a Mr. Eliot**.

（有一位名叫艾略特的先生打電話給你。）

### （i）慣用句

She made the list **in a hurry**.

（她匆促地製作名單。）

**All of a sudden**, the computer stopped working.

（突然之間，電腦當機了。）

其它還有 at a loss（困惑不解）、com [draw] to an end [close]（結束）、put a stop to（制止～）、as a rule（通常）、once upon a time（從前）、a little [few]（少量的）、a great many（很多）等等。

## （3）定冠詞的用法

MP3
020

### （a）指之前出現過的名詞

I bought a shirt and a tie. **The** shirt is white and **the** tie is blue.

（我買了一件襯衫和一條領帶。襯衫是白的，領帶是藍的。）

### （b）指說話的人和聆聽的人之間都能夠了解的事物

Will you close **the** window?

（你把那扇窗戶關起來好嗎？）

## （c）表示獨一無二的事物

**The** moon circles around **the** earth every 27 days and 8 hours.

（月亮每２７天又８個小時繞行地球一周。）

其它還有 the sun（太陽）、the world（世界）、the universe（宇宙）、the sky（天空）、the sea（海）、the North Pole（北極）、the equator（赤道）、the north（北方）、the right（右邊）等等。

〔注意〕 表示「一個狀態」時加上不定冠詞。a new moon（新月）、a half moon（半月）、a full moon（滿月）等等。

## （d）接續最高級、序數或者 only / same 等名詞

We had **the** best sales in August.

（八月份的業績達到巔峰。）

The sales department is on **the** fifth floor.

（業務部在五樓。）

You are **the** only person I can trust.

（你是我唯一可以信任的人。）

Don't make **the** same mistake again.

（別再犯同樣的錯誤。）

## （e）片語與名詞子句也可以加 the

Washington, D.C. is **the** capital of the United States.

（華盛頓是美國的首都。）

This is **the** telephone bill that I received yesterday.

（這是我昨天收到的電話帳單。）

## （f）表示全體國民的名詞

**The** Japanese are hardworking.

（日本人是勤勉的。）

### （g）表示種類全體

**The** elephant is the largest living land animal.

（大象是居住在陸地上體積最大的動物。）

### （h）用「the＋形容詞〔分詞〕」變成表示特定人群的複數名詞

We have to do something for **the** poor.

（我們必須為窮人做些什麼。）

其它還有 the old（老人）、the young（年輕人）、the rich（有錢人）、the dead（死者）、the wounded（傷者）等等。

### （i）用「by the＋名詞」表示單位

We are paid by **the** hour.

（我們以時薪來計算薪資。）

### （j）身體的部位

Don't hit him on **the** head.

（別打他的頭。）

### （k）慣用句

It will be profitable in **the long run**.

（從長遠來看，那是有利益的。）

## （4）冠詞的位置

名詞中含有冠詞，且後面接形容詞或副詞時，一般的語序為「冠詞＋形容詞＋名詞」或「冠詞＋形容詞＋名詞」。

a **[the]** matter（問題）

a **[the]** serious matter（嚴重的問題）

a **[the]** very serious matter（非常嚴重的問題）

但是，以下的例子是例外。

**（a）what [such, quite, half]＋a [an]＋（形容詞）＋名詞**

What **a** sloppy report !

（真是一份草率的報告！）

I did not say such **a** thing.

（我沒說那樣的話。）

This is quite **a** surprise.

（這真是令人十分驚訝。）

I'll be back in half **an** hour.

（我３０分鐘後回來。）

**（b）so [too, as]＋形容詞＋a [an]＋名詞**

You cannot master typing in so short a time.

（你在那麼短的時間內無法精通打字。）

This is too big a risk to take.

（這實在太冒險了。）

She is as attractive a person as you.

（她像你一樣，是個有魅力的人。）

**（c）all [both, half, double]＋the＋名詞**

I walked all **the** way home.

（我一路走回家。）

Both (**the**) workers were promoted.

（這兩個員工都晉升了。）

Half **the** work is done.

（工作已完成一半。）

He gave me double **the** pay.

（他付給我兩倍的工資。）

3

**45**

**（5）冠詞的重複**

以 and 連結的兩個名詞表示「**同一種東西**」時，只要在第一個名詞加上冠詞即可。但是，表示「**其它的東西**」時，原則上名詞各自加上冠詞。

I was introduced to **a** musician and lawyer.

（我被介紹給一位既是音樂家、也是律師的人。）

I was introduced to **a** musician and **a** lawyer.

（我被介紹給一名音樂家以及一名律師。）

I saw **a** black and white dog.

（我看見一隻毛色黑白相間的狗。）

I saw **a** black and **a** white dog.

（我看見一隻黑狗和一隻白狗。）

〔**參考**〕以 and 連結的兩個東西視為**一組**時，只要在第一個名詞加上冠詞即可。這個時候當作單數處理，and 的發音變成 [n]。

**the** bread and butter（塗上奶油的麵包）

**a** cup and saucer（附上茶托的杯子）

**a** watch and chain（加上鍊子的錶）

**the** whiskey and soda（威士忌加上蘇打水稀釋）

**（6）冠詞的省略**

以下情形中，冠詞會被省略。

**（a）表示呼喚的名詞**

How is he, Doctor?

（醫生，請問他的身體怎麼了？）

**（b）表示家人或親戚的名詞**

Mother answered the phone.

（媽媽去接電話了。）

## （c）表示身分、官職的名詞，當作稱號、專有名詞的同格或補語使用時

President Bush（布希總統）〔稱號〕

Professor Morgan（摩根教授）〔稱號〕

Alex Haley, author of Roots, died of a heart attack. 〔同格〕

（《根》的作者──艾力克斯・哈雷死於心臟病發作。）

Mr. Wilson is president of the company. 〔補語〕

（威爾森先生是這家公司的董事長。）

〔參考〕指身份、官職等特定名稱，並想要強調其意時，有時會加上冠詞或所有格。

## （d）建築物等等的名詞，表示原本的目的、功能時

Do you go to **school** on Saturday?

（你星期六要上學嗎？）

She goes to **church** on Sundays.

（她星期天去教會。）

其它還有 go to bed（就寢）、appear in court（出庭）、go on to college（進入大學）、at school（求學）、at home（在家）、watch television（看電視）、by train（搭火車）等等。

## （e）運動、遊戲、用餐等等的名詞

Let's play **tennis** this weekend.

（這個周末一起去打網球吧。）

I played chess with Tom after **supper**.

（我在晚餐後跟湯姆一起下西洋棋。）

## （f）兩個名詞形成對句時

She's getting better **day by day**.

（她一天比一天變得更好。）

**3**

其它還有 man and woman（男女）、husband and wife（夫妻）、young and old（老少）、mother and child（母子）、day and night（日夜）、day after day（日復一日）、from door to door（挨家挨戶地）、face to face（面對面）、step by step（逐步地）、side by side（肩並肩地）等等。

## （g）相對於動物與神表示「人類」、相對於女性表示「男性」的 man

**Man** is mortal.

（凡人都會死。）

**Man** is stronger than woman.

（男人比女人強壯。）

## （h）慣用句

Where did the accident **take place**?

（事故是在哪裡發生的？）

其它還有 take part in（參加～）、by accident（偶然地）、by mistake（錯誤地）、at night（在夜裡）、at noon（在中午）、at hand（在手邊）、at first（最初）、at last（最後、終於）、in fact（事實上）等等。

# 練習題

請在以下各題目的(A),(B),(C),(D)之中選出最適合的答案填入空格之中。

**1. These men are all of _____.**
    (A) kind         (B) their kind
    (C) a kind      (D) the kind

**2. Gas is about 125 yen _____.**
    (A) a liter      (B) liter
    (C) liters       (D) the liter

**3. It's been _____ since I saw you last.**
    (A) while       (B) a while
    (C) long time    (D) for long

**4. London is _____ of the United Kingdom.**
    (A) the capital    (B) their capital
    (C) a capital     (D) the capitals

**5. The count of _____ reached 128.**
    (A) wound     (B) a wound
    (C) wounding    (D) the wounded

**6. We rent bicycles by _____.**
    (A) an hour     (B) the hour
    (C) some hours   (D) hours

**7. The guard grabbed the man by _____.**
    (A) the arm     (B) one arm
    (C) arms       (D) their arms

**8. That is quite _____ unique idea.**
    (A) that       (B) an
    (C) a        (D) the

3

**9.** This is too big _____ to put in the trunk.
    (A) boxes            (B) the box
    (C) box             (D) a box

**10.** In _____, I prefer to go alone.
    (A) fact             (B) a fact
    (C) facts           (D) the facts

**11.** "The First Strike" was made in _____, and much of the script was written during filming.
    (A) hurry          (B) a hurry
    (C) hurries        (D) to hurry

**12.** "It would be _____ to be considered for the position" of chief administrative officer, said Mr. David Duncan.
    (A) honor         (B) an honor
    (C) honors        (D) a honor

**13.** This small island, 70 miles north of _____ in Southeast Asia, is one of the most beautiful places to visit or live.
    (A) equator       (B) an equator
    (C) equators     (D) the equator

**14.** The two retailers stock merchandise from _____ wholesalers.
    (A) a same        (B) same
    (C) the same      (D) this same

**15.** Sales of sport utility vehicles and pickup trucks are also on _____.
    (A) the increase    (B) increase
    (C) an increase    (D) increases

3

16. On _____ , it will only accelerate job losses in the travel industry.

    (A) contrary         (B) a contrary

    (C) contraries       (D) the contrary

17. _____ rises in the east and sets in the west.

    (A) A sun          (B) The sun

    (C) Sun            (D) The suns

18. Mary had to go all _____ to the airport to pick up her lost baggage.

    (A) way           (B) a way

    (C) the way       (D) ways

19. Mr. Conway was elected _____ of the Committee on the Budget.

    (A) chairman      (B) a chairman

    (C) the chairman    (D) chairmen

20. In her new position, Mary got pressured _____.

    (A) a day after a day   (B) day after day

    (C) day after days     (D) days after days

# 正確解答

1-(C) a kind 的 a 表示「同一個」。

2-(A) a liter 的 a 表示「每～」。

3-(B) a while 的 a 表示「有點～」。

4-(A) of the United Kingdom 修飾 the capital。

5-(D)「the＋形容詞（分詞）」表示人。

6-(B) by the hour 表示「時間上」的單位。

7-(A) arm 由於是指身體的部位，所以加上 the。

8-(C) unique 的 u，發音是子音。

9-(D) 變成「too＋形容詞＋a [an]＋名詞」的語順表現方式。

10-(A) in fact 是表示「事實上」的慣用句。the 被省略。

11-(B) in a hurry 是片語，意思是「匆忙地」。

12-(B) honor 的字首雖然是 h，可是發音是以母音起始的單字，所以
　　　冠詞必須是用 an。It would be an honor to... 的意思是「很榮
　　　幸去做～」。

13-(D) equator（赤道）是世上唯一的東西，所以加上 the。

14-(C) same 之前一定會加上 the。

15-(A) 片語 on the increase 的意思是「增加」。不可以省略冠詞。
　　　此外，也不可以使用 a。

16-(D) 片語 on the contrary 的意思是「正好相反」。

17-(B)「太陽」通常以 the sun 表示。

18-(C) 片語 all the way 有「相當遙遠」的意思。

19-(A) chairman 是表示身分、官職的用語，在本句中被當作補語使
　　　用，所以前面不需要加冠詞。chairmen 是 chairman 的複數
　　　形，但句子的主詞是單數，所以 chairmen 是錯誤答案。

20-(B) day after day 是兩個名詞形成的對句片語，不可以用冠詞。

# 練習題的中文翻譯

1. 這些男人都是同一種類型。
2. 汽油每公升約１２５日幣。
3. 有一陣子沒有看到你了。
4. 倫敦是英國的首都。
5. 傷者的人數達到１２８人。
6. 自行車以一個小時為單位租借。
7. 警衛抓住那名男子的手臂。
8. 那是非常獨特的想法。
9. 這個箱子太大了，放不進車子後面的行李箱。
10. 事實上，我傾向一個人去。
11. 「The First Strike」是在匆忙之中拍攝的，大部份的劇本都是在拍攝期間寫出來的。
12. 大衛鄧肯先生表示自己非常榮幸能被考慮擔任最高行政官員的職務。
13. 位於赤道以北７０公里處的這座東南亞小島，是個適合觀光、居住的最美地點之一。
14. 這兩間門市是從同一個批發商進貨。
15. 多功能運動休旅車與小型貨車的銷售業績同時成長。
16. 正好相反，這只會加速觀光產業工作機會的流失。
17. 太陽從東邊昇起，從西邊落下。
18. 瑪麗為了取回遺失的行李，必須專程到機場一趟。
19. 康威先生當選為預算委員會的會長。
20. 在新的職務上，瑪麗每天都處於壓力中。

# 4th Day 代名詞（1）
## （人稱代名詞、指示代名詞）

**4**

It's my fault, not yours. ——————————「人稱代名詞」
（這是我的責任，不是你的。）

This is fresh, but that is rotten. ——————「指示代名詞」
（這個是新鮮的，但那個是腐壞的。）

## （1）代名詞的種類

代名詞主要是為了避免反覆使用同一個名詞的用語，共有**人稱代名詞、指示代名詞、不定代名詞、疑問代名詞、關係代名詞**五種。

### （a）人稱代名詞

人稱代名詞是指第一人稱（說話者）、第二人稱（聆聽者）、第三人稱（話題中出現的人及物），**用來區別人稱的代名詞**，包括 I, you, we, he, she, it, they 等等。此外，人稱代名詞的特殊用法，包括所有格代名詞與反身代名詞。

### （b）指示代名詞

指示代名詞是**明白表示人或物的代名詞**。包括 this, that, these, those, such, so, same 等等。

### （c）不定代名詞

不是具體指出特定的事物，而是指**模糊不清與不特定的人或物的代名詞**，稱為不定代名詞。one, some, all, any, none, other, another, each, both, either, neither 都可以當作不定代名詞。

### （d）疑問代名詞

這是表示**疑問的代名詞**，包括 what, who, which 等等。

# 代名詞（1）（人稱代名詞、指示代名詞）

## （e）關係代名詞

**兼具代名詞與連接詞功能**的代名詞，包括 who, which, that 等等。

## （2）人稱代名詞「格」的變化

| 人稱 | 單複數 | 主格 | 所有格 | 受格 | 所有代名詞 | 反身代名詞 |
|------|--------|------|--------|------|------------|------------|
| 第一人稱 | 單數 | I | my | me | mine | myself |
| | 複數 | we | our | us | ours | ourselves |
| 第二人稱 | 單數 | you | your | you | yours | yourself |
| | 複數 | you | your | you | yours | yourselves |
| 第三人稱 | 單數 | he | his | him | his | himself |
| | | she | her | her | hers | herself |
| | 複數 | it | its | it | — | itself |
| | | they | their | them | theirs | themselves |

## （3）人稱代名詞的用法

MP3
025

### （a）主格被做為主詞與主格補語

**He** is good at bargaining. 〔主詞〕

（他擅長談判。）

It's **she**. 〔補語〕

（是她。）

〔注意〕 在口語中使用受格，例如 It's her. 與 It's me.。

### （b）所有格是表示之後名詞的所有關係。

It's **my** mistake.

（這是我的錯。）

### （c）受格成為動詞與介系詞的受詞

Don't compare **me** with Cathy.

（請不要拿我與凱西比較。）

I'm very proud of **you**.

（我非常以你為榮。）

## （4）表示一般人的 we, you, they

we, you, they 有時候泛指一般人

**We**'re going to have a short rainy season this year.

（今年會有一個短暫的梅雨季節。）

**You** never can tell.

（誰都想像不到。）

**They** speak English in Jamaica.

（在牙買加是說英語。）

## （5）it 的特別用法

### （a）泛指時間、天候、距離、明暗、冷暖等等，當作主詞使用。

How long will **it** take to get there?

（到那裡需要多久的時間？）

**It** will rain in the afternoon.

（下午應該會下雨。）

How far is **it** from here to the airport?

（從這裡到機場有多遠？）

**It**'s very dark here.

（這裡很暗。）

**It**'s very cold outside.

（外面非常冷。）

# 代名詞（1）（人稱代名詞、指示代名詞）

## （b）當作表示狀況的主詞使用

**It** can't be helped.

（無能為力。）

**It**'s all over for me.

（我已經完蛋了。）

## （c）當作虛主詞，代替後面的不定詞片語、**that** 子句、動名詞。

**It** is possible to reduce working hours.

（縮減工作時數是可能的。）

**It** is certain that he'll get a promotion.

（他升職是已確定的事。）

**It**'s no use scolding him.

（責罵他也無濟於事。）

## （d）當作虛受詞，代替後面的不定詞片語、**that** 子句、動名詞。

They found **it** difficult to meet the target.

（他們發現達成目標是困難的。）

He took **it** for granted that she was married.

（他完全以為她已婚。）

I find **it** very dangerous crossing the street.

（我認為橫越那條路非常危險。）

find something + adj.

## （e）用於 **It is [was]...that...** 的強調句型

**It** was Jack that **[who]** made the long-distance call.

（撥打長途電話的人是傑克。）

### （6）所有格代名詞的用法

這是表示「～的東西」的代名詞，mine（我的東西）、ours（我們的東西）、yours（你的東西）、yours（你們的東西）、his（他的東西）、hers（她的東西）、theirs（他們的東西）。

#### （a）用於避免名詞重覆使用

This is my passport. Where is **yours**?

（這是我的護照，你的在哪裡呢？）

#### （b）變成「a [the, this, etc.]＋名詞＋of＋所有格代名詞」的語順

He is a friend of **mine**.

（他是我的朋友。）

〔參考〕a friend of mine 泛指朋友中的一個，my friend 是指特定的友人。

#### （c）所有格代名詞的慣用表現

All good wishes to you and **yours.** [= your family]

（也代我向你的家人問好。）

I have received **yours** of September 5th. [= your letter]

（我已經收到你 9 月 5 日寄出的信。）

### （7）反身代名詞的用法

反身代名詞是在人稱代名詞的所有格或受格加上 -self（單數）、-selves（複數）組合而成，表示「本身」的意思。

#### （a）反身用法

Don't blame **yourself**.

（不要自責。）

Help **yourself** to some cookies.

（請隨意取用餅乾。）

Take care of **yourself**.

（你好好保重。）

## （b）強調用法

反身代名詞可以用來強調名詞或代名詞。其與主詞、受詞同格。

He drove to the airport **himself**. 〔與主詞同格〕

（他自己開車去機場。）

She went to see the president **himself**. 〔與受詞同格〕

（她去見社長本人。）

## （8）指示代名詞的用法

### （a）基本的用法

較近的東西用 this [these]，較遠的東西用 that [those]。

**This** is my desk and **that** is Tom's.

（這張是我的桌子，那張是湯姆的。）

**These** are mine and **those** are yours.

（這些是我的，那些是你的。）

### （b）為了避免重複使用名詞，可以使用 that [those]

The number of crimes per capita in Detroit is greater than **that** in New York.

（底特律的每人犯罪數比紐約的還多。）

Working conditions in Japan are worse than **those** in the U.S.

（日本的工作條件比美國差。）

### （c）要表示之前已經出現過的內容，可以使用 this 或是 that

I forced her to work overtime, but **this** was a mistake.

（我強迫她加班，但這樣是錯的。）

The American economy is looking up, and **that** is good.

（美國的景氣有起色，這是一件好事。）

### （d）為了指以下敘述的內容可以使用 this

The truth is **this**: he miscalculated the total cost of the project.

（事實是這樣的：他算錯專案所需的費用。）

### （e）such 的用法

指示代名詞的 such 用來表示「**那樣的人〔或物〕**」。
**Such** is life.

（人生就是這樣。）

He is a celebrity, and likes to be treated as **such**.

（他是個名人，他也喜歡被當作名人對待。）

### （f）so 的用法

原本 so 是副詞，但是與 believe, do , expect, hope, say, suppose, think 等動詞合併，當作代名詞使用。
I think **so**, too.

（我也是這麼認為。）

I like weak coffee. ─ **So** do I.

（我喜歡喝淡咖啡。── 我也是。）

### （g）same 的用法

通常會加上 the 表示「相同的東西（事物）」。
I'll have the **same**.

（我要一樣的東西。）

The **same** applies to your case.

（同樣的事適用於你的情況。）

# 練習題

請在以下各題目的(A),(B),(C),(D)之中選出最適合的答案填入空格之中。

**1.** I'm not proud of _____.   *D*

    (A) me               (B) I

    (C) my              (D) myself

**2.** She is an old friend of _____.   *C*

    (A) my               (B) me

    (C) mine            (D) myself

**3.** Help _____ to tea or coffee.   *B*

    (A) you             (B) yourself

    (C) your            (D) yours

**4.** Isn't the _____ true of Japanese cars?   *D*

    (A) so               (B) such

    (C) that            (D) same

**5.** Come and see for _____.   *A*

    (A) yourself       (B) you

    (C) your            (D) yours

**6.** Is the company going to lay off more workers? － I'm afraid _____.   *D*

    (A) such           (B) same

    (C) them          (D) so

**7.** I was influenced a lot by _____ opinion.   *B*

    (A) the            (B) his

    (C) him           (D) himself

**8.** We haven't found a replacement for _____ yet.   *A*

    (A) her           (B) she

    (C) hers          (D) herself

**4**

9. Your words make me happier than _____ of anyone else.
   (A) it
   (B) that
   (C) these
   (D) those

10. The president _____ showed the buyers around the factory.
   (A) him
   (B) his
   (C) he
   (D) himself

11. The prices were set a bit lower than _____ of imported brand items.
   (A) it
   (B) one
   (C) those
   (D) that

12. _____ took the new employee two whole days to make an invoice for the goods.
   (A) It
   (B) That
   (C) This
   (D) They

13. The sales representatives _____ very difficult to market American dishwashers in Japan.
   (A) found
   (B) found it
   (C) found that
   (D) found them

14. The job applicant _____ for granted that he could get three weeks of paid vacation every year at the company.
   (A) took one
   (B) took
   (C) took out
   (D) took it

15. _____ is no use discussing anything with the stubborn product sales manager.
   (A) This
   (B) That
   (C) It
   (D) Such

# 代名詞（1）（人稱代名詞、指示代名詞）

16. The development manager blamed _____ for the project failure.

    (A) himself                (B) he

    (C) his                    (D) to him

17. "The quality of our products is much higher than _____ of any manufacturer in this country," said the president.

    (A) one                    (B) that

    (C) it                     (D) those

18. You are our most valued customer, and _____, we would like to offer you a 30% discount off the list price.

    (A) as to                  (B) as of

    (C) as if                  (D) as such

19. _____ not surprising that the majority of skilled programmers are seeking jobs overseas.

    (A) It's                   (B) This is

    (C) That's                 (D) Those are

20. Yesterday the United States and _____ allies tried to prop up the American currency by buying huge numbers of dollars on world markets,

    (A) it                     (B) its

    (C) their                  (D) they

# 正確解答

1-(D) 主詞是 I，所以後面用反身代名詞 myself。

2-(C) an old friend of mine 是指「老朋友中的一人」。

3-(B) Help yourself to... 的意思是「請自己隨意……」。

4-(D) 在前面有 the，所以選擇 same。true of 的意思是「對……而言是適當的」。

5-(A) Come and see for yourself. 是「請你自己確認」的意思。

6-(D) I'm afraid so. 的意思是「很可惜地、恐怕如此」。I hope so. / I suppose so. / I think so. 等都是一樣的說法。

7-(B) 由於是名詞 opinion 之前，所以用所有格 his。

8-(A) 變成介系詞 for 的受詞，所以受格的 her 是正確答案。

9-(D) words 是複數形，所以 those 是正確答案。

10-(D) himself（他本身）的強調用法。

11-(C) prices 是複數形，對應的代名詞也必須是複數形，所以（C）those 是正確答案。

12-(A) 從句子後半部的 to make an invoice... 可以看出這是使用虛主詞（it）的句子。

13-(B) 從主詞＋found...＋補語（very difficult）＋to market... 的語順可以看出這是使用受詞（it）的句子。Market 在這裡並不是當作名詞而是動詞，意思是「銷售」。

14-(D) 這是使用 take if for granted that...（把……視為理所當然）的句子。

15-(C) 使用 It is no use doing 表示「無論做……也無濟於事」。

16-(A) 從文脈來看，blamed（責備）的對象是「他本身」，所以（A）himself 是正確解答。

17-(B) 請注意，成為比較對象的是 quality，而不是 products。quality 是單數，所以空格應該填入 that。

18-(D) 從文脈來看，空格應該填入表示「就其本身而論」的 as such。as to 是「關於～」、as of 是「現在～」、as if 是「猶如」的意思。

19-(A) 從 not surprising（補語）that... 可以看出這是使用虛主詞的

句子。真正的主詞是 that 子句。

20-(B) 空格填入所有格。the United States 的 States 是複數形，但是由於是國名，必須當作單數處理，所以這個所有格是 its。

# 練習題的中文翻譯

1. 我並不以自己為榮。
2. 她是我的一個老朋友。
3. 請隨意取用紅茶、咖啡。
4. 這難道不適合日本車嗎？
5. 請您親自確認。
6. 公司是否打算裁減更多員工呢？恐怕是如此。
7. 他的意見影響我很深。
8. 我們還沒找到人可以取代她。
9. 你的話比任何人的話都令我開心。
10. 社長親自帶買家們參觀工廠。
11. 價格設定比進口名牌商品更低。
12. 那位新進員工花了整整兩天製作商品發票。
13. 銷售員們發現在日本銷售美式洗碗機是一件非常困難的事。
14. 那位求職者以為在這家公司，每年可以有三週有薪休假。
15. 跟這位頑固的商品銷售經理爭論也無濟於事。
16. 開發部經理對於這個計劃的失敗感到相當自責。
17. 社長說：「本公司的商品品質，是我國所有製造商中最優秀的。」
18. 您是本公司最重要的客戶，因此，我們將提供您定價的七折優惠。
19. 大多數的資深程式設計師應徵海外的工作，這並不令人驚訝。
20. 昨天，美國與其盟國試著在國際市場購買巨額美元，企圖支撐美元匯率。

## 5th Day 代名詞（2）
### （不定代名詞、疑問代名詞）

**MP3 031**

I'll take this one. ——————————— 「不定代名詞」
（我要買這個。）

Some of the glasses were broken. ———— 「不定代名詞」
（有一些杯子破掉了。）

Both of them quit their job. ————— 「不定代名詞」
（他們兩個都辭掉了工作。）

What happened to him? ——————— 「疑問代名詞」
（他究竟發生什麼事了？）

Who wrote this report? ——————— 「疑問代名詞」
（這份報告是誰寫的？）

Which would you prefer, pork or beef? ——— 「疑問代名詞」
（你要豬肉還是牛肉？）

如前所述，不定代名詞是指不特定事物的代名詞，主要有 one, some, all, any, none, other, another, each, both, either, neither 等等。此外，疑問代名詞是指表示疑問語氣的代名詞，包括 what, who, which 等等。接下來會針對各個不定代名詞與疑問代名詞的用法進行解說。

### （1）one 的用法

**MP3 032**

#### （a）代替前面出現過的不特定「可數名詞」

Jack bought a nice bicycle. I want to buy **one**, too.

（傑克買了一輛好自行車。我也想要買一台。）

#### （b）以「a [an]＋形容詞＋one」（單數）、「形容詞＋ones」（複數）的形態，避免重複使用之前用過的普通名詞。

# 代名詞（2）（不定代名詞、疑問代名詞）

Nancy bought an expensive camera, but **I** bought a cheap **one**.

（南西買了一台高價相機，不過我買了一台便宜的相機。）

Sorry, the black wallets are all sold out. We have only brown **ones**.

（不好意思，黑色的錢包賣完了，只剩下褐色的。）

### （c）在 one 加上 the 表示特定的事物

Which CD player would you like? — I'd like the smaller **one**.

（你喜歡那一種 CD 播放器？ — 我喜歡小一點的。）

### （d）用來泛指「世上一般的人」

這個時候不能使用複數形的 ones。

**One** should do one's duty.

（每個人必須盡自己的義務。）

〔注意〕one 可以用 one's 和 oneself來接續，但是在美式英語中，大多使用 him 及 himself 來接續。

## （2）none 的用法

### （a）代替前面出現過的名詞，意思是「完全沒有」

這個時候，如果該名詞是單數，則當作**單數處理**，如果是複數，則當作**複數處理**。

Is there any milk in the carton? — No, there is **none**.

（箱子裡有奶粉嗎？ — 沒有，裡面完全沒有奶粉。）

Are there any guests in the living room? — No, there are **none**.

（有客人在客廳裡嗎？ — 沒有，一個客人也沒有。）

### （b）none of 表示比 no... 更強烈的否定

這個時候的一般用法是，後面接續的名詞是單數時，則當作**單數處理**，複數時，則當作**複數處理**。

None of her work has been done.

（她的工作沒有一項是完成的。）

None of us have received any letters.

（我們之中沒有人收到信件。）

### （c）慣用語法

It's none of your business.

（這不關你的事。）

## （3）all 的用法

### （a）用來表示「所有的人〔或物〕」的意思

表示「**數**」時，當作**複數處理**，表示「**量**」時，當作**單數處理**。

All who hear him speak are very impressed.

（聽過他說話的人全都感到印象深刻。）

All you have to do is press this button.

（只要按這個按鈕即可。）

### （b）慣用語法

He decided not to go after all.

（結果，他決定不去了。）

He is good-looking, intelligent, and above all, generous.

（他長得英俊、聰明，最重要的是他為人寬厚。）

This model isn't selling at all.

（這個機種完全賣不出去。）

That comes to 75 dollars in all.

（全部總計７５美金。）

# 代名詞（2）（不定代名詞、疑問代名詞）

## （4）both 的用法

both 的意思是「**兩者都**」，**通常當作複數處理。**

Both of their daughters are married.

（他們倆各自的女兒都已經結婚。）

〔**注意**〕all 以及 both 接續否定詞時，表示部份否定，意思分別是
「並不限全部～」、「並不限兩者都～」。

He didn't invite **all** the people.

（他並沒有邀請所有的人。）

She did not throw **both** of them away.

（她並沒有兩個都捨棄。）

## （5）each 的用法

each 的意思是「**各自、分別**」，**通常當作單數處理。**

**Each** of the students has his or her own locker.

（每個學生都擁有自己的置物櫃。）

They know a lot about **each** other.

（他們非常了解對方。）

〔**注意**〕each 與 every 是意思非常相近的單字，不過 each 是當作
代名詞、形容詞及副詞使用，相對地，every 只能當作形容
詞使用。

**Each** participant must bring five pictures. 〔形容詞〕

（每個參加者必須帶五張相片。）

I gave them ten dollars **each**. 〔副詞〕

（我給他們一人十塊美金。）

He tried **every** approach he could think of. 〔形容詞〕

（他試過每一個他能想到的方法。）

## (6) either 與 neither 的用法

either 以及 neither 分別表示兩人或是兩件事物中的「**任一、每一個**」及「**兩者皆不**」。這兩個單字都當作**單數處理**。但是，在**口語**上有時候會當作**複數使用**。

**Either** will do.

（這兩個任一個都可以。）

**Either** of them would do well in this job.

（他們兩個中任何一個人都應該能做好這件事。）

**Neither** of us answered the phone.

（我們兩個都沒有接電話。）

〔**注意**〕I don't like either of them. 與 I like neither of them 意思相同，表示「他們兩個我都不喜歡」。

## (7) other 與 another 的用法

other 的複數形是 others。此外，another 可以視為 an＋other，所以當作單數處理。

### (a) one － the other:（兩件事物中的）一個 — 剩下的那個

I have two cars: **one** is an ordinary passenger car, and **the other** is a sports car.

（我有兩台車：一台是普通的轎車，另一台是跑車。）

### (b) one － another:（眾多之中的）一個 — 剩下的任何一個

I don't like this **one**. Will you show me **another**?

（我不喜歡這一個。麻煩拿其它的給我看好嗎？）

### (c) some [a few, etc.] － the others:（眾多之中的）幾個 — 剩下的全部

**Some** of them were for the proposal, but **the others** were against it.

（他們之中有幾個贊成那個提案，但是剩下的人全部反對。）

# 代名詞（2）（不定代名詞、疑問代名詞）

## （d）some － some [others]：（眾多之中的）幾個 — 其它幾個

There are many kinds of workers. **Some** are hardworking, and **some** are lazy.

（有許多種勞工。其中有一些勤奮工作，有一些很怠惰。）

**Some** experts say the economy is looking up, and **[but] others** say it's getting worse.

（有一些專家說景氣會變好，有一些專家說景氣會變差。）

## （e）others：其它的人們

Don't speak ill of **others** behind their backs.

（別在背後說別人的壞話。）

## （f）慣用語法

To know is **one thing**; to teach is quite **another**.

（了解是一回事，教又是另一回事。）

They are cursing **each other**.

（他們互相詛咒對方。）

The guests said goodbye to **one another**.

（客人相互道別。）

He opened the boxes **one after another**.

（他一個一個開箱。）

## （8）some 與 any 的用法

some 與 any 表現「數」時，都當作**複數處理**，表示「量」時，當作**單數處理**。原則上，some 用於**肯定句**，any 用於**否定句、疑問句**及**條件句**。

**Some** of the requests were granted. 〔肯定句〕

（有幾個要求被採納了。）

**Some** of the money was used for buying a gift. 〔肯定句〕

（那些錢有一部分用在購買禮物。）

I don't like **any** of these. 〔否定句〕

（我討厭這些東西。）

Do **any** of you know? 〔疑問句〕

（你們有任何人知道嗎？）

If **any** of you want to come with me, please let me know. 〔條件句〕

（如果你們之中有人想跟我去，請讓我知道。）

〔注意〕在否定句與疑問句中，有時也可以使用 some。

I don't like **some** of them.

（我討厭他們之中的一些人。）

Would you like **some**?

（你想要來一些嗎？）

此外，即使是肯定句，表示「無論如何～」、「任何一個」、「任何人」時也可以使用 any。

**Any** of these will do.

（這些中的任何一個都可以。）

### （9）包含 every, some, any, no 的組合單字用法

包含這些單字的代名詞有 everyone, someone, anyone, no one, everybody, somebody, anybody, nobody, everything, something, anything, nothing 等等。這些字的用法幾乎與 every, some, any, none 的用法一樣。

**Everyone** was sick.

（大家都生病了。）

# 代名詞（2）（不定代名詞、疑問代名詞）

**Somebody** has to do this.

（必須有人去做這件事。）

**Anybody** can do this work.

（任何一個人都能做這件事。）

**No one** agreed with him.

（沒有人同意他的想法。）

Let me tell you **something**.

（請讓我告訴你一些事。）

I have **nothing** to say.

（我沒有什麼話可說。）

## （10）who 的用法

變成**主詞**、動詞以及介系詞的**受詞**、**補語**。**主格**是 who，**所有格**是 whose，**受格**是 whom。

**Who** came while I was out? 〔主詞〕

（我外出時有誰來過嗎？）

**Whom [Who]** did you invite? 〔受詞〕

（你邀請誰？）

**Whom [Who]** is she angry with? 〔介系詞的受詞〕

（她在生誰的氣？）

**Who** is that beautiful lady? 〔補語〕

（那位漂亮的女士是誰？）

**Whose** suitcase is this? 〔所有格〕

（這是誰的手提箱？）

## （11）what 的用法

變成主詞、動詞以及介系詞的**受詞**、**補語**。主格、受格都是 what，沒有所有格。

**What** made you say so? 〔主詞〕

（你為什麼那麼說？）

**What** did you say to her? 〔受詞〕

（你對她說了什麼？）

**What** is that? 〔補語〕

（那是什麼？）

## （12）which 的用法

變成主詞、動詞以及介系詞的**受詞**、**補語**。**主格**與**受格**都是 **which**，沒有所有格。

**Which** of you started the argument? 〔主詞〕

（是誰開始這場爭吵的？）〔是誰先開始吵的？〕

**Which** would you prefer, tea or coffee? 〔受詞〕

（你想要紅茶還是咖啡？）

**Which** is her real name, Linda or Julia? 〔補語〕

（她的真名是琳達還是茱麗葉？）

## 練習題

請在以下各題目的(A),(B),(C),(D)之中選出最適合的答案填入空格之中。

**1. These are too expensive. May I see some cheaper _____?**

    (A) one                (B) other

    (C) any                (D) ones

**2. Would you like to take a look at this _____?**

    (A) none              (B) one

    (C) some             (D) ones

**3. _____ that glitters is not gold.**

    (A) None              (B) All

    (C) Both              (D) Either

**4. We don't have much to say to _____ other.**

    (A) every            (B) all

    (C) both             (D) each

**5. _____ of her students have received the award.**

    (A) Each             (B) Every

    (C) One              (D) None

**6. I haven't read _____ of his two letters.**

    (A) either            (B) ones

    (C) others          (D) the others

**7. Some say one thing and _____ another.**

    (A) another        (B) other

    (C) any              (D) others

**8. You won't find _____ willing to sell their stock.**

    (A) all                (B) who

    (C) anyone         (D) whom

9. _____ fault is it?

    (A) Whose           (B) Who

    (C) Whom          (D) Who's

10. _____ of the customers were you talking to?

    (A) Who            (B) Anyone

    (C) Which         (D) What

11. "Once and for _____, I will quit drinking," promised the bus driver to his supervisor.

    (A) one            (B) some

    (C) none          (D) all

12. _____ do you think will be appointed to lead the irrigation project in the region?

    (A) Whom         (B) Whose

    (C) Who           (D) Of whom

13. To take a dip in the city's newest public pool will cost $3. At _____ of the city's other pools, swimming is free.

    (A) any            (B) every

    (C) that          (D) another

14. He has tried everything to improve company efficiency, but _____ has worked.

    (A) anything      (B) everything

    (C) nothing       (D) something

15. The boss took up _____ of the two proposals made at the meeting.

    (A) either         (B) all

    (C) any           (D) neither

16. _____ who wants to apply for the new position in the Silver Spring plant, must contact the human resources department by the end of May.

    (A) Someone           (B) Anyone

    (C) They              (D) All people

17. Many airlines allowed children to fly free last summer, and _____ are still offering substantial discounts.

    (A) someone           (B) who

    (C) some               (D) anyone

18. Forcing employers to bear the cost of healthcare will reduce _____ employment and wages.

    (A) each               (B) both

    (C) either             (D) neither

19. We have two manufacturing plants in Latin America; one is in Mexico and _____ is in Brazil.

    (A) some              (B) other

    (C) others            (D) the other

20. _____ of the two cost-cutting programs is more effective?

    (A) Either             (B) Both

    (C) Which            (D) What

5

# 正確解答

1-(D) 在前面有 some，所以用複數形的 ones 來代替。

2-(B) 在前面有 this，所以用單數形的 one 來代替。

3-(B) All that glitters is not gold. 是句諺語，意思是「中看的不一定中用。」

4-(D) each other 的意思是「互相」。

5-(D) 述語動詞是 have received，所以表示單數的 each 及 one 不適合填入空格。Every 是形容詞，並不是代名詞。

6-(A) 由於是 two letters，所以 ones, others, the others 不適合填入空格。I haven't read either of his two letters. 的意思是「他寄來的兩封信我都還沒看。」

7-(D) 前半部的主詞是複數，變成 some say，所以應該選擇對應 some say 的複數不定代名詞。題目的意思是「不同的人說不同的話。」

8-(C) 題目的意思是「應該沒有人是心甘情願賣掉他的股份」。

9-(A) 在題目中 fault 是當作「責任」使用。「Whose fault is it?」的意思是「那是誰的責任？」

10-(C) Which 的意思是「那個人」，也能用來指人。

11-(D) 片語 once and for all 的意思是「最後一次」。for 的後面必須是 all。

12-(C) do you think 是插入句。will be appointed 可以判斷其為述語。空格應該填入主詞，所以選擇主格的 Who。irrigation 的意思是「灌溉」。

13-(A) every 是形容詞，所以在 every 前面不可以加上 of。that（那個）是指示代名詞，前面的句子沒有 that 所指的東西，所以為錯誤答案。another 的意思是「再一個」，是單數的用語，

所以語意上不自然。「～之中的任一個」，即 any 是正確答
案。dip 的意思是「浸一下」。

14-(C) 從文脈來看，空格應該填入「沒有任何～」意思的單字。has
worked 的部份沒有否定詞，所以選擇否定意思的 nothing 是
正確答案。

15-(D) either（任一）在句意上不適合。針對兩件事物不可以用 all。
題目是肯定句，而且 any 在句意上不適合。因此，選擇具有
「兩者都不～」之意的 neither 是正確解答。

16-(B) who 後面的動詞是第三人稱單數現在式，所以 who 的先行詞
必須是單數。They 與 All people 都是複數形。從文脈來看，
空格應該填入具有「任何一個人」之意的單字。選擇 anyone
（無論誰〔放在肯定句中〕）是正確答案。

17-(C) 空格填入接續 are 的主詞，是複數名詞。someone 與 anyone
是單數形，不是正確答案。some 可以用於複數，所以是正
確答案。題目不是疑問句，而且當作關係代名詞也沒有先行
詞，所以 who 也是錯誤答案。

18-(B) 連結 employment 與 wages 的連接詞是 and，所以 both 是正
確答案。

19-(D) two manufacturing plants 是指剩下的兩個東西，所以答案是
the other。

20-(C) 首先掌握住這是疑問句。從 be動詞的位置可以判斷這是使用
疑問詞的疑問句。這是詢問兩個東西中的一個，所以用 which
是正確答案。

# 練習題的中文翻譯

1. 這些太貴了。可以拿便宜一點的給我看嗎？

2. 你想要看看這個嗎？

3. 中看的不一定中用。

4. 我們沒有太多話跟對方講。

5. 她的學生中，沒有人得到獎學金。

6. 他寄來的兩封信我都還沒看。

7. 各說各話。

8. 應該沒有人會心甘情願賣掉他的股份。

9. 那是誰的責任呢？

10. 你是跟那一位客人說話？

11. 巴士司機向上司保證：「這是最後一次，我會戒酒。」

12. 你認為誰會被任命成為這個地區的灌溉計劃領導者？

13. 最新的市立游泳池，游一次泳要 3 塊美金。市內的其它游泳池則是免費。

14. 他為了提高公司的效率嘗試了所有方法，但是沒有一個方法有效。

15. 在會議上提出的兩個提案都沒有被上司採納。

16. 想要應徵 Silver Spring 工廠新職務的求職者，請於五月底以前連絡人事部。

17. 去年的夏天有許多航空公司免費讓兒童搭乘，現在仍有幾家公司提供大幅度的折扣。

18. 強迫雇員負擔醫療費用可減少雇用及薪資。

19. 該公司在中南美洲有兩間製造工廠；一間在墨西哥，另一間在巴西。

20. 這兩個刪減經費的計劃那一個比較有效？

# Note

# 6th Day 形容詞

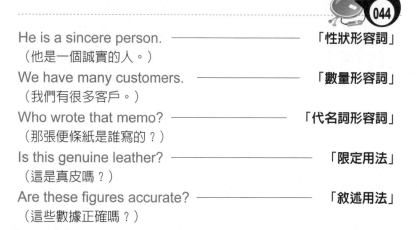

He is a sincere person. ——————— 「性狀形容詞」
（他是一個誠實的人。）

We have many customers. ——————— 「數量形容詞」
（我們有很多客戶。）

Who wrote that memo? ——————— 「代名詞形容詞」
（那張便條紙是誰寫的？）

Is this genuine leather? ——————— 「限定用法」
（這是真皮嗎？）

Are these figures accurate? ——————— 「敘述用法」
（這些數據正確嗎？）

## （1）形容詞的種類

形容詞是用來修飾名詞及代名詞，也可當作動詞的補語。形容詞從意思及用法來看，可以區分為以下三類。

### （a）敘述形容詞

表示人或事物的**性質**、**狀態**、**種類**的形容詞，稱為「**性狀形容詞**」，其中包括非從其它品詞轉變而成的性狀形容詞，這種原本形態便為性狀形容詞的詞，稱為「**敘述形容詞**」。另外，也包含了從專有名詞衍生的「**專有形容詞**」，從動詞的現在分詞、過去分詞衍生的「**分詞形容詞**」，從物質名詞衍生的「**物質形容詞**」。

They are trying to put out a good product. 〔敘述形容詞〕

（他們努力試著生產更優良的產品。）

They are trying to avoid buying **Japanese** products. 〔固有形容詞〕

（他們試著避免購買日本製商品。）

There is a **growing** demand for American cigarettes. 〔分詞形容詞〕

（美國菸的需求增加。）

The **proposed** abolition of the system is a welcome move.
〔分詞形容詞〕

（廢止那項系統的提案是受歡迎的措施。）

**Glass** fiber is used to build boats and car bodies.　〔物質形容詞〕

（玻璃纖維被用於製造船體及車體。）

### （b）數量形容詞

這是表示**數**、**量**、**程度**的形容詞，包括泛指「數」與「量」大小的**「不定數量形容詞」**與**「數詞」**兩種。

There are **many** tax barriers. 〔不定數量形容詞〕

（有許多關稅障礙。）

He doesn't have **much** experience in sales. 〔不定數量形容詞〕

（他沒有什麼業務經驗。）

Japanese employees work an average of **1,853** hours a year.
〔數詞〕

（日本上班族平均一年工作１，８５３個小時。）

### （c）代名詞形容詞

將代名詞當作形容詞使用，包括「**所有格形容詞**」、「**指示形容詞**」、「**不定形容詞**」、「**疑問形容詞**」、「**關係形容詞**」等五種。

Will you take this to **his** office, please? 〔所有格形容詞〕

（可以幫我把這個拿去他的辦公室嗎？）

I need **that** report by the end of the day. 〔指示形容詞〕

（在今天下班前，我需要那份報告書。）

Give him **another** chance. 〔不定形容詞〕

（請再給他一次機會。）

**Which** number should I call? 〔疑問形容詞〕

（我應該打那一支電話號碼？）

I lent him what (little) money I had. 〔關係形容詞〕

（我把僅有的一點錢都借給他了。）

## （2）形容詞的兩種用法

形容詞有兩種用法，第一種是直接接續名詞、代名詞的「**限定用法**」，第二種是當作動詞補語的「**敘述用法**」。大部份的形容詞都是屬於這兩種用法之一。

It's a very **attractive** proposition. 〔限定用法〕

（那是個非常吸引人的提案。）

The proposition is very **attractive**. 〔敘述用法〕

（那個提案非常吸引人。）

## （3）只能使用限定用法的形容詞

### （a）表示上下前後的形容詞

my **elder** [**older**] brother （哥哥）
the **former** president （前社長）
the **latter** half （後半）
the **upper** class （上流階級）
the **lower** class （下層階級）

### （b）表示程度的形容詞

a **mere** child （只是個孩子）
the **only** job （唯一的工作）
the **sole** survivor （唯一的生存者）
**sheer** nonsense （完全胡說八道）

### （c）「名詞＋-en」的形容詞

the **golden** rule （黃金定律）

her **maiden** name （結婚前的姓氏）

a **wooden** table （木頭桌子）

an **earthen** vessel （陶器的器皿）

## （4）只能使用敘述用法的形容詞

許多此類的形容詞以 a 為字首。

| | |
|---|---|
| afraid（害怕的） | aware（知道的） |
| asleep（睡著的） | alone（單獨的） |
| akin（同類的、同族的） | well（健康的） |
| ashamed（羞愧的） | awake（清醒的） |
| alive（活著的） | alike（相似的） |
| worth（有價值的） | content（滿足的） |

## （5）在限定用法與敘述用法時，意思不同的形容詞

The **present** management is not so bad.

（現在的管理沒有那麼糟。）

Our chairman was **present** at the ceremony.

（我們公司董事長出席了典禮。）

I agree with him to a **certain** degree.

（在某個程度上，我同意他的想法。）

I'm **certain of** your success.

（我確信你一定會成功。）

## （6）限定用法中形容詞的位置

### （a）「冠詞或是代名詞形容詞＋形容詞＋名詞」

a major issue （重大的問題）

these new models （這些新型號）

**（b）「冠詞或代名詞形容詞＋數量形容詞＋性狀形容詞＋名詞」**

those two new secretaries（那兩個新任秘書）

**（c）兩個以上的性狀形容詞重複出現時，原則上，依下列順序排列——「①大、小＋②形狀＋③性質、狀態＋④顏色＋⑤年齡、新舊＋⑥材料、專有形容詞」。**

a big black wooden table（又大又黑的木頭桌子）

a tall good-looking young executive（身材高大，長相十分俊俏的年輕董事）

**（d）數量形容詞重複出現時，依照「序數詞＋基數詞」的順序排列**

the first two items on the agenda（議程最前面的兩個事項）

## （7）「the＋形容詞」的用法

### （a）變成表示人物的複數普通名詞

The rich must be considerate of **the poor**.

（有錢人必須體諒貧窮的人。）

其它還有 the young（年輕人）、the old（老年人）、the living（活著的人）、the dead（死者）、the injured（傷者）、the sick（病人）、the wicked（壞人）等等。

〔注意〕「the＋形容詞」被當作對句使用時不加上 the。

Young and old enjoyed the game.

（不論是年輕人還是老年人，都喜歡玩這個遊戲。）

### （b）變成抽象名詞

This hotel has become a symbol of **the elegant** and **refined**.

（這個飯店成為優雅與精緻的象徵。）

### （c）表示事物的部份

She eats only **the lean** of beef.

（她只吃牛肉無脂肪的部位。）

其它還有 the whites of one's eyes（眼白）、the white of an egg（蛋白）、the middle（正中）等等。

## （8）慣用語法

MP3 052

The kidnapper is still **at large**.

（綁架犯還沒被抓到。）

其它還有 in short（總而言之、簡言之）、for certain（肯定地）、for sure（確切地）、in particular（特別地）、for good（永久地）、in general（一般地）、in full（充分地）、before long（不久之後）等等。

## （9）不定數量形容詞的種類

MP3 053

這一類的形容詞，依據後面接續的名詞，可以分為三個種類。

### （a）接續可數名詞的不定數量形容詞

many（多的）                    several（幾個的）
few（少的）

### （b）接續不可數名詞的不定數量形容詞

much（多的）                    little（少的）

### （c）可以接續可數名詞及不可數名詞的不定數量形容詞

some（某些）                    all（所有的）
a lot of（許多）                 plenty of（許多）
more（更多的）                  any（若干）
enough（足夠的）                lots of（許多的）
no（沒有）                       most（最多、大部份的）

## （10）不定數量形容詞的用法

MP3 054

### （a）many 與 much 的用法

many 表示「數」，加在可數名詞的複數形之前。much 表示「量」與「程度」，加在不可數名詞之前。

Smoking is forbidden in **many** public places.

（許多公共場所已經禁菸。）

I didn't pay **much** attention to what he said.

（我沒有注意聽他說的話。）

### （b）few, a few, little, a little 的用法

**Few** people realized the importance of the matter.

（幾乎沒有人發現事情的重要性。）

I've been to your country **a few** times.

（我去過你的國家幾次。）

**Quite a few** people participated in the workshop.

（有相當多的人參加講習會。）

**Not a few** people donated their blood to the child.

（為了那個小孩，有很多人捐血。）

It will have **little** effect on gas prices.

（這對於汽油的價格根本沒什麼影響。）

There is still **a little** hope.

（仍有一絲希望。）

**Not a little** effort was put forth to accomplish the task.

（花了很大的心力達成那個任務。）

### （c）some 與 any 的用法

I'd like to ask **some** personal questions.

（我想要問一些私人的問題。）

I really need **some** sleep.

（我真的需要一些睡眠。）

I haven't received **any** reports on it.

（我沒有收到任何關於該事件的報告。）

Do you have **any** information on it?

（你有任何關於那個事件的資訊嗎？）

If you have **any** suggestions, please let me know.

（如果你有任何建議，請提出來。）

〔注意〕any 表示「無論～都可以」、「任何的」時，可以用在肯定
句。

**Any** plan will do.

（任何計劃都可以。）

I'll take **any** job.

（無論什麼工作我都願意做。）

### （d）enough 的用法

enough 的意思是「足夠的」，可以接續可數名詞，也可以接續不可
數名詞。可以放在名詞前面，也可以放在名詞後面，不過放在名詞
前面時，是強調的用法。

We have **enough** chairs for the guests.
We have chairs **enough** for the guests.

（我們已經有足夠的椅子給客人坐。）

We have **enough** gas to get there.

（我們有足夠的汽油開到那裡。）

### （e）no 的用法

no 表示「沒有」、「很少」時，可以接續可數名詞或是不可數名詞
其中一個。

There is **no** rule without exceptions.

（有規則必有例外。）

He's got **no** brains.

（他腦筋不好。）

There's **no** hurry.

（沒有必要著急。）

## （11）數詞的種類

數詞包括表示「數量」的基數詞，與表示「順序」的序數詞。

one, two, three, four, five 〔基數詞〕

first, second, third, fourth, fifth 〔序數詞〕

The company laid off about **150** employees.

（公司資遣１５０名員工。）

The company went into the red for the **first** time in **20** years.

（公司２０年來第一次出現赤字。）

## （12）包含基數詞的表現

### （a）數字等級的唸法

hundred（100） million（一百萬）

thousand（1,000） billion（十億）

123 = one hundred (and) twenty-three

5,678,901 = five million, six hundred (and) seventy-eight thousand, nine hundred (and) one

### （b）小數點的唸法

小數點唸作 point，小數點以下的數字，只要一個一個照數字唸法唸出即可。

0.3 = (zero) point three

23.45 = twenty-three point four five

### （c）年號的唸法

以１００的等級與１０的等級為區隔唸出來。

1900 = nineteen hundred
1993 = nineteen ninety-three
2000 = two thousand

### （d）時間的唸法

3:00 = three o'clock
4:15 = four fifteen 或是 a quarter past four
5:30 = five thirty 或是 half past five
6:45 = six forty-five 或是 a quarter to seven

### （e）電話號碼的唸法

一個一個照數字唸法唸出即可。

03-3456-7089 = oh **[zero]**, three, **(pause)** three, four, five, six, **(pause)** seven, oh **[zero]**, eight, nine

### （f）溫度的唸法

28℃ = twenty-eight degrees Celsius [centigrade]
75°F = seventy-five degrees Fahrenheit

## （13）包含序數詞的表現

### （a）分數的唸法

1／2 = a half 或是 one-half
1／3 = a third 或是 one-third
2／3 = two-thirds
3　4／5 = three and four-fifths

### （b）日期的唸法

7月3日 = July (the) third 或是 the third of July

### （14）慣用語法

#### （a）泛指多數

They collected **thousands of** empty cans.

（他們收集了幾千個空罐。）

其它還有 dozens of...（幾十個）、scores of...（幾十個）、hundreds of...（幾百個）、millions of...（幾百萬個）等等。

#### （b）表示年代

表示年代時，把１０的等級變成複數。

He is still in his **thirties**.

（他現在仍是三十幾歲。）

It became popular in the **1960s** [nineteen sixties].

（那是１９６０年代開始流行的。）

#### （c）基數詞用連字號接續單數名詞以修飾其它名詞。

They started a **three-year** program.

（他們開始進行三年計劃。）

# 練習題

請在以下各題目的(A),(B),(C),(D)之中選出最適合的答案填入空格之中。

**1. There has been _____ discussion within the government.**

    (A) many                (B) any

    (C) a few              (D) no

**2. I'd be very happy to come down to your office _____ time.**

    (A) any                 (B) no

    (C) other               (D) most

**3. That's the _____ thing I want you to do.**

    (A) late                (B) later

    (C) last                (D) latter

**4.The automaker reported that it lost a _____ $4.5 billion in 2005.**

    (A) record            (B) recording

    (C) recorded        (D) recorder

**5. Is it a _____ concert?**

    (A) life                (B) live

    (C) living             (D) alive

**6. He gave away _____ money he had earned.**

    (A) quite a few      (B) such a

    (C) which           (D) what

**7. _____ information was gathered on the microcomputer.**

    (A) A few           (B) Not a few

    (C) Quite a lot of    (D) Dozens of

8. The _____ were taken to several local hospitals, both civilian and military.
   (A) wound
   (B) wounds
   (C) wounding
   (D) wounded

9. We cannot make a prediction, as we do not have _____ information.
   (A) sufficiency
   (B) suffice
   (C) sufficient
   (D) sufficiently

10. In _____, people spend too much time watching TV.
    (A) a general
    (B) the general
    (C) general
    (D) generally

11. In addition to chocolate, Goldman Co. makes cereal, cheese, and _____ of other items.
    (A) hundred
    (B) hundreds
    (C) one
    (D) dozen of

12. By one estimate, as many as 10% of _____ business trips include children.
    (A) another
    (B) each
    (C) some
    (D) all

13. Most attendees at the _____ conference were environmentalists.
    (A) two days
    (B) two-day
    (C) two-days
    (D) someday

14. No _____ explanation for the planned pay cut was given by the management.
    (A) convince
    (B) conviction
    (C) convinced
    (D) convincing

15. There is _____ possibility that his employer might hire someone to replace him.
    (A) few                (B) little
    (C) many              (D) plenty

16. The _____ output of the new production line is 1,000 units.
    (A) hourly            (B) hours
    (C) hour               (D) by hour

17. Brown Woodhouse, the San Francisco-based accounting firm, has named _____ in its Washington office.
    (A) new four partners   (B) four partners new
    (C) four new partners   (D) new partners four

18.        We have already received _____ telephone calls inquiring about the new product.
    (A) number        (B) numbers
    (C) numerous     (D) numerously

19. Will you inform me of the _____ status of affairs?
    (A) present       (B) presenting
    (C) presentation   (D) presented

20. "Initial employment could be _____ hundred workers," said the vice president at the meeting.
    (A) few            (B) enough
    (C) much          (D) several

# 正確解答

1-(D) no 可以修飾單數名詞及複數名詞。

2-(A) any time 的意思是「隨時」。

3-(C) 題目的意思是「那是我最不希望你做的事」。

4-(A) record 當作形容詞使用時，意思是「創記錄的」。

5-(B) 請注意 concert 是演唱會。live concert 是「現場演唱會」。

6-(D) 題目的意思是「他把賺到的錢全都捐贈出來」。

7-(C) information 是不可數名詞。

8-(D) 「the＋形容詞」表示「複數的人」。the wounded 是「傷者」。

9-(C) 選擇意思是「足夠」的形容詞。

10-(C) in general 的意思是「一般的」，請注意不要加冠詞。

11-(B) 請務必了解 hundreds of...（幾百的）的片語。(D) 如果是 dozens of...（數十的）的話，也是正確解答。

12-(D) 空格之後接續複數形的 business trips，所以表示單數的 another 與 each 都不是正確答案。從句意來看，some 不適合。

13-(B) 填入空格的詞必須可以用來修飾 conference。形容詞 two-day 的意思是「兩天的」。由於有連字號，所以 day 不變成複數形。

14-(D) 在空格填入修飾 explanation 的詞。convinced 是過去分詞，具有被動意味，convincing 是現在分詞，具有主動意味。從句意（有說服力的）來看，選擇 convincing 為正確答案。

15-(B) possibility 是單數形，所以 little 是正確答案。few 與 many 接續複數名詞。沒有 plenty possibility 這種說法。

16-(A) 在空格之前有 The，在空格之後有 output of...，所以填入空

格的必須是修飾 output 的詞。形容詞 hourly 以 -ly 結尾，意思是「每小時的」。

17-(C) 依據「數量形容詞＋性狀形容詞＋名詞」的詞序，four new partners 是正確答案。

18-(C) 只有 numerous 是形容詞。

19-(A) the present status of affairs 是指「現在的狀態」。就意思來說，presenting 及 presented 都不適合。

20-(D) several hundred 的意思是「數百的」。沒有 few hundred workers 以及 enough hundred workers 這種說法。much 是用來修飾不可數名詞。

6

# 練習題的中文翻譯

1. 在政府內部沒有進行任何討論。

2. 隨時樂意到您的辦公室拜訪。

3. 那是我最不希望你做的事。

4. 那間汽車公司宣告於２００５年創記錄虧損４５億日幣。

5. 那是現場演唱會嗎？

6. 他將賺到的錢全部捐贈給別人。

7. 在那台微電腦上收集非常多的資訊。

8. 傷者被送到當地的幾個民間以及軍方醫院。

9. 我們無法預測，因為沒有足夠的資訊。

10. 一般來說，人們浪費太多時間在看電視上。

11. Goldman 公司除了巧克力以外，還生產麥片、乳酪等其它幾百種商品。

12. 根據某項估算，所有出差旅行的人當中，有１０％的人會帶著小孩。

13. 為期兩天的會議，出席者大部份是環境保護論者。

14. 針對薪資被刪減，經營團隊沒有提出任何有說服力的說明。

15. 他的雇主幾乎不可能雇用其它人來取代他。

16. 新的生產線每個小時的產量是一千個。

17. 總公司位於舊金山的 Brown Woodhouse 會計師事務所，已經在華盛頓分公司任命四名新合夥人。

18. 我們已經接到許多針對這項新產品的詢問電話。

19. 可以告訴我現在的狀況嗎？

20. 副總裁在會議上說：「一開始的雇用人數將達到數百人」。

# Note

# 7th Day 副詞

I sometimes go to work by car.
（我有時會開車去上班。）

Can I park my car here?
（我可以把車停在這裡嗎？）

When does the contract expire?
（合約的截止日是什麼時候？）

## （1）依據用法分類的副詞種類

副詞主要是用來修飾動詞、形容詞以及其它副詞的詞。依據用法來區分，可分為「**普通副詞**」、「**疑問副詞**」、「**關係副詞**」三個種類。

### （a）普通副詞

普通副詞是除了疑問副詞及關係副詞以外的副詞，大部份的副詞都屬於普通副詞。

This copy machine **often** breaks down.

（這台影印機經常故障。）

### （b）疑問副詞

表示疑問的副詞，包括 when, where, why, how 等等。

**Where** are you going to meet him?

（你要去哪裡見他？）

### （c）關係副詞

兼具連接詞作用的副詞，包括 when, where, why, how 等等。針對關係副詞的部份，將會在12th Day 的關係詞中詳細說明。

This is the house **where** John F. Kennedy was born.

（這間房子是約翰・F・甘迺迪出生的地方。）

## （2）依據意思分類的副詞種類

依據意思之不同，可將副詞分類如下：

**表示時間的副詞**：now, ago, before, early, soon, recently, yesterday 等等。

**表示場所的副詞**：here, there, near, far, up, down, somewhere 等等。

**表示頻率的副詞**：sometimes, often, always, again, seldom, rarely 等等。

**表示量、程度的副詞**：only, very, much, too, enough, little, almost 等等。

**表示狀態的副詞**：well, fast, quickly, slowly, kindly, fluently 等等。

**表示順序的副詞**：first, second(ly), third(ly), next, last 等等。

**表示理由、結果的副詞**：therefore, so, consequently, accordingly 等等。

**表示肯定、否定的副詞**：yes, no, not, certainly, perhaps, maybe 等等。

**表示讓步的副詞**：anyway, anyhow, however, nevertheless 等等。

## （3）副詞的用法

副詞主要是用來修飾動詞、形容詞以及其它的副詞，此外，有時也能修飾名詞、代名詞、片語、子句或整個句子。

### （a）修飾動詞

The economy is **slowly** recovering.

（景氣正慢慢地恢復。）

**（b）修飾形容詞**

You are **absolutely** right.

（你說的完全正確。）

**（c）修飾副詞**

The negotiation is going **very** well.

（談判進行非常順利。）

**（d）修飾名詞**

**Even** John could not persuade him.

（即使是約翰也無法說服他。）

**（e）修飾代名詞**

**Only** he can use the computer.

（只有他才能使用那台電腦。）

**（f）修飾片語**

We are very busy, **especially** in the afternoon.

（我們很忙，特別是下午的時候。）

**（g）修飾子句**

She quit her job **simply** because she didn't like her boss.

（她辭掉工作，只因為她不喜歡她的上司。）

**（h）修飾整個句子**

**Probably** the economy will improve this year.

（或許今年景氣就會好轉。）

## （4）副詞的詞形

### （a）「形容詞＋ly」

The company finally went bankrupt.

（這家公司終於破產了。）

其它還有 kindly, safely, simply, easily, fully, truly, probably 等等。

### （b）與形容詞同形的副詞

It's **hard** work. 〔形容詞〕

（這是很難的工作。）

He worked very **hard**. 〔副詞〕

（他很努力工作。）

其它還有 early（早的、提早）、fast（快的、快）、late（遲的、遲到）、long（長的、長久地）、daily（每日的、每日）等等。

### （c）同時具有與形容詞同形，以及以「形容詞＋-ly」呈現的兩種詞形，但意思卻不同的副詞。

He tried very **hard** to please her.

（他拚命地取悅她。）

I **hardly** knew him.

（我幾乎不清楚他的事。）

其它還有 late（遲到）－ lately（最近）、high（高）－ highly（非常地）、pretty（相當）－ prettily（漂亮地）等等。

## （5）副詞的位置

句子中副詞擺放的位置相當自由，不過大致上依據下述原則排列：

### （a）修飾形容詞、副詞、片語、子句時，副詞位置放在被修飾詞之前。

We were **very** lucky.

（我們非常幸運。）

He finished the work **quite** fast.

（他非常快地完成了工作。）

She came **just** before the lunch break.

（剛好在午休前她到了。）

**但是，enough 修飾形容詞、副詞時，放在被修飾詞之後。**

A week is long **enough** to finish the work.

（一個星期的時間足以完成那項工作。）

She didn't run fast **enough** to catch the train.

（她跑得不夠快，所以趕不上電車。）

**（b）表示狀態的副詞修飾動詞時，將副詞放在動詞之後，不過動詞有受詞時，則可將副詞放在動詞之前。**

They argued **loudly**.

（他們大聲地爭吵。）

She studied it **carefully**.
She **carefully** studied it.

（她仔細地研究這個東西。）

**（c）表示頻率以及否定的副詞 sometimes, usually, often, always, constantly, seldom, scarcely, hardly, never 等副詞修飾動詞時，將副詞放置在動詞之前。**

有 be 動詞與助動詞時，則將副詞放在動詞之後。

I **usually** drink tea in the morning.

（我通常在早上喝紅茶。）

He is **seldom** at home on weekends.

（他週末幾乎都不在家。）

She has **almost** finished her work.

（她的工作幾乎已經完成了。）

**（d）not, never, always 等副詞修飾不定詞時，將副詞放置在不定詞之前。**

He told her **not** to call him at his office.

（他告訴她不要打電話到他的辦公室找他。）

**（e）以「動詞＋副詞」片語形式出現的「及物動詞」將代名詞當作受詞時，將代名詞放置在動詞與副詞之間。**

She **turned** it **on**.

（她把它打開了。）

**（f）有表示時間與場所（片語）的副詞時，依照「場所＋時間」的順序排列**

I'll meet you **in the lobby at nine o'clock**.

（我們九點在大廳見面。）

**（6）應該注意的副詞用法**

**（a）very 與 much**

very 修飾形容詞、副詞、現在分詞、原級。much 修飾動詞、過去分詞、比較級、最高級。

She is **very** considerate. 〔形容詞〕

（她非常體貼。）

She spoke **very** fast. 〔副詞〕

（她說話非常快。）

I don't like her attitude **much**. 〔動詞〕

（我非常不喜歡她的態度。）

His idea is **very** interesting. 〔現在分詞〕

（他的想法非常有趣。）

I'm **much** obliged to you. 〔過去分詞〕

（非常感謝你。）

但是，如果是 tired, pleased, excited, worried 等形容詞化的過去分詞，一般是使用 very 來修飾。

He was very tired.

（他非常疲倦。）

This printer is very **small**. 〔原級〕

（這台印表機非常小。）

This printer is **much** smaller than that one. 〔比較級〕

（這台印表機遠比那一台小。）

Jim is **much** the smartest boy in the class. 〔最高級〕

（吉姆是班上最聰明的男孩。）

〔注意〕very 與 much 一樣可以修飾最高級，但是必須特別注意「the very＋最高級」與「much the＋最高級」的詞序不同。

Jim is the **very** smartest boy in the class.

（吉姆是班上最聰明的男孩。）

### （b）ago 與 before

ago 是以現在為基點，表示「在（現在）之前」，使用過去式。
before 是以過去或是未來某個時間點為基點，表示「在（那時候）之前」，使用過去完成式或是未來式。before 單獨被使用時表示「目前為止的過去」或是「在過去某個時間點之前」，分別可以使用過去式、現在完成式、過去完成式。

He left the office ten minutes **ago**. 〔過去〕

（他在十分鐘之前離開辦公室。）

Yesterday I found out that she had left the apartment a week **before**. 〔過去完成式〕

（昨天我才發現，她在一星期之前已經離開公寓。）

I (have) met him **before**. 〔過去、現在完成式〕

（我以前遇見過他。）

He said he had met her **before**. 〔過去完成式〕

（他說他以前遇見過她。）

〔注意〕被單獨使用的 since，使用現在完成式時，表示「從那時候開始到現在」。

She moved to Chicago last year, and I haven't heard from her **since**.

（去年她搬到芝加哥。從那時開始，我就沒有聽過她的消息。）

〔注意〕ago 不能被單獨使用。

**(c) still, yet, already**

still 的意思是「仍然、還」，表示持續。

She's **still** talking on the phone.

（她還在講電話。）

yet 的意思是「已經……了嗎？」、「還沒……」，分別用於疑問句及否定句。

Has the president arrived **yet**?

（總裁已經到了嗎？）

The buyer hasn't come **yet**.

（買家還沒來。）

在肯定句中，yet 與 still 意思幾乎一樣，這時候 yet 的意思是「依然還沒……」，表示未完成的意思。

This issue is **yet** to be discussed.

（這個議題還沒有被討論。）

already 的意思是「已經……」，表示完成，用於肯定句。有時候也會用於疑問句，用來表示驚訝，意思是「已經做……了嗎？」

The conference has **already** started.

（會議已經開始了。）

Have the results come out **already**?

（結果已經出來了嗎？）

### （d）too 與 either

too 的意思是「也」，用於肯定句。either 的意思是「也不～」，用於否定句。

I can drive, and she can drive **too**.

（我會開車，她也會開車。）

I can't drive, and she can't drive **either**.

（我不會開車，她也不會開車。）

### （e）just 與 just now

just 的意思是「剛好」，用於現在式與現在完成式。just now 的意思是「剛才」，用於現在式與過去式。通常 just now 不能被用於現在完成式。

The movie is **just** starting.

（電影剛好開始。）

The movie has **just** started.

（電影才剛開始。）

Mr. Scott is very busy **just now**.

（史考特先生現在非常忙碌。）

Mr. Scott came in **just now**.

（史考特先生才剛到。）

## 練習題

請在以下各題目的(A),(B),(C),(D)之中選出最適合的答案填入空格之中。

**1. Things are _____ looking up.**

    (A) general              (B) generality

    (C) generate            (D) generally

**2. We need to watch the financial market _____.**

    (A) just                 (B) closely

    (C) nearby             (D) hard

**3. These rooms are _____ for executives.**

    (A) exclusive          (B) excluding

    (C) exclusively       (D) exclusion

**4. The new system is working _____ well.**

    (A) pretty              (B) prettily

    (C) much              (D) approximately

**5. They haven't come to a conclusion _____.**

    (A) just now          (B) never

    (C) yet                 (D) ago

**6. More than 20,000 Japanese now travel between the two countries _____ via Hong Kong, Bangkok, or Singapore.**

    (A) annually         (B) annual

    (C) recently          (D) lately

**7. I'm kind of busy today. Can you come _____ away?**

    (A) immediately     (B) right

    (C) soon              (D) shortly

**8. They are _____ drunk or crazy.**

    (A) once              (B) either

    (C) neither           (D) nor

9. I _____ had time to prepare for my presentation.
    (A) slight              (B) shortly
    (C) hard               (D) scarcely

10. The value of the property is _____ to be assessed.
    (A) yet                (B) sometimes
    (C) final              (D) very

11. The visitors were asked to turn off their cellular phones, but some of them _____.
    (A) left on them     (B) left them
    (C) left them on     (D) left to it

12. The new office on Sunset Ave. is _____ more spacious than the one on Canon Dr.
    (A) much           (B) so
    (C) such          (D) very

13. He is a famous financial advisor as well as a best-selling author. I have attended one of his workshops _____.
    (A) before        (B) previous
    (C) ago          (D) last year

14. Mr. Lee was _____ to achieve the target when he was appointed to the job.
    (A) enough confidence  (B) confidence enough
    (C) confidently enough  (D) confident enough

15. The construction company is regarded _____ likely to win the bid.
    (A) high         (B) highly
    (C) height       (D) higher

16. The new system is known for its _____ high efficiency and relatively low cost.
    - (A) comparative
    - (B) compare
    - (C) comparison
    - (D) comparatively

17. There are some scratches in the windshield, but they are _____ noticeable.
    - (A) hardly
    - (B) hardness
    - (C) hard
    - (D) hardened

18. The soft drink maker _____ stopped supplying all public schools with its sugar-sweetened soft drink.
    - (A) volunteer
    - (B) voluntary
    - (C) volunteering
    - (D) voluntarily

19. The guide told the group of students _____ exhibits in the museum.
    - (A) touch not to
    - (B) to not touch
    - (C) not to touch
    - (D) touch to not

20. The electronics company has set up a wholly owned subsidiary in Malaysia _____.
    - (A) ago
    - (B) last month
    - (C) recently
    - (D) just now

7

# 正確解答

1-(D) 題目的意思是「局勢大體來說有起色」。generally 的意思是「一般地、如往常地」。

2-(B) financial market 是「金融市場」。closely 是「仔細地、嚴密地」。

3-(C) 選項中只有 exclusively 是副詞，意思是「排他的、獨佔地」。

4-(A) pretty 當作副詞時，意思是「相當」。而 prettily 是「可愛地、適合地」。

5-(C) 否定句中的 yet 是「尚未」的意思。

6-(A) annually 的意思是「每年一次、每年」。recently 與 lately 通常不用於現在式的動詞。

7-(B) 片語 right away 的意思是「馬上」。

8-(B) eithe...or... 的意思是「……或者……、不是……就是……」。

9-(D) 在空格填入修飾動詞 had 的詞。只有表示「幾乎沒有」的副詞 scarcely 為適合的答案。

10-(A) 被用於肯定句的 yet 表示「仍然、還沒」，具有未完成的意思。property 是「財產」，assess 是「估價」。

11-(C) 當作受詞的代名詞，放在動詞與副詞之間。

12-(A) 請注意這是比較級的句子。修飾比較級時使用 much。

13-(A) 這是完成式的句子，不可以用 ago 以及 last year。形容詞 previous 的意思是「之前的」。

14-(D) enough 修飾形容詞、副詞時，放在被修飾詞之後。

15-(B) 副詞 highly 的意思是「非常」。從句意來看，空格的部份應該填入修飾likely（很可能）的詞。選項中只有 highly 是副詞，可以用來修飾形容詞。

16-(D) 空格應該填入修飾 high（高的）的詞。副詞 comparatively 的意思是「比較地」，可以用來修飾形容詞。

17-(A) 空格填入修飾 noticeable（顯而易見的〔形容詞〕）的詞。選項中只有副詞 hardly（幾乎沒有）是適合的詞。

18-(D) 接續在空格之後的是動詞 stopped，所以空格應該填入副詞。voluntarily（自發性地）是副詞。

19-(C) 副詞修飾不定詞時，副詞放置在不定詞之前。成為 not to...的詞序。

20-(C) 題目是完成式的句子，所以不可以用 ago, last month, just now。

7

# 練習題的中文翻譯

1. 局勢大體來說有起色。
2. 我們必須仔細留意金融市場。
3. 這些房間是董事們專用的。
4. 新系統運轉地非常順利。
5. 他們還沒有達成結論。
6. 現在每年有超過二萬名的日本人,在旅行兩個國家時,會經由香港、曼谷或新加坡轉機。
7. 我今天有點忙。你可以馬上過來嗎?
8. 他們不是喝醉了就是瘋了。
9. 我幾乎沒有時間準備簡報。
10. 那項資產的價值還在估算中。
11. 訪客被要求關閉他們的手機,但是有一部份訪客仍然開著手機。
12. 在日落街的新辦公室比在卡農大道的辦公室還更寬敞。
13. 他不僅是暢銷作家,也是著名的投資顧問。我以前曾經參加過他的研討會。
14. 李先生被任命這項工作時,十分有自信能達成目標。
15. 這家建設公司被認為很有可能得標。
16. 那項新系統以較好的效率及較低的價格而聞名。
17. 擋風玻璃雖然有幾處擦傷,不過並不明顯。
18. 那間清涼飲料製造商,主動停止供應其生產的含糖飲料給全部公立學校。
19. 警衛告訴學生們不要用手觸摸博物館的展示品。
20. 那間電子公司最近在馬來西亞設立百分之百獨資的子公司。

# Note

# 8th Day | 比較級

This material is as hard as a diamond.
（這個物質跟鑽石一樣硬。）

Americans are more competitive than Japanese.
（美國人比日本人競爭意識更強烈。）

Japan is the most peaceful country in the world.
（日本是世界上最和平的國家。）

形容詞與副詞比較其性質、狀態、數量差異時，詞形會有所變化。
比較式的詞形變化，可以區分為「**原級**」、「**比較級**」、「**最高
級**」三個種類。

## （1）規則的比較變化

### （a）變成 -er, -est 的詞形

一個音節（發音的母音數量只有一個）的單字、兩個音節，但語尾
是以 -er, -le, -ly, -y, -ow 結尾的詞、重音落在後面兩個音節的單字變
成比較級時，語尾會變成 -er，表最高級時，語尾則變成 -est。

tall, taller, tallest（高的）

fast, faster, fastest（快的）

clever, cleverer, cleverest（聰明的）

humble, humbler, humblest（謙遜的）

early, earlier, earliest（早的）

narrow, narrower, narrowest（狹窄的）

〔注意〕以-e 結尾的單字加上 -r, -st（例如：safe, safer, safest）。
以「單母音＋子音」結束的單字則重覆子音、加上 -er,
-est（例如：big, bigger, biggest）。以「子音＋y」結尾

的單字將 y 改成 i，再加上 -er, -est（例如：busy, busier, busiest）。

## （b）加上 more, most 的單字

兩個音節且以 -ful, -less, -ous, -ive, -ing, -ish, -ed 結尾的單字、三個音節以上的單字、除了 early 以外的以 -ly 結尾的副詞，在原級之前加上 more, most，則變成比較級與最高級。

careful, more careful, most careful（仔細地）
careless, more careless, most careless（不小心地）
famous, more famous, most famous（有名的）
active, more active, most active（活潑的）
expensive, more expensive, most expensive（貴的）
slowly, more slowly, most slowly（緩慢地）

## （2）不規則的比較變化

8

不規則的比較變化有以下幾個單字：
good, better, best（好的）
well, better, best（健康的、精通的）
bad, worse, worst（壞的）
ill, worse, worst（生病的、惡意的）
many, more, most（多的）
much, more, most（多的、非常）
little, less, least（少的、幾乎沒有）

## （3）擁有兩個不同變化形態的單字

old, older, oldest（年齡）
old, elder, eldest（兄弟間的年長、年幼）
late, later, latest（時間）
late, latter, last（順序）
far, farther, farthest（距離）
far, further, furthest（程度、距離）

〔注意〕在口語上，farther 與 further 大多被當作相同的詞意使用。

## （4）使用原級的句型

### （a）as＋原級＋as（和～一樣……）

California is **as big as** many countries.

（加州和許多國家一樣大。）

### （b）not as＋原級＋as（不如……）

He does **not** work **as hard as** he used to (work).

（他不像以前一樣努力工作。）

### （c）...times as＋原級＋as（～是～的…倍）

The United States is about **25 times as big as** Japan.

（美國大約是日本的２５倍大。）

### （d）as＋原級＋as possible [as one can]（盡可能～）

Start working on it **as soon as possible**.

（盡可能快一點進行那件工作。）

Compile the news **as fast as you can**.

（請盡可能快一點編輯新聞。）

### （e）nothing [no (other)＋名詞]is as＋原級＋as（沒有比～更～）

**Nothing is as important** as education.

（沒有什麼比教育更重要。）

**No (other) employee** in this section **works as hard as** Jack.

（在這個部門裡沒有比傑克更努力工作的人。）

### （f）as＋原級＋as ever（依舊）

He is **as busy as ever**.

（他依舊很忙。）

（g）as＋原級＋as any (other)（完全不亞於～、十分、非常）

It was **as good** a factory **as any**.

（這是一間非常好的工廠。）

（h）not so much A as B（與其說是 A，不如說是 B）

He is **not so much** a writer **as** a businessman.

（與其說他是作家，不如說他是一個商人。）

**（5）使用比較級的句型**

**（a）比較級＋than（比～還～）**

John is **more aggressive than** Jim.

（約翰比吉姆還積極。）

Mary can type **faster than** Nancy.

（瑪麗打字速度比南希快。）

This watch is **more expensive than** that one by 20 dollars

（這支手錶比那支貴２０美金。）

This watch is 20 dollars **more expensive than** that one.

（這支手錶比那支貴２０美金。）

**（b）superior [inferior, senior, junior] + to**

（優於～〔劣於、年長於、年少於〕）

German cars are **superior to** Japanese cars in many ways.

（德國汽車在許多方面都優於日本車。）

**（c）比較級＋than any other＋單數名詞（比其它任何一個都～）**

Jack is **more diligent than any other employee** in this section.

（傑克比這個部門裡的其他員工更勤勉。）

(d) no (other)＋名詞＋is＋比較級＋than（沒有比～更～）

**No other secretary** in the personnel section **is more efficient than** Mary.

（在人事課裡，沒有比瑪麗做事更有效率的秘書。）

(e) nothing is＋比較級＋than（沒有什麼比～更～）

**Nothing is more important than** health.

（沒有什麼比健康更重要。）

(f) 比較級＋and＋比較級（越來越～、逐漸）

Business is getting **worse and worse**.

（景氣越來越差。）

(g) less＋原級＋than（比～還不～）

Going by train **is less expensive than** going by plane.

（坐火車去比坐飛機更便宜。）

（6）使用最高級的句型

(a) the＋最高級＋of all [in]....（在～之中是最～）

Mr. Johnson is **the most decisive of all** the executives.

（強生先生是所有的董事中最果決的一個。）

Mr. Gates is **the richest** man in the U.S.

（蓋茲先生是美國最有錢的人。）

(b) the＋序數詞＋最高級（表示第幾名）

This is **the second tallest** building in Japan.

（這是日本第二高的建築物。）

〔注意〕以下情況在最高級上不加 the：

(c) 副詞的最高級

I like your proposal **best**.

（我最喜歡你的提案。）

在現代的英語中有時候會加上 the。

I like your proposal **the best**.

**（d）針對同一個人或物，比較部份時的最高級。**

The swimming pool is **deepest** here.

（游泳池這裡是最深的。）

Jack is **happiest** when he is working.

（傑克在工作時覺得最快樂。）

**（e）將 most 當作「大致上的、大部份的」的意思使用時**

**Most** female workers in this office have no wish to be promoted.

（在這個辦公室裡的女性大部份不期望可以晉升。）

**（f）當作「非常地」表示強烈意思的最高級**

This is a **most** important matter.

（這是非常重要的問題。）

8

# 練習題

請在以下各題目的(A),(B),(C),(D)之中選出最適合的答案填入空格之中。

**1. I'd like to see as _____ samples as possible.**

    (A) more                (B) most

    (C) many              (D) a lot of

**2. Japanese workers' wages are among the _____ in the world.**

    (A) high                (B) highest

    (C) most highly       (D) as high

**3. Japanese companies must be _____ aggressive in pursuing market share.**

    (A) less                (B) worse

    (C) little              (D) far

**4. The drop is the second _____ in the company's history.**

    (A) most               (B) largest

    (C) low                (D) worse

**5. Major-leaguers are _____ skilled than professional baseball players in Japan.**

    (A) most               (B) more highly

    (C) highest           (D) most highly

**6. Some experts say the problem may have become _____ than expected.**

    (A) worse             (B) bad

    (C) little              (D) least

7. The new model can process visual information twice as _____ as the old model.

    (A) faster             (B) fastest

    (C) very fast        (D) fast

8. Industrial production showed the _____ growth in five years.

    (A) as low as       (B) low

    (C) lower than      (D) lowest

9. The German and Japanese markets are _____ to our operation.

    (A) further important    (B) most important

    (C) importance       (D) less important than

10. Japanese goods are _____ competitive on world markets than those produced in the West.

    (A) very            (B) most likely

    (C) most            (D) more

11. The company spokesman went no _____ than stating its current financial plight.

    (A) far              (B) further

    (C) as far as        (D) furthest

12. Buyers may find _____ homes on the market that appeal to them than last year.

    (A) little          (B) few

    (C) fewer         (D) fewest

13. The per capita GNP of the Japanese people is one of the _____ in the world.

    (A) height        (B) high

    (C) higher        (D) highest

8

14. The company's losses in the second quarter were _____ than the previous quarter.

    (A) bad              (B) too bad

    (C) worse          (D) worst

15. Buying a new car consistently ranks as one of the _____ enjoyable experiences people have to go through.

    (A) little            (B) less

    (C) lesser          (D) least

16. The hurricane was described as the _____ natural disaster to strike the country in its history.

    (A) badness        (B) worse

    (C) worst          (D) bad

17. The net profit of Pamko Inc. , leading supplier of sporting goods, had jumped more _____ twofold over a year earlier.

    (A) to              (B) from

    (C) than           (D) through

18. According to a new survey, a woman's workweek is now half a day _____ than it was five years ago.

    (A) long            (B) longer

    (C) longest        (D) length

19. The chief director's salary is five times as _____ as the sales manager's.

    (A) bigness        (B) big

    (C) bigger         (D) biggest

20. _____ married female workers carry the double burden of work outside the home and inside the home.

    (A) Most           (B) More

    (C) The most      (D) At most

# 正確解答

1-(C) as many... as possible 的意思是「盡可能更多的……」。

2-(B) 從 the... in the world（在世界上）可以知道這是最高級的句子。wages 是「工資」。

3-(A) aggressive 的意思是「積極的、攻擊的」。less...than 的意思是「不比～還～」，表示劣等比較。題目是省略了 than they are now。

4-(B) the second largest 的意思是「第二大的」。

5-(B) 句子中有 than，所以使用比較級。副詞 highly是「高度地、非常」。

6-(A) 句子中有 than，所以使用 bad 的比較級 worse。

7-(D) 比較句型 twice as... as 的意思是「兩倍……」。as 與 as 之間使用原級。

8-(D) 從 in five years（在五年之間）可以看出這是最高級表現句型。

9-(B) 在句中沒有 the，所以 most important 是正確答案。這個時候的最高級是「非常地」的意思。

10-(D) 因為有 than，所以可以先把句子當作是比較級。

11-(B) 因為在空格之後馬上出現 than，由此可以判斷這是使用比較級的句子。far 的比較級是 further。

12-(C) 在句中有 than，可以判斷這是使用比較級的句子。fewer 是 few 的比較級。

13-(D) 在空格前後出現 one of the... in the world，所以可以判斷這是使用最高級的句子。highest 是 high 的最高級。

14-(C) 在空格之後馬上出現 than，可以判斷這是使用比較級的句子。bad 的比較級是 worse。

15-(D) 只要看選項，就能了解這是比較的題目。在比較的題目中只
要句中有 one of the...，十之八九一定是最高級的句子。

16-(C) 句中有 in its history（史上），所以很容易可以判斷出這是使
用最高級的句子。

17-(C) 句中有比較級 more，所以空格填入 than。

18-(B) 請注意，在空格之後馬上出現 than，所以空格應該填入比較
級。

19-(B) as... as 之間填入原級。

20-(A) 從句意可以明白這並不是比較的句子。most 當作最高級使用
時，意思是「最」，修飾名詞時意思是「大部份的」。在本
題中後者的用法是正確解答。但是，在這個用法中不加冠詞
（不使用 the）。

8

# 練習題的中文翻譯

1. 我想盡可能多看一些樣品。
2. 日本的勞工薪資是世界上最高的。
3. 日本企業必須對一昧地追求市場佔有率一事有所節制。
4. 這次業績衰退，是這家公司史上第二大衰退。
5. 大聯盟的選手在技巧上比日本的職業棒球選手更優異。
6. 部份的專家說這個問題可能會比預測值更惡化。
7. 新型號和舊型號比較起來，可以用加倍的速度處理視覺資訊。
8. 工業產量顯示出這五年間最低的成長率。
9. 德國與日本市場對我們的經營來說是最重要的。
10. 日本製商品和西方各國製造的商品比較起來，在世界上更有競爭力。
11. 公司的發言人沒有更進一步說明現在財務的窘境。
12. 買家喜歡的待售房屋或許比去年更少。
13. 日本的每人平均國民生產總額是世界上最高的國家之一。
14. 這間公司的第二季損失比第一季更加惡化。
15. 購買新車，是人們必須經歷的最令人厭煩的經驗之一。
16. 那場颶風被形容為史上襲擊該國的最強大的自然災害。
17. 運動用品主要供應商 Pamko 公司的淨利，比前年急速增加兩倍以上。
18. 根據新的調查顯示，現在女性的每週工作時間，比五年前多半天。
19. 一級主管的薪水比業務經理的薪水多 5 倍。
20. 大多數已婚女性工作者，同時背負家庭內與家庭外的雙重負擔。

8

## 9th Day 動詞

He refused to take responsibility. ——————— 「規則動詞」
（他拒絕承擔責任。）

He lay down on the grass. ——————— 「不規則動詞」
（他躺在草地上。）

Time flies. ——————— 「不及物動詞」
（時間飛逝。）

We had to modify our plan. ——————— 「及物動詞」
（我們必須修正計畫。）

One thousand dollars is a lot of money. ——————— 「呼應」
（一千元美金是一大筆錢。）

### （1）動詞的活用

動詞是描述事物的動作、狀態、性質的詞。動詞詞形變化分為**原形、現在式、過去式、過去分詞、現在分詞**等五種，不過**原形、過去式以及過去分詞**是**動詞主要的詞形**。

| 原形 | 現在式 | 第三人稱單數 | 過去式 | 過去分詞 | 現在分詞 |
|------|--------|------------|--------|----------|----------|
| be | am, are | is | was, were | been | being |
| have | have | has | had | had | having |
| do | do | does | did | done | doing |
| make | make | makes | made | made | making |

### （a）規則動詞

在原形加上 -(e)d，變成過去式、過去分詞的動詞稱為「規則動詞」。通常是原形加上 -ed，但是以 e 結尾的動詞只加上 -d，以「子

音＋y」結尾的動詞，將 y 改成 i 再加上 -ed，以「單母音＋子音」
結尾的單音節的動詞，重覆該子音後加上 -ed，即使是以「單母音＋
子音」結尾的兩個音節以上的動詞、重音在最後一個音節的動詞，
都必須重覆該子音後再加上 -ed。

live － lived － lived
try － tried － tried
stop － stopped － stopped
omit － omitted － omitted

語尾的 -(e)d 的發音：①在 [t], [d] 之後發音為 [id]，②在 [t] 以外的
無聲音之後發音為 [t]，③在 [d] 以外的有聲音之後發音為 [d]。

① wanted [wɑntɪd]　　　　　needed [nidɪd]
② helped [hɛlpt]　　　　　　looked [lʊkt]
③ loved [lʌvd]　　　　　　　closed [klozd]

### （b）不規則動詞

① A－B－B 型

make － made － made　　　hear － heard － heard
send － sent － sent

② A－B－A 型

run － ran － run　　　become － became － become
come － came － come

③ A－B－C 型

go － went － gone　　　write － wrote － written
see － saw － seen

### （c）容易混淆的動詞變化

lie － lay － lain （躺）
lay － laid － laid （放）
lie － lied － lied （說謊）
wind － wound － wound （捲繞）
wound － wounded － wounded （受傷）
find － found － found （發現）

found － founded － founded（創立）
hang － hung － hung（懸掛）
hang － hanged － hanged（絞死）

## （2）不及物動詞與及物動詞

沒有受詞的動詞是不及物動詞，有受詞的動詞稱為及物動詞。有許多動詞可以當作不及物動詞、也可以當作及物動詞，所以必須注意句中是否有受詞。

He can **run** fast. 〔不及物動詞〕
My father **runs** a restaurant. 〔及物動詞〕

（他的父親經營餐廳。）

### （a）容易被誤用為不及物動詞的及物動詞

They **discussed** about the problem. 〔錯誤〕
They **discussed** the problem. 〔正確〕
Mary **married** with Jack. 〔錯誤〕
Mary **married** Jack. 〔正確〕
I **attended** to the meeting. 〔錯誤〕
I **attended** the meeting. 〔正確〕
We can **reach** to the airport in an hour. 〔錯誤〕
We can **reach** the airport in an hour. 〔正確〕

### （b）容易被誤用為授與動詞的完全及物動詞

Jane **suggested** the group that they should visit the museum.
〔錯誤〕
Jane **suggested** to the group that they should visit the museum.
〔正確〕

（珍恩建議那一群人應該去參觀博物館。）

The secretary **admitted** her boss that she had forgotten to mail the letter. 〔錯誤〕
The secretary **admitted** to her boss that she had forgotten to mail the letter. 〔正確〕

（秘書向她的上司承認她忘了寄信。）

其它還有 explain, introduce, announce, prove 等等。

**（3）動詞片語**

有時候動詞會與其它的品詞連結後，當作一個動詞來使用，這被稱為「動詞片語」，組合的形式如下，請將以下當作片語熟記。

**（a）「動詞＋副詞」＝不及物動詞的功能**

His plane **took off** ten minutes ago.

（他的班機已經在十分鐘前起飛。）

**（b）「動詞＋副詞」＝及物動詞的功能**

Don't forget to **turn off** the TV.

（別忘了關電視。）

**（c）「動詞＋介系詞」＝及物動詞的功能**

What does M.B.A. **stand for**?

（M.B.A 是什麼的簡寫？）

**（d）「動詞＋名詞」＝不及物動詞的功能**

The festival is scheduled to **take place** in Boston Sept. 2nd-7th.

（這個節慶從 9 月 2 日開始到 7 日為止於波士頓舉行。）

**（e）「動詞＋副詞＋介系詞」＝及物動詞的功能**

I can't **put up with** his rudeness anymore.

（我再也無法忍受他的無禮了。）

**（f）「動詞＋名詞＋介系詞」＝及物動詞的功能**

He **made fun of** her.

（他取笑她。）

## （4）主詞與動詞的呼應

動詞的詞形變化與主詞的人稱及單複數一致。主詞如果為單數時，則使用單數形的動詞，如果主詞為複數，則使用複數形的動詞，這是基本原則，不過必須注意以下的情況：

### （a）即使是複數形的名詞，表示一個東西時，仍然使用單數形的動詞

**Mathematics is** my favorite subject.

（數學是我喜歡的科目。）

### （b）兩個以上的東西即使用 and 連結，但表示同一事物，或將整體視為一個集合體時，使用單數形態的動詞

**Ham and eggs is** Jack's usual breakfast.

（火腿與蛋是傑克平常的早餐。）

### （c）時間、距離、金額等等的單位使用單數形的動詞

**Twenty years is** a long time.

（二十年是一段很長的時間。）

但是，表示時間的經過時，使用複數形的動詞。

**Twenty years have passed** since Jim graduated from college.

（吉姆自從大學畢業之後已經過了二十年。）

### （d）集合名詞將其構成要素視為個別要素時，使用複數形動詞；將全體視為一個集合體時，則使用單數形動詞

**Half of the class are** girls.

（那一班有一半是女生。）

**The class is** very small.

（那個班級人數非常少。）

## 練習題

請在以下各題目的(A),(B),(C),(D)之中選出最適合的答案填入空格之中。

**1. He was _____ over 80 kph when he was stopped by the policeman.**

    (A) holding            (B) accelerating

    (C) taking              (D) doing

**2. Mr. Lee has been in a bad mood all day. I wonder what's _____ him.**

    (A) holding            (B) keeping

    (C) eating              (D) soothing

**3. Dick has to _____ five years in prison for robbery.**

    (A) arrive              (B) inhabit

    (C) reside              (D) serve

**4. I don't need much money. Twenty dollars will _____.**

    (A) do                (B) make

    (C) amount            (D) count

**5. Mr. Young always finds _____ his staff.**

    (A) mistakes to         (B) fault with

    (C) defects of          (D) disadvantage with

**6. The mayor submitted a proposal to do _____ the school lunch program in high schools.**

    (A) up to             (B) down with

    (C) close to           (D) away with

**7. This contract still _____ good.**

    (A) does              (B) holds

    (C) lasts              (D) stays

9

8. After all, you have disregarded your family for so long, it
_____ you right if your wife divorces you.
   (A) holds (B) serves
   (C) gets (D) has

9. Selling everything from diapers to telephones, American
companies are _____ in foreign markets.
   (A) expanding (B) expansion
   (C) expanded (D) expanse

10. The Tokyo consumer price index _____ at 97. 3 against
the 2000 base of 100.
   (A) stood (B) stayed
   (C) sat (D) got

11. The research institute was _____ to promote the
translation of theory to practical applications in economic
forecasting.
   (A) found (B) founding
   (C) find (D) founded

12. We recommend that you _____ the workshop with a
laptop to make the most of it.
   (A) attend (B) attend to
   (C) attending (D) to attend

13. The book says that measles _____ a disease that people
usually get in childhood.
   (A) is (B) be
   (C) are (D) they are

14. Mr. Williams found that the new accountant had _____
on a time sheet, claiming 15 extra hours of overtime.
   (A) laid (B) lie
   (C) lied (D) lain

15. The relationship between automakers and parts manufacturers _____ loosening.
    (A) be
    (B) is
    (C) are
    (D) were

16. It is needless to say that each of us _____ to avoid waste and save energy.
    (A) to need
    (B) need
    (C) needs
    (D) needing

17. On-time delivery anywhere in the United States _____ guaranteed, or there's no charge.
    (A) be
    (B) is
    (C) being
    (D) are

18. Many Americans believe that Japanese industry _____ away both jobs and markets from American firms.
    (A) to take
    (B) take
    (C) taking
    (D) takes

19. Once again I _____ the customer service representative why I was calling.
    (A) explain
    (B) explained
    (C) explained to
    (D) explanation

20. The course will _____ when we have a minimum of 10 people interested.
    (A) take place
    (B) take a place
    (C) taken the place
    (D) taking places

9

# 正確解答

1-(D) do 的意思是「以……的速度前進」。80kph 是「時速８０公里」。

2-(C) eat 的意思是「使煩惱」。

3-(D) serve 當作及物動詞，意思是「服刑」。robbery 是「強盜」。

4-(A) do 當作不及物動詞，意思是「足夠、夠用」。

5-(B) find fault with 的意思是「挑剔」。

6-(D) do away with 的意思是「廢止」。school lunch program 是「學校營養午餐計畫」。

7-(B) hold good 是「有效、適用」。

8-(B) serve 也有「報答」的意思。serve...right 的意思是「理所當然（帶有負面意味）」。

9-(A) expand 的意思是「擴大、擴展」。diapers 是「尿布」。

10-(A) stand 的意思是「在（某個狀態）」。consumer price index 是「消費者物價指數」。against the 2000 base of 100 是「把２０００年當作１００來看的話」。

11-(D) find 與 found 是意思完全不同的動詞，前者是「發現」，後者是「設立」。find 的變化形是 find, found, found；found 的變化形是 found, founded, founded。The research institute（研究所）是主詞，在空格之前有 was，所以本句是被動式，選擇 founded 是正確答案。

12-(A) attend 是及物動詞，所以與受詞之間不會有介系詞。在 recommend 的 that 子句之中，動詞須使用原形，所以 attending 與 attend 不是適合的答案。

13-(A) measles 是「麻疹」的意思。雖然是複數形，仍然當作單數處理。

**動詞**

14-(C) 從句意可以判斷，空格應該填入意思為「說謊」的單字。在空格之前有 had，所以應該填入「說謊」的過去分詞。lie（說謊）的變化形是 lied, lied；lie（橫躺）的變化形是 lay, lain；lay（放）的變化形是 laid, laid。

15-(B) 主詞是單數形的 relationship，所以選擇單數形的動詞 is。請不要被空格前的 manufacturers 的複數形所誤導。

16-(C) each of... 當作單數處理。呼應的動詞是第三人稱單數現在式。

17-(B) 主詞是 on-time delivery，是單數，不要被空格前的 the United States 的複數形所誤導。

18-(D) that 子句的主詞是單數名詞 Japanese industry，所以動詞選擇「第三人稱單數的現在式」為正確答案。

19-(C) 當作及物動詞的 explain 用「explain＋直接受詞＋to＋間接受詞」的句型或是「explain＋to＋間接受詞＋直接受詞」的句型。此外，用 that 子句或 why 子句當作受詞時，使用「explain＋to＋間接受詞＋that 子句（或是 why 子句）」。

20-(A) 助動詞 will 之後是用原形動詞，所以選項中的 take place 或是 take a place 其中一個是正確答案。片語 take place 的意思是「舉行」，take a place 的意思是「佔位置」，從句意來看，take place 是正確答案。

9

137

# 練習題的中文翻譯

1. 他被警察攔下來時，時速超過８０公里。

2. 李先生一整天心情不佳。究竟有什麼事情困擾著他？

3. 迪克因為強盜罪，必須坐五年牢。

4. 我不需要很多錢。只要二十美金就夠了。

5. 楊先生總是挑剔他的員工。

6. 市長提案廢除高中營養午餐計畫。

7. 這個合約依然有效。

8. 畢竟你已經有很長一段時間忽略你的家人了，如果你的太太跟你離婚，也是理所當然的。

9. 美國企業積極在海外市場拓展勢力，販售的東西從尿布到電話都有。

10. 東京的消費者物價指數，若以２０００年作為１００來看的話，現在則是９３．３。

11. 這個研究所是為了將經濟預測的理論，轉化成實際應用而設立的。

12. 我們建議你帶筆記型電腦到研討會上，以發揮最大效用。

13. 書上說麻疹通常是人類在孩童時代會罹患的疾病。

14. 威廉先生發現新任會計造假工作時間表，多報了額外的１５小時加班時數。

15. 汽車製造商與零件工廠之間的關係是緩和的。

16. 我們每個人必須避免浪費並且要節省能源，這是無須贅言的。

17. 保證準時送達美國境內任何地方，否則不收費。

18. 許多美國人認為日本企業奪走美國企業的工作機會及市場。

19. 我再一次向客戶服務人員說明我為什麼打電話進來。

20. 至少要有十個人課程才會開班。

# Note

## 10th | Day  時態

I play tennis every Sunday. ──────── 「現在式」
（我每個星期天打網球。）

Mr. Morgan called ten minutes ago. ──── 「過去式」
（十分鐘之前，摩根先生打電話來。）

I'll take care of it. ──────── 「未來式」
（我會處理這件事。）

He has just come back from London. ── 「現在完成式」
（他才剛從倫敦回來。）

I had never talked to her before then. ── 「過去完成式」
（我之前從來沒有和她說過話。）

英語的時態有１２個種類，分別是現在式、過去式、未來式、現在進行式、過去進行式、未來進行式、現在完成式、過去完成式、未來完成式、現在完成進行式、過去完成進行式、未來完成進行式。其中現在式、過去式以及未來式，稱為三種基本時態。

### （1）現在式

#### （a）現在的動作與狀態

Here **comes** our bus.

（巴士來了。）

I **know** Mr. Clark very well.

（我非常了解克拉克先生。）

#### （b）現在的習慣與反覆動作

I **go** jogging in the park every morning.

（我每天早上去公園慢跑。）

I often **stop** at that shop on my way home.

（我在回家途中經常去那一家店。）

### （c）一般的真理

The sun **rises** in the east.

（太陽從東邊出來。）

History **repeats** itself.

（歷史不斷重演。）

### （d）確定未來的預定與計畫

Mr. Benson **leaves** for San Francisco next Friday.

（班森先生下個星期五將出發前往舊金山。）

### （e）用表示時間或條件的副詞子句表示未來

I'll wait till he finishes his phone call.

（我會等他打完電話。）

I'll give her your message when she **calls**.

（她打電話來時，我會把你的留言轉告給她。）

We'll stay home if it **rains** tomorrow.

（如果明天下雨，我們會待在家裡。）

〔注意〕I don't know if it will rain tomorrow. 的 if it will rain tomorrow
是名詞子句，所以用 will。

## （2）過去式

MP3
079

### （a）過去式的動作與狀態

The movie **started** ten minutes ago.

（電影在十分鐘之前開始。）

I **stayed** at home all day yesterday.

（我昨天一整天都待在家裡。）

### （b）過去的習慣與反覆動作

In those days I **went** golfing every weekend.

（在那些日子裡，我每個周末都會去打高爾夫球。）

### （c）過去完成式的代用

根據 before 與 after 等等的連接詞，清楚了解時間的前後關係時，可以用來取代過去完成式。

The show **started** [= had started] before I got to the theater.

（到達劇場之前，表演已經開始。）

### （d）時態一致的過去式

He said he **was** quite satisfied with the results.

（他說他十分滿意結果。）

## （3）未來式

### （a）單純未來與意志未來

在未來式中，有單純表示未來事物的單純未來式，以及表示說話者意志，或是尋問對方意志的未來意志之表現方式。

Nancy **will** be 15 next month. 〔單純未來式〕

（南希下個月就15歲了。）

She **will** get well soon. 〔單純未來式〕

（她馬上就會好轉。）

I **will** ask him to stay. 〔未來意志〕

（我會要求他留下來。）

**Will** you answer the phone? 〔未來意志〕

（你要接電話嗎？）

**Shall** we take a coffee break? 〔未來意志〕

（要不要休息一下，喝杯咖啡？）

#### （b）表示未來的其它表現

① be going to＋動詞的原形

**I'm going to** stay in London for three weeks.

（我將在倫敦停留三週。）

② 用現在進行式表示不久的未來

They **are arriving** tomorrow.

（他們將於明天抵達。）

③ be to＋動詞的原形

He **is to** have a physical checkup next week.

（他預定下個星期接受健康檢查。）

④ be about to＋動詞原形

**I'm about to** leave the office.

（我剛好要離開公司。）

### （4）現在完成式

現在完成式的句型是「have [has]＋過去分詞」，表示過去的動作及狀態，在某些意思上與現在關連的某件事。現在完成式分別有表示完成、結果、經驗、繼續等等的用法。

#### （a）完成、結果

這種情況大多會伴隨 just, now, already, yet, recently 等等的副詞。

I **have** just **finished** my work.

（我剛好完成了工作。）

**Have** you **finished** typing the letter already?

（你信件打好了嗎？）

**I've lost** my watch.

（我弄丟了手錶。）

### （b）到目前為止的經驗

這種情況大多伴隨 ever, never, once, before 等等的副詞。

I **have been** to that art museum before.

（我曾經去過那間美術館。）

**Have** you ever **played** squash?

（你曾經打過回力球嗎？）

### （c）持續到現在為止的狀態

We **have lived** here for nearly ten years.

（我們已經在這裡住了將近十年。）

I **have known** him since he was a little boy.

（我在他小時候就已經認識他了。）

### （d）未來完式的代用

在表示時間或是條件的副詞子句中，表示未來完成。

Come to my office when you **have finished** your work.

（工作結束的話，請到我的辦公室。）

I'll take you to the mall if you **have finished** your homework.

（如果你寫完功課，我就帶你去購物中心。）

### （e）不能使用現在完成式的情況

現在完成式不可以與 just now, ...ago, last... 等清楚表示過去的詞，或者與 when, what time 等疑問詞一起使用。

The movie **has finished** just now. 〔錯誤〕

The movie has just finished. 〔正確〕

（電影剛剛結束。）

The movie **finished** just now. 〔正確〕

（電影剛剛結束。）

When **have** you **started** smoking? 〔錯誤〕

When **did** you **start** smoking? 〔正確〕

（你是從什麼時候開始抽菸的？）

## （5）過去完成式

過去完成式的句型是「had＋過去分詞」，以過去某個時點為基準，用來敘述當時為止的經驗、持續到當時的動作及狀態。

### （a）完成、結果

The symposium **had** already **started** when I got to the hall.

（到達會館時，研討會已經開始了。）

### （b）經驗

I **had** never **skied** till then.

（到當時為止，我沒滑過雪。）

### （c）繼續

John **had lived** in Boston for five years before he moved to New York.

（約翰搬到紐約之前，在波士頓住了五年。）

### （d）表示兩個突發事件時間前後關係的過去完成式

表示一個動作比其它動作更早發生的用法

I broke the camera which I **had bought** the day before.

（我前天買的相機弄壞了。）

〔注意〕描述事件的發生順序時，可以同時使用過去式。

I **bought** a camera the other day, but I **broke** it.

（我前天買了相機，但是弄壞了。）

### （e）利用時態一致表示過去完成

She said that she **had** never **seen** it before.

（她說她從來沒有看過它。）

## （6）未來完成式

未來完成的句型是「will [shall] have＋過去分詞」，以未來某個時間點為基準，表示到那個時點之前已完成的動作、結果、經驗、繼續。

### （a）完成、結果

They **will have arrived** in Miami by tomorrow morning.

（他們明天早上將會到達邁阿密。）

### （b）經驗

If I watch this movie again, I **will have watched** it five times so far.

（如果我再看一次這部電影，那麼我到現在為止就看了五遍了。）

### （c）繼續

By next month, I **will have worked** for this company for ten years.

（到下個月，我就已經在這間公司工作十年了。）

## （7）現在進行式

### （a）表示現在進行中的動作

Mr. Brown **is talking** on the phone.

（布朗先生正在講電話。）

### （b）強調反覆的行為

這種情況通常伴隨 always, constantly 等等的副詞。

Jim **is** always **criticizing** his co-workers.

（吉姆總是批評他的同事。）

### （c）表示不久的未來

表示往來以及出發、到達的動詞，例如用 go, come, start, leave, arrive 等等的進行式來表示不久的未來。

I'm **leaving** tomorrow morning.

（我將在明天早上出發。）

## （8）過去進行式

### （a）表示在過去進行中的動作

He **was reading** the report when the phone rang.

（電話響的時候他正在看報告。）

### （b）強調過去的反覆行為

They **were** always **arguing** over little things.

（他們過去總是為了一些小事吵架。）

### （c）在過去的某一個時間點表示「當時打算……」

I **was leaving** my office when you called me.

（你打電話給我時，我正打算離開公司。）

## （9）未來進行式

### （a）表示在未來進行中的動作

I **will be cooking** when you come.

（當你來的時候我應該正在煮飯。）

### （b）表示未來的計劃行動

We **will be having** dinner with Mr. Williams this Friday.

（本週五我們預計和威廉斯先生一起吃飯。）

## （10）現在完成進行式

這個時態是用於強調到現在為止的持續動作。

I **have been writing** the report all day today.

（我今天一整天都在寫這份報告。）

## （11）過去完成進行式

使用於強調「一直持續到過去某個時間點的舉動或動作」。

She **had been waiting** for two hours when he finally showed up.

（她已經等了兩個小時了，他才終於出現。）

## （12）未來完成進行式

這個時態是用於強調未來某個時間點之前的持續動作

By tomorrow, I **will have been waiting** for his answer for two weeks.

（到了明天，我已經等他的回覆等了兩個星期了。）

# 練習題

請在以下各題目的(A),(B),(C),(D)之中選出最適合的答案填入空格之中。

**1. We are still _____ all the various options.**

    (A) discuss            (B) discussing

    (C) discussed         (D) discussion

**2. Mr. Clark _____ your name before.**

    (A) mentions         (B) would mention

    (C) has mentioned    (D) was mentioning

**3. Well, hello, Mr. Baker. I _____ expecting you.**

    (A) am               (B) was

    (C) have been       (D) had been

**4. May I borrow the magazine when you _____ reading it?**

    (A) will finish       (B) have finished

    (C) had finished     (D) to finish

**5. Bart _____ for Edwin Trust Company for ten years when he left the company.**

    (A) had worked     (B) was working

    (C) have worked    (D) will have been working

**6. So far, these efforts _____ very successful.**

    (A) is not          (B) were not

    (C) have not been    (D) won't be

**7. If I call Ralph at his office once more, I _____ him seven times today.**

    (A) called        (B) have called

    (C) had called     (D) will have called

10

8. I have _____ to your country a few times.

    (A) visit             (B) trip

    (C) been going     (D) been

9. I'm sorry, Mr. Smith _____ just stepped out for lunch. Could I take a message?

    (A) had            (B) has

    (C) was           (D) will have

10. Honda Motor Co. _____ begin selling two U. S. -made Accord vehicles in Japan starting Friday.

    (A) has            (B) is to

    (C) will have        (D) has been to

11. Mr. Adams _____ back, but I'm sure he will show up any moment now.

    (A) doesn't come      (B) didn't come

    (C) won't come       (D) hasn't come

12. About 30 percent said they _____ holiday gifts last year on the Internet.

    (A) purchase        (B) are purchasing

    (C) purchased       (D) have purchased

13. According to a recent study, three in ten Americans _____ to a gym or health club.

    (A) belong          (B) are belonging

    (C) have been belonging (D) will be belonging

14. I _____ an e-mail just now telling me that I passed the job interview.

    (A) get            (B) got

    (C) have gotten      (D) had gotten

15. Will you give this memo to Mr. Nelson when you _____ him this afternoon?

(A) saw          (B) will see

(C) have seen      (D) see

16. When _____ Mr. Morris come back from his business trip to Bangkok?

    (A) had           (B) has

    (C) will           (D) is

17. The tax burden for the average family _____ since the last election.

    (A) rise          (B) rose

    (C) is rising      (D) has risen

18. In all, by the year 2015, Mercury Motors Corporation _____ its workforce to half the size it was in 2005.

    (A) will have cut      (B) will cut

    (C) have cut         (D) cuts

10

19. We _____ applications for the positions of manager and part-time sales associate.

    (A) will currently accept    (B) currently accept

    (C) are currently accepting   (D) have currently accepted

20. Production of hybrid vehicles _____ on the rise in recent years.

    (A) is           (B) was

    (C) has been      (D) had been

# 正確解答

1-(B) 從 We are still（我們仍然……）可以判斷這是進行式。

2-(C) 題目的意思是「克拉克先生之前提過你的名字」。句子中有 before，所以不可以用 was mentioning。

3-(C) 題目的意思是「恭候大駕」。之前和 Baker 先生說過話之後「一直等待～」，所以用現在完成進行式。

4-(B) 在副詞子句中現在完成式用來代替未來完成式。

5-(A) 以 when he left the company 的時間點為基準，所以用過去完成式。

6-(C) So far 的意思是「到目前為止（up to now）」，所以用現在完成式。

7-(D) 題目的意思是「如果再打一次電話給勞夫，我就已經打了七次電話給他了。」這樣的情況下使用未來完成式。

8-(D) 「曾經去～」表示經驗，使用 have been to。

9-(B) 請注意 just stepped out 的 just。表示完成、結果的現在完成式，通常會出現 just, now, already 等等的副詞。

10-(B) 首先，請注意動詞是原形 begin。「be to＋動詞原形」可以表示未來。題目的意思是「本田公司從星期五開始，在日本銷售美國製的兩種雅哥車種」。

11-(D) but 之後使用現在式與未來式的 I'm sure he will show up，由此可知亞當斯先生在現在這個時間點還沒出現。由於是指到目前為止的事件，所以空格的部份填入現在完成式。

12-(C) 主要子句的動詞是過去式，可以判斷從屬子句中為使用過去式或是過去完成式。原形 purchase、現在進行式 are purchasing、現在完成式 have purchased 這三個完全不適合。

13-(A) belong 不能用進行式。

10

14-(B) 請注意句中有 just now。just now 不能用在現在完成式、過去完成式的句子。在現在式中不能用 I get...just now。

15-(D) 表示時間及條件的現在式副詞子句，可以用於表示未來。所以正確答案是(D) see。

16-(C) 在現在完成式、過去完成中不能用疑問詞 when，所以(A) 與 (B) 是錯誤答案。在莫里斯先生之後有動詞 come，所以(D) is 是錯誤答案。

17-(D) 在空格之後馬上接續 since（自～以來），所以選擇完成式是正確解答。

18-(A) 本題目是以未來的時間點 by the year 2015 為基準，所以選擇未來完成式為正確解答。

19-(C) currently（現在）通常與現在進行式一起使用。

20-(C) 因為句中有 in recent years（這幾年），所以選擇現在完成式是正確答案。

10

# 練習題的中文翻譯

1. 我們仍然針對各種選項做討論。

2. 克拉克先生以前提過你的名字。

3. 你好，午安，貝克先生。恭候大駕。

4. 你看完之後那本雜誌可以借我嗎？

5. 巴特辭去艾德溫信託公司的工作時，他已經在那裡工作十年了。

6. 到目前為止，這些努力還沒有什麼回報。

7. 如果再打一次電話到勞夫的公司，我就已經打了七次電話給他。

8. 我曾經去過你的國家幾次。

9. 不好意思，史密斯先生現在正好出去吃午飯。請問要留言嗎？

10. 本田公司預計從星期五開始，在日本銷售美國製的兩種雅哥車種。

11. 亞當斯先生還沒回來，不過我確信他隨時會出現。

12. 據說，去年大約有３０％的人在網路上購買聖誕節禮物。

13. 根據最近的調查，十個美國人之中有三個人參加健身房或是健身俱樂部。

14. 我剛剛接到一封電子郵件，告訴我通過求職面試了。

15. 今天下午如果遇到尼爾森先生，可以幫我把這張備忘便條紙交給他嗎？

16. 莫里斯先生什麼時候從曼谷出差回來的？

17. 上次選舉之後，平均的家庭稅務負擔增加了。

18. Mercury 汽車公司在２０１５年前，預計將全公司員工數量減至２００５年 的一半數量。

19. 本公司現在正在招募經理職位以及兼職銷售人員的職位。

20. 近年來，環保雙動力車的生產數量正在增加。

# Note

# 11th Day 助動詞

Will you do me a favor?
（您能幫我一個忙嗎？）

I can handle it myself.
（我自己可以處理這件事。）

May I use the telephone?
（我可以借用一下電話嗎？）

You must answer my question.
（你必須回答我提出的問題。）

I ought to call my boss.
（我必須打電話給上司。）

## （1）助動詞的種類

助動詞除了原本是動詞的 be, have, do 之外，還有 will, would, shall, should, can, could, may, might, must, ought (to), need (to), dare (to), used (to) 等等。

## （2）助動詞的特徵

### （a）在助動詞之後接續原形動詞

Perhaps we **can** change his mind.

（或許我們可以改變他的心意。）

### （b）即使是第三人稱單數也不加上 -(e)s

Peter **will** pick you up at the station.

（彼得會到車站接你。）

## （c）疑問句時將助動詞放在句首

**Will** you take our order, please?

（麻煩您，我們要點餐。）

## （d）否定句時在助動詞之後加上 not

You **must not** tell anyone about this.

（你絕對不能告訴任何人這件事。）

### （3）can 的意思與用法

## （a）能力「可以……」

I **can** adapt to any circumstances.

（我可以適應任何環境。）

## （b）許可「可以……」

**Can** I leave now?

（我現在可以離開嗎？）

## （c）可能性「可能……」

It **can** happen.

（這可能會發生。）

## （d）強烈懷疑「果然是……吧？」

**Can** it be true?

（那是真的嗎？）

It **cannot** be true.

（那不可能是真的。）

過去的懷疑使用「Can...have＋過去分詞、「cannot have＋過去分詞」等句型。

**Can** he **have been** sick?

（他之前是不是生過病？）

He **cannot have said** such a thing.

（他不可能說過那樣的話。）

使用 could 比 can 表示現在時間點的更強烈懷疑。

**Could** it be true?

（那是真的嗎？）

**（e）could 是比 can 更客氣的表現**

**Could** you move over a little?

（您可以坐過去一點嗎？）

**（f）慣用語法**

**cannot help doing（忍不住、不得不～）**

I **couldn't help laughing**.

（我忍不住大笑。）

**cannot but...（忍不住、不得不～）**

I **could not but** laugh.

（我忍不住大笑。）

**cannot... too＋形容詞或副詞**

You **cannot** be **too careful** when you drive.

（你開車時越小心越好。）

**（4）may 的意思與用法**

**（a）許可「可以……」**

**May** I come in?

（我可以進來嗎？）

## （b）推測「或許……」

He **may** be busy right now.

（他現在或許正在忙。）

過去的推測以「may have＋過去分詞」的句型表現。

He **may** not have seen her.

（他或許沒有見到她。）

might 表示比 may 可能性更低的推測

I **might** have a chance, too.

（或許我也有一次機會。）

## （c）祈願「祈求……」

**May** he succeed!

（祝他成功！）

## （d）慣用語法

**may well...**（〔表示有充分理由〕完全能……、大概會……吧）

You **may well** get angry with Mary, but she is doing her best.

（你有充分理由生瑪麗的氣，但是她已經盡了全力。）

She **may well** turn down your offer.

（她大概會拒絕你的提議吧。）

**may as well...**（不妨、最好……）

We **may as well** start the meeting because it's already ten past two.

（已經 2 點 1 0 分了，我們最好開始進行會議吧。）

**might (just) as well...**（或許最好……）

We **might (just) as well** call him now.

（我們或許最好現在打電話給他。）

11

## （5）must 的意思與用法

### （a）必要、義務「必須……」

I **must** finish addressing these letters by two o'clock.

（我必須在兩點之前寫完這些信件的收件人姓名及地址。）

表示這種情況的過去與未來時，分別使用 had to 與 will have to。此外，否定句型為 don't have 或是 need not, mustn't，則表示「禁止」。

I **had to** stay at my office till ten.

（我必須在辦公室待到十點。）

You**'ll have to** stay home for a couple of days.

（你必須待在家裡幾天。）

You **mustn't** bother him now.

（你現在不可以去煩他。）

### （b）當然的推測「一定……」

You **must** be tired after such a long drive.

（你開了那麼久的車，一定累了吧。）

推測過去已發生的事時，可以用「must have＋過去分詞」（一定……）

He **must have studied** abroad.

（他一定留過學。）

### （c）主張「無論如何……、不得不」

Jack **must** always have his own way.

（傑克總是非得按照自己的做法不可。）

## （6）ought (to) 的意思及用法

### （a）義務「應該……」

You **ought to** apologize to him.

（你應該向他道歉。）

否定的句型是 ought not to（不應該）

You **ought not to** talk so loud.

（你不應該那麼大聲說話。）

### （b）當然的推測「應該……」

He **ought to** know how to deal with it.

（他應該知道如何處理。）

## （7）used (to) 的意思與用法

### （a）過去的習慣行動「過去一向……」

I **used** to walk two miles every morning.

（我過去一向每天早上走兩英里的路。）

否定句型 didn't used to 比 usedn't to 更常被使用。

He **didn't used to** eat breakfast.

（他過去一向不常吃早餐。）

疑問句是「Used＋主詞＋to」，但是「Did＋主詞＋used to」比較常被使用。

**Did** he **used to** drink a lot?

（他過去經常喝酒嗎？）

### （b）過去的狀態「以前是……」

There **used to** be an elementary school here.

（以前這裡有一間小學。）

## （8）would 的特別用法

### （a）客氣的請託「可以幫我……嗎？」

Would you hold this bag, please?

（可以幫我拿這個包包嗎？）

### （b）推測

這是比 will 更客氣的表現方式。

It would be best to maintain silence.

（保持沉默是最好的方式。）

### （c）過去不固定的習慣

She and I would often have lunch together.

（她經常與我一起吃午餐。）

### （d）過去強烈的意志

She would not listen to me.

（她不會聽我說的話。）

### （e）慣用語法

would like to（想要……）

I would like to see Mr. Wilson.

（我想要見威爾森先生。）

would rather... than...（與其……不如……）

I would rather go by train than by plane.

（與其搭火車，我寧願搭飛機。）

## （9）should 的特別用法

### （a）義務、勸告「應該……」

You should tell him about it.

（你應該告訴他那件事。）

應該要做（但沒做）與沒有被實現的過去義務、勸告用「should

have＋過去分詞」來表示。

You should have called her again.

（你當時應該再打一次電話給她。）

### （b）當然、推測（一定……吧、應該……）

The pictures should be ready by now.

（照片應該已經準備好了。）

### （c）當然、意外等等的感情判斷

It is a pity（可惜）、It is natural（當然）、It is surprising（令人驚訝）等片語之後使用「that＋主詞＋should」的句型。

It is natural that he should get angry with you.

（他生你的氣是理所當然的。）

### （d）接續表示命令、主張、提案、決定等等的主要子句

demand, insist, suggest, decide 等單字之後，接續「that＋主詞＋should」。在美式英語中，通常省略 should，而直接使用原形動詞。

He suggested that someone **should** help her.

（他建議應該有人幫助她。）

He suggested that someone help her. 這是美式英語〔省略掉should〕

### （e）與疑問詞一起使用，表示驚訝、意外（反問法）

Who **should** trust him?

（誰會相信他呢？）

### （f）委婉的表現

I **should** say she is not fit for the job.

（我猜想她不適合那份工作。）

# 練習題

請在以下各題目的(A),(B),(C),(D)之中選出最適合的答案填入空格之中。

**1.** _____ you hold the elevator, please?

    (A) May              (B) Should

    (C) Shall            (D) Could

**2.** We _____ heed these voices.

    (A) could have       (B) ought

    (C) used            (D) should

**3.** Excuse me. You _____ be Mr. Hamilton. I'm Roy Jones from ABC Communications.

    (A) can              (B) will

    (C) must            (D) ought to

**4.** What he is saying seems very foolish, but it _____ happen.

    (A) must have       (B) can

    (C) should have     (D) be

**5.** She _____ have done such a foolish thing in front of all those important guests.

    (A) shall           (B) cannot

    (C) should         (D) ought to

**6.** I _____ not but help the old lady when I saw her struggling to carry a big bag.

    (A) can              (B) may

    (C) could          (D) must

**11**

7. It's a pity that you _____ leave our company after having worked here only a month.

    (A) might            (B) may

    (C) should          (D) could

8. You _____ be too careful when you start a joint venture.

    (A) ought           (B) might not

    (C) must            (D) cannot

9. We _____ to do something to block the takeover by the Japanese company.

    (A) might           (B) can

    (C) ought          (D) should have

10. I didn't know you walked all the way from the station. You _____ called me from there.

    (A) might           (B) must have

    (C) should         (D) should have

11. We _____ do our utmost to publicize the site and keep it running for as long as possible.

    (A) are             (B) need

    (C) will            (D) have

12. Nancy _____ not admit that she sent the invoice to the wrong client.

    (A) do             (B) would

    (C) has           (D) would have

13. Online retail book sales _____ nearly double over the next three years.

    (A) will            (B) do

    (C) didn't         (D) will have

11

14. We _____ set up workplace education programs in order to increase morale within our organization.

    (A) able to                (B) ought

    (C) are used to         (D) should

15. It _____ cost $80 million for the city to renovate the school buildings in the district.

    (A) is                  (B) should be

    (C) could have been    (D) would

16. I think we _____ let the client have a little more time to decide by himself.

    (A) has                (B) ought not

    (C) had better        (D) would have been

17. Yesterday the manager _____ apologize to the board for letting production fall behind.

    (A) had better to     (B) had to

    (C) must              (D) used to

18. Mary is not liked very much by her co-coworkers because she _____ always have her own way.

    (A) must             (B) can

    (C) will              (D) ought to

19. Boating accidents are often the result of negligence and _____ result in serious injuries.

    (A) must             (B) does

    (C) can              (D) should have

20. The company _____ laying off some 200 employees as part of the cost-cutting efforts.

    (A) will             (B) ought to

    (C) had better      (D) couldn't help

11

# 正確解答

1-(D) 題目是表示請託的句子。使用 could 是比使用 can 更客氣的表現方式。hold the elevator 的意思是「暫停電梯」。

2-(D) heed these voices 的意思是「傾聽這些意見」。從句意來看，正確答案是表示義務、勸告的 should。

3-(C) must 可以用來表示「一定」。

4-(B) can 可以用來表示「可能性」。

5-(B) 「cannot have＋過去分詞」的意思是「不可能……」。可以從句意來判斷正確答案。

6-(C) 請注意句中有 but。所以 cannot but...（不得不、忍不住……）是正確答案。請注意句子是使用過去式。

7-(C) it's a pity that... 句子中使用 should。

8-(D) 「cannot be too＋形容詞或是副詞」的意思是「越……越好」。

9-(C) 請注意 to do 的 to；ought 後面接 to。

10-(D) 句意應該是「你應該在那裡打電話給我的（但是沒有打）」。should have 是正確解答。

11-(C) 請注意空格之後有 do。沒有 are do 這種說法。need 就像 need to do 一樣必須有 to，have 也是一樣，have to do 必須有 to。選擇 will 是正確答案。助動詞之後接續動詞原形。

12-(B) 主詞 Nancy 是第三人稱單數，所以 do 是錯誤答案。動詞 admit 是原形，所以(C) 與(D) 是錯誤答案。在主詞 Nancy 及動詞 admit 之後，必須接續過去分詞，所以這個句子的 would not... 表示過去強烈意志，意思是「不打算……」。

13-(A) over the next three years（在今後三年）表示未來的期間，所以選擇表示未來的 will 是正確答案。

11

14-(D) 選項(A) 必須有 be動詞（We are able to...）。(B) 必須
有 to（We ought to...）。(C) are used to 的意思是「習
慣……」，在 to 之後必須接續名詞或是動名詞，所以(C) 也
是錯誤答案。

15-(D) 請先了解句首的 It 是表示 to 以下的虛主詞。cost 是動詞，
意思是「花費」。所以在 cost 前面放置助動詞 would（大
概……）為正確答案。從(A) 到(C) 的選項都有 be動詞，所以
句子變成被動式，不符合句意。

16-(C) 只要了解表示「最好……」的「had better＋原形」的句型，
就能選出正確答案。選項(A) 無法呼應動詞，必須有 to，(B)
也必須有 to。(D) 的 would have been（大概已經……）不符
合句意。

17-(B) 在句首有 Yesterday，所以這是過去式的句子。must 沒有過
去式，所以使用 had to。(A) 不需要 too，had better 是用來
描述現在的事情，所以是錯誤答案。(D) used to 的意思是
「過去一向」，用來表示過去的習慣行為，所以在句意上不
適合。

18-(A) 在句中有 always have her own way（總是依照自己的想法，
我行我素），所以使用表示主張的 must，意思為「無論如
何……一定」。

19-(C) can 除了可以表示能力「可以……」之外，也可以用來表示可
能性「可能……」。從句意來看，(C) 是正確答案。選項(A)
在句意上不符，(B) 無法呼應主詞（accidents 是複數形），
(D) 是動詞的變化形（必須是過去分詞），所以是錯誤答案。

20-(D) 請注意在空格之後有 laying off 與 -ing 形（動名詞或是現在分
詞）。只要知道 cannot help doing 的意思是「不得不、忍不
住」，那麼應該就能選出正確答案(D)。

# 練習題的中文翻譯

1. 可以先將電梯按停嗎？
2. 我們應該把這些聲音留在心中。
3. 不好意思，您一定是漢米敦先生吧。我是 ABC 通訊公司的羅瓊斯。
4. 雖然他說的話聽起來很荒謬，但是十分可能發生。
5. 她應該不會在那麼重要的客人面前做那樣的蠢事。
6. 當我看到老婆婆費力地拿著大包包時，我忍不住去幫了她。
7. 你只在我們公司工作一個月就辭職，實在太可惜了。
8. 開始經營合資公司時，越小心越好。
9. 我們應該做些什麼，來阻止日本企業的收購行動。
10. 我不知道你自己從車站走回來。如果你在那裡打電話給我，讓我去接你就好了。
11. 我們盡最大的努力宣傳這個網站，並且盡可能維持網站的運作。
12. 南希不打算承認自己把發票寄給錯誤的客戶。
13. 線上零售書籍的數量，在三年後將會倍數成長。
14. 為了提高組織內士氣，應該增設職場教育課程。
15. 市政府花了八千萬美金，改善這個地區的學校校舍。
16. 我認為最好再給客人一點時間，讓他自己決定。
17. 昨天，經理為生產延遲一事向董事會道歉。
18. 瑪麗總是我行我素，所以不太受同事歡迎。
19. 划船事故通常起因於疏忽，而且可能造成重傷。
20. 那家公司為了努力刪減費用，不得不解雇大約２００名員工。

11

# 12th Day 關係詞

The man who is talking on the phone is Mr. Hall. 「關係代名詞」
（正在講電話的人是霍爾先生。）

Did you read the memo which I gave you? ── 「關係代名詞」
（你看過我給你的備忘便條紙嗎？）

The lion that escaped from its cage was caught. 「關係代名詞」
（從獸籠逃走的獅子被捕獲了。）

This is the building where I work. ──────── 「關係副詞」
（這是我工作的大樓。）

That's why I came here. ──────────── 「關係副詞」
（這就是我為什麼來這裡的原因。）

## （1）關係詞的種類

關係詞包含同時具備連接詞及代名詞功用的**關係代名詞**，以及具備連接詞及副詞功用的**關係副詞**。此外，也包含關係形容詞，也就是有時候會被用為形容詞使用的關係代名詞。

## （2）代名詞的種類

關係代名詞有以下幾種，具備與普通代名詞一樣，有格的變化。

| 先行詞 | 主格 | 所有格 | 受格 |
|--------|------|--------|------|
| 人 | who | whose | whom |
| 物、動物 | which | whose of which | which |
| 人、物、動物 | that | ─ | that |
| 包含先行詞 | what | ─ | what |

## （3）who 的用法

用於先行詞是「人」的時候

The gentleman **who** is smoking over there is Mr. Sullivan. 〔主格〕

<The gentleman is Mr. Sullivan. + He is smoking over there.>

（在那裡抽菸的人是蘇利文先生。）

That is the man **whose** wife is a senator. 〔所有格〕

<That is the man. + His wife is a senator.>

（那位先生的太太是參議員。）

The lady **whom** you met at the airport is the president's wife. 〔受格〕

<The lady is the president's wife. + You met her at the airport.>

（你在機場遇見的女士是社長的太太。）

## （4）which 的用法

用於先行詞除了「人」之外的「動物」及「物品」

This is the dog **which** bit the child. 〔主格〕

（這是咬了小孩的那隻狗 。）

This is the book **of which** pages are missing. 〔所有格〕

（這是那本掉頁的書。）

She bought a table the surface **of which** was scratched.〔所有格〕

= She bought a table whose surface was scratched.

（他買了一張表面有刮傷的桌子。）

These are the documents **which** Mr. Brown left in my office.
〔受格〕

（這些是布朗先生遺留在我辦公室的文件。）

## （5）that 的用法

### （a）人、動物、物品中任何一個當作先行詞時

that 可以用於任何一種先行詞。沒有所有格。

The robber **that** stole 100 million from the bank was arrested.
〔主格〕

（從銀行搶劫一億元的強盜已經被逮捕。）

His pet is a special type of pig **that** comes from Vietnam. 〔主格〕

（他的寵物是越南產的特殊品種小豬。）

Did you receive the parcel **that** I sent to you the day before yesterday? 〔受格〕

（前天寄出的包裹是否已經收到？）

### （b）先行詞包括「人與物」時

They rescued the boy and his dog **that** had fallen into the hole.
〔主格〕

（他們救出掉進那個洞穴裡的少年與他的狗。）

### （c）先行詞接續最高級與序數詞 the only, the same, the very, every, all 等詞組時

She is the most beautiful woman **that** I've ever seen. 〔受格〕

（他是我到目前為止見過最美的女性。）

Nancy is the only person **that** can speak French in our section.
〔主格〕

（南希是我們部門裡唯一會講法語的人。）

### （d）在 that 之前有 who 及 which 等等的疑問詞時

Who is the lady **that** was here a few minutes ago? 〔主格〕

（幾分鐘前在這裡的女性是誰？）

12

## （6）what 的用法

what 本身包含先行詞，表示「～的事物」。關係代名詞 what 不可以用於人的先行詞。

**What** is worth doing is worth doing well. 〔主格〕

（如果這件事值得去做，那麼就值得你把它做好。）

Did you believe **what** he said? 〔受格〕

（你相信他說的話嗎？）

what 後面馬上接名詞時被當作關係形容詞使用。

You can wear **what** dress **[= any dress that]** you like to the party.

（你可以穿任何你喜歡的衣服去參加那場派對。）

He gave her **what** money **[= all the money that]** he had.

（他把他所有的錢都給了她。）

## （7）關係代名詞與介系詞

有時候變成介系詞的受詞，使用「介系詞＋關係代名詞」句型

This is the hammer **with which** the boy broke the car windows.

（這是那個少年打壞車窗所使用的鐵鎚。）

This is the gentleman **from whom** Jack borrowed $1,000.

（就是這位紳士，借了傑克一千元美金。）

〔注意〕關係代名詞的 that 不能馬上接續在介系詞之後。

## （8）關係代名詞的省略

### （a）當作動詞的受詞時

This is the memo I got from Mike.

（這是從邁可那裡拿到的備忘便條紙。）

### （b）當作介系詞的受詞時

這個時候把介系詞放到句尾時可以省略。

This is the bookstore I used to stop by.

（這是我經常光顧的書店。）

### （c）關係代名詞接續在 There is 與 Here is 之後時

There is a gentleman wants to see you.

（有一位紳士想要見你。）

### （d）變成補語時

Paul is not the man he used to be.

（他已經不是以前的保羅了。）

## （9）限定用法與非限定用法

### （a）限定用法

關係代名詞的引導子句限定、修飾先行詞時稱為「限定用法」。這個時候，在關係詞之前不需逗號。

I like a worker **who** works very hard.

（我喜歡努力工作的員工。）

Jack has two daughters **who** are high school teachers.

（傑克有兩個在當高中老師的女兒。）

### （b）非限定用法

針對先行詞做補充說明時，會在關係詞之前放置逗號。that 與 what 沒有非限定用法，請務必注意。

I like the worker, **who** works very hard.

（我喜歡那個員工。因為他很努力工作。）

Jack has two daughters, **who** are high school teachers.

（傑克有兩個女兒。兩個女兒都是高中老師。）

### （c）非限定用法的 which 有時候指前面句子的一部份或是整個句子。

Mary wouldn't apologize, **which** made her boss very angry.

（瑪麗不打算道歉，這令她的上司非常生氣。）

## （10）其它的關係代名詞

### （a）as

關係代名詞的 as 與 same , such , as 等等一起搭配使用。

You made the same mistake **as** I made.

（你犯了與我一樣的錯誤。）

Lend me as much money **as** you have, will you?

（你可以把你所有的錢借給我嗎？）

關係代名詞的 as，有時指前面的句子或是後面整個句子。

**As** is often the case, he made a customer angry.

（雖然這是經常發生的情況，但是他還是讓客人生氣了。）

### （b）but

but 承接包含否定詞的先行詞，意思是「沒有……不」

There is no rule **but** has some exceptions.

（有規則必有例外。）

There is no mother **but** loves her children.

（沒有不愛自己孩子的母親。）

### （c）than

than 承接接續比較級修飾詞的先行詞

Don't withdraw more money **than** is necessary.

（請不要提領所需以外的錢。）

12

## （11）複合關係代名詞

關係代名詞的 who, whom, which, what 接續 -ever 組合而成的單字稱為複合關係代名詞。與 what 一樣，複合關係代名詞包含先行詞。

### （a）引導名詞子句

I'll take **whoever** wants to come with me.

（任何想跟我去的人，我都會帶他去。）

You can invite **whomever** you like.

（你可以邀請任何你喜歡的人。）

Take **whichever** you like better.

（請拿走你比較喜歡的那一個。）

Do **whatever** you want.

（做任何你想做的事。）

### （b）引導表示讓步的副詞子句

**Whoever** calls, tell him I'm out.

（不管任何人打電話來都說我不在。）

**Whichever** you choose, you'll find it satisfactory.

（不管你選擇那一個，你都會感到滿意。）

**Whatever** you say, he won't get angry.

（不管你說什麼，他都不會生氣。）

### （c）whichever 與 whatever 被當作關係形容詞使用

**Whichever** way you do it, the result will be the same.

（不管用那一種方法，都是一樣的結果。）

He won't forgive you, **whatever** reason you have.

（不管你有什麼理由，他都不會原諒你。）

## （12）關係副詞

主要的關係副詞有 where, when, why, how 四個。關係副詞中也有沒有先行詞的用法，請務必小心。

This is the place **where** the treaty was signed.

\<This is the place. + The treaty was signed here.\>

This is **where** the treaty was signed.

（這是條約簽定的地點。）

請特別注意 where 除了「場所」以外，也會用於「立場」、「場合」、「狀態」等等的先行詞。

I'm not in a position **where** I can comment on that.

（我沒有立場針對那件事發言。）

This is one case **where** you have to be very careful.

（這是你必須注意的情況之一。）

They have reached the point **where** they cannot give in to each other.

（他們到了互不相讓的地步。）

She was born in the year **when** Tokyo held the Olympic Games.

（她在東京舉辦奧運的那一年出生。）

Tell me **why** you did it.

（告訴我，你為什麼那麼做？）

That's **how** he made the deal.

（那是他交易的方式。）

## （13）複合關係副詞

where, when, how 接續 -ever 組合成的單字稱為複合關係副詞。複合關係副詞大多用來引導表示讓步的副詞子句。

Eat **wherever** you like.

（在任何你喜歡的地方吃飯。）

**Wherever** you go, I'll go with you.

（我會跟隨你到任何你想去的地方。）

You can come **whenever** you like.

（歡迎你隨時來這裡。）

**Whenever** you visit him, he's busy.

（不管你什麼時候拜訪他，他都十分忙碌。）

**However** hard you work, you won't be promoted this year.

（不管你多努力工作，你今年應該不會升官。）

# 練習題

請在以下各題目的(A),(B),(C),(D)之中選出最適合的答案填入空格之中。

1. Pets _____ are unusual in one country are sometimes common in other countries.

    (A) who           (B) that

    (C) they          (D) whom

2. I have to go to the hotel _____ the reception is being held by three o'clock tomorrow.

    (A) when         (B) for which

    (C) at the place     (D) where

3. Peter didn't really try his best to improve sales, _____ made Mr. Brown very disappointed.

    (A) that          (B) what

    (C) which        (D) and they

4. Let me see _____ you have.

    (A) at that       (B) what

    (C) of which      (D) where

5. There is no worker _____ appreciates a pay raise.

    (A) which       (B) whose

    (C) he          (D) but

6. You have to be careful not to buy more meat _____ is necessary.

    (A) than         (B) what

    (C) of which      (D) which

7. _____ I call him at his office, the line is always busy.

    (A) At which      (B) Whoever

    (C) Whenever     (D) Whomever

12

8. Were you at the site _____ the accident took place?

    (A) which          (B) that

    (C) whenever     (D) where

9. Who is the man _____ contributed $10,000 to the charity?

    (A) which          (B) that

    (C) what          (D) whose

10. That appears to be _____ is happening now.

    (A) which          (B) that

    (C) but          (D) what

11. We cannot expect the dramatic sales growth _____ we have enjoyed in the past few years.

    (A) what          (B) of which

    (C) that          (D) whom

12. The proposals, _____ were approved by the advisory body, were then sent to the subcommittee.

    (A) which          (B) that

    (C) what          (D) whichever

13. Quite a few business leaders _____ in important positions have urged cautious handling of the matter.

    (A) are          (B) they are

    (C) whoever     (D) who are

14. There are aspects of the phenomenon _____ I am quite pleased, but I am disturbed by other facets.

    (A) that          (B) with which

    (C) what          (D) whose

15. There is little possibility that crude oil prices will fall below the present level _____ is already low.

    (A) that          (B) at which

    (C) where          (D) what

16. The moves stem from intensified price-cutting in the U. S. computer market, _____ major makers have marked down their laptop computers.

    (A) that              (B) whatever

    (C) in which        (D) wherever

17. Company officials blamed the decline largely on _____ they called a "worse than expected" slump in sales and price falls for the company's main line of products.

    (A) what            (B) which

    (C) where          (D) that

18. The number of executives _____ pay totaled $1 million or more declined to 85 from 100 last year.

    (A) who             (B) their

    (C) whose         (D) of which

19. That's _____ we have developed a new solution to this old problem.

    (A) which          (B) what

    (C) whichever     (D) why

20. The removal of an organ in the state of brain death should be limited to cases _____ the person in question had clearly expressed a will to approve such action.

    (A) what           (B) which

    (C) where         (D) how

12

# 正確解答

1-(B) 請注意先行詞是動物。

2-(D) 首先，注意先行詞是場所。思考 the hotel 與 the reception 的關係，應該就能明白空格應該填入表示場所的關係副詞。

3-(C) 在空格前有逗號，所以這是非限定用法。關係代名詞的 that 與 what 沒有非限定用法。

4-(B) 首先，先明白題目句意是「請讓我看你擁有的東西」。what 已經包含先行詞。

5-(D) 請注意先行詞 no worker 中有否定詞。這個時候可以用表示「沒有……不」的關係代名詞 but。appreciate 的意思是「感謝、感激」。

6-(A) 請注意先行詞中有比較級的修飾詞。

7-(C) 題目的意思是「不管什麼時候打電話去他的辦公室，電話線都佔線」。表示「不管什麼時候……」的關係副詞是 whenever。

8-(D) 思考先行詞 site（現場）與 the accident 的關係，應該就能發現空格應該填入表示場所的關係副詞。

9-(B) 在空格之前有 who 與 which 等等的疑問詞時，使用關係代名詞 that。

10-(D) 題目的意思是「那看起來似乎是現在發生的事」。「現在發生的事」是 the thing which is happening now. 也就是 what is happening now。

11-(C) dramatic sales growth 是先行詞。what 已經包含先行詞，所以(A) 是錯誤答案。of which（那個……）之後必須是名詞或是取代名詞的詞。在空格之後接續 we have enjoyed，所以(B) 是錯誤答案。whom 的先行詞必須是人。

12-(A) 在空格之前有逗點，所以可以知道這是關係代名詞的非限定

用法。that 與 what 中沒有非限定用法。whichever 在句意上不適合。

13-(D) 只要能判斷出句子的主詞是 business leaders，述語是 have urged，那麼，就知道(A) 是錯誤答案。(B) 不可以接續在 leaders 之後。(C) whoever 在意思上與 quite a few business leaders 互相矛盾。

14-(B) 請注意 I am quite pleased。「喜歡、樂意～」是 be pleased with [about,at]，所以(B) with which 是正確答案。

15-(A) 空格之前的 present level（現在的等級）是先行詞。在空格之後接續 is already low，所以選擇(A) 是正確答案。(B) 與(C) 之後不可以接續動詞。(D) 是包含先行詞的關係代名詞。

16-(C) 先行詞 the U.S. computer market（美國的電腦市場）與空格之後的 major makers have marked down their laptop computers（主要製造商調降筆記型電腦價格），所以思考前後關係，應該用「因此」來連接。(C) in which 是正確答案。

17-(A) 請注意空格之後的 they called。這個時候表示「他們認為……」，所以(A) what 是正確答案。

18-(C) 在空格之後的 pay 接續 totaled，所以是名詞（薪水）而不是動詞（支付）。由此可知(A) who 是錯誤答案。(B) their 很明顯是錯誤答案。(D) of which 不可以把人當作先行詞。

19-(D) 只要先了解 That's why...（那就是為什麼……）的意思，就能很容易地解題。

20-(C) 先行詞 cases 是指「情況」，所以使用關係副詞 where 為正確答案。

12

# 練習題的中文翻譯

1. 對某個國家來說，極為珍貴的「寵物」，有時對其它國家來說，只是一般的寵物。

2. 我必須在明天三點之前抵達飯店，參加招待會。

3. 彼得並沒有盡全力增加營業額，這讓布朗先生感到失望。

4. 請讓我看你擁有的東西。

5. 沒有員工不感謝加薪。

6. 你必須注意不要買超過需求的肉。

7. 不管什麼時候打電話去他的辦公室，電話線都佔線。

8. 你在事故發生現場嗎？

9. 捐獻一萬美金給那家慈善機構的男性是誰？

10. 那看起來似乎是現在發生的事。

11. 不能再期待像過去幾年，可以看到戲劇性的營業額成長。

12. 這些提案被諮詢委員會認可，接下來送到分科委員會。

13. 相當多重要的企業領導者主張必須更小心地處理這個問題。

14. 那個現象有非常令人高興的一面，也有令人擔心的一面。

15. 已經很便宜的原油價格，幾乎不可能降的比現行水準更低。

16. 這個變化是因為在美國市場大幅調降售價，造成主要製造商調降筆記型電腦的價格。

17. 公司的員工們把業績不振的主要原因歸究於公司主力商品銷售不如預期以及價格下跌。

18. 薪資總額超過１００萬美金的員工總數從去年的１００名減少為８５名。

19. 那就是為什麼我們對舊問題發展出新的解決方式。

20. 在腦死狀態進行器官摘除時，僅限捐獻者已經清楚表明接受該行為後，方能進行。

12

# Note

# 13th Day 語態

The telephone was invented by Alexander Graham Bell.
（電話是亞歷山大‧格拉漢姆‧貝爾所發明。）

He is called a computer wizard by his friends.
（他被朋友稱為電腦天才。）

Rose was laughed at by her co-workers.
（羅絲被她的同事嘲笑。）

Linda was seen to take out the confidential document by her boss.
（琳達被上司看見她帶走機密文件。）

## （1）主動語態與被動語態

語態中包括**主動語態**與**被動語態**。「A 對 B 做～」，**主詞對人或事物做出某種動作**時，我們將主詞與動詞的關係稱為「**主動語態**」。「B 被 A～」，當**主詞是接受其它外來動作的一方**時，主詞與動詞的關係就稱為「**被動語態（被動式）**」。被動語態通常是用「be 動詞＋過去分詞」的句型來表示。

Mr. Scott scolded Jane. 〔主動語態〕

（史考特先生責罵珍恩。）

Jane was scolded by Mr. Scott. 〔被動語態〕

（珍恩被史考特先生罵。）

## （2）被動語態的時態

被動語態的時態是根據 be 動詞的變化來判斷。

**現在式**──is [am, are]＋過去分詞

**過去式**──was [were]＋過去分詞

**未來式**──will [shall] be＋過去分詞

**現在完成式**──have [has] been＋過去分詞

**過去完成式**──had been＋過去分詞

**未來完成式**──will [shall] have been＋過去分詞

**現在進行式**──is [am, are] being＋過去分詞

**過去進行式**──was [were] being＋過去分詞

## （3）被動語態與句型

**MP3 113**

變成被動語態後，主動語態的句型也會改變。

John **wrote** this letter. 〔第三句型＜S＋V＋O＞〕

（約翰寫這封信。）

This letter **was written** by John. 〔第一句型＜S＋V＞〕

（這封信是約翰寫的。）

Miss Adams **teaches** us German. 〔第四句型＜S＋V＋IO＋DO＞〕

（亞當斯小姐教我們德文。）

We **are taught** German by Miss Adams. 〔第三句型＜S＋V＋O＞〕

（我們被亞當斯小姐教德文。）

German **is taught** us by Miss Adams. 〔第三句型＜S＋V＋O＞〕

（德文是亞當斯小姐教我們的。）

German **is taught** to us by Miss Adams. 〔第一句型＜S＋V＞〕

（德語是亞當斯小姐教我們的。）

The members **elected** Mr. Baker chairman.
〔第五句型＜S＋V＋O＋C＞〕

（委員們選貝克先生為議長。）

Mr. Baker **was elected** chairman by the members.
〔第二句型＜S＋V＋C＞〕

（貝克先生被委員們推選為議長。）

**13**

### （4）句子中有助動詞的被動語態

變成助動詞＋be＋過去分詞的句型

This paper must be signed by Mr. Clark.

（這個文件必須由克拉克先生簽名。）

The trip may be canceled.

（旅行或許會被取消。）

### （5）被動語態的否定句

be 的變化形之後放置 not。

Jack's suggestions were not adopted by the committee.

（傑克的提案沒有被委員會採用。）

That kind of behavior must not be tolerated.

（那樣的行為不被允許。）

### （6）被動語態的疑問句

變成 be 的變化形＋主詞＋過去分詞的句型

Was he laid off?

（他被解雇了嗎？）

By whom was this order made?

（這張訂單是誰下的？）

What is this system called?

（這個系統的名稱是什麼？）

### （7）主動語態的主詞為表示一般人的 we, you, they, people 等等時

這個時候，by us, by you, by them, by people 等等被省略。

They speak Portuguese in Brazil.

Portuguese is spoken in Brazil.

（在巴西說葡萄牙語。）

### （8）應該注意的被動語態

#### （a）片語動詞（動詞＋介系詞等等）的被動語態

這個時候使用「be動詞＋過去分詞＋介系詞等等」的句型。

The meeting was put off till next Wednesday.

（會議延至下週三。）

The cat was run over by a car.

（那隻貓被汽車輾過去。）

#### （b）感官動詞與使役動詞，將動詞原形當作受詞的補語時

這個時候，原形補語變成 to「不定詞」。

Gary saw the boy steal the toy.

（蓋瑞看到那個少年偷走玩具。）

The boy was seen to steal the toy by Gary.

〔注意〕請注意受詞的補語不是「不定詞 to」的情況

Barbara saw him speaking to the president.

（芭芭拉看見他跟社長說話。）

He was seen speaking to the president by Barbara.

Mark made her wait for hours.

（馬克讓她等了好幾個小時。）

She was made to wait for hours by Mark.

### （c）行為者用 by 以外的介系詞來表示時

He is very interested in the software.

（他對於那個軟體非常感興趣。）

He was disappointed with **[about]** the results.

（他對於結果感到失望。）

She was satisfied with the raise in salary.

（她對於加薪感到十分滿意。）

其它還有 be surprised at, be covered with, be known to, be pleased at [with, about], be annoyed with [at], be filled with 等等。

# 練習題

請在以下各題目的(A),(B),(C),(D)之中選出最適合的答案填入空格之中。

**1. The text is _____ on 8-cm CD-ROMs.**
    (A) store           (B) storing
    (C) stored         (D) storage

**2. What is this device _____?**
    (A) calling         (B) called
    (C) to call         (D) call

**3. The baseball game was _____ because of rain.**
    (A) off called       (B) calling off
    (C) being called     (D) called off

**4. The man was seen _____ into the shop by the guard.**
    (A) to break       (B) broke
    (C) had broken     (D) break

**5. The mountaintop was _____ snow.**
    (A) covered at     (B) covering with
    (C) covered by     (D) covered with

**6. We are _____ that Japan is seen as an arrogant country.**
    (A) concerning     (B) concerned
    (C) concern       (D) concerned about

**7. The index is _____ from a base of 100% for 2000.**
    (A) measurement     (B) measuring
    (C) to measure     (D) measured

**8. The total cost of the annex _____ at $5 million.**
    (A) has estimated     (B) is estimated
    (C) has estimation     (D) is to estimate

**9. Miss Davis _____ to deputy manager of the section.**

13

(A) was promoted      (B) was promoting

(C) was promotive      (D) had promoted

10. A new shopping mall is _____ in the town.

     (A) constructing      (B) construction

     (C) been constructed      (D) being constructed

11. Smoking is strictly _____ in any part of the building.

     (A) forbid      (B) forbidding

     (C) forbidden      (D) forbidder

12. The secretary was made _____ for the phone call she made to her friend in London, by her boss.

     (A) payment      (B) pay

     (C) to pay      (D) paying

13. Consumption of marine products _____ to grow three times faster between now and 2020 than in the last 10 years.

     (A) expecting      (B) expectation

     (C) is expected      (D) has expected

14. The lid can be easily _____ by simply loosening the hinge pin with a screwdriver.

     (A) remove      (B) removable

     (C) removing      (D) removed

15. The cause of the problem _____ and corrected.

     (A) identified      (B) identity

     (C) has been identified      (D) has been identifying

16. The shipbuilders were _____ into three groups because no single group could build all seven tankers in the time required for delivery.

     (A) divide      (B) divided

     (C) division      (D) divisible

17. Reservations must _____ 24 hours in advance by calling Sunshine Airlines at the reservation number below.

    (A) be reconfirmed    (B) reconfirm

    (C) to reconfirm    (D) confirmation

18. Charles Rayner, who is to replace Tom Spencer as chief software architect at Miraclesoft Corp. Next week, is _____ as an innovator.

    (A) know    (B) to know

    (C) knowing    (D) known

19. Michael Goldsmith, Vice President, Chief information Office, will _____ a base salary of $280,000 and is eligible for a target annual bonus equal to not less than 45% of base salary.

    (A) pay    (B) have paid

    (C) be paid    (D) being paid

20. Dogs are not _____ in any of the communal internal areas and must be on a lead when being taken to the bedrooms.

    (A) permission    (B) permit

    (C) permitting    (D) permitted

13

# 正確解答

1-(C) 被動語態用「be動詞＋動詞的過去分詞」句型來表示。text 的意思是「本文」、store 是「儲存」。

2-(B) 題目的意思是「這個裝置怎麼被稱呼」。這是包含疑問詞的被動語態。

3-(D) 片語動詞是由詞組組成，被當作一個及物動詞使用。call off 的意思是「中止」。

4-(A) 在使用感官動詞與使用動詞的被動語態中，補語變成不定詞 to。break into 的意思是「打斷、闖入」。

5-(D) 「用……覆蓋」是 be covered with...，介系詞是 with，不是 by。

6-(B) 「擔心是否……」是 be concerned that...。arrogant 是「傲慢的」。

7-(D) index 之後有 is，不能是被動語態。題目的意思是「指標以 2000年為100%來測量」。

8-(B) 題目的意思是「擴建的總工程費被估算為五百萬美金」。

9-(A) 在中文中，「晉升」可以用主動語態表示，但是在英語中 promote 是及物動詞，所以必須變成被動語態 was promoted。deputy manager 是「副理」。

10-(D) 被動語態的進行式用「is [am, are] being＋過去分詞」來表示。

11-(C) 在空格之前有 strictly（嚴格地），所以或許會覺得困難。只要當作是 Smoking is...就可以。「被禁止」是被動式，所以 (C) forbidden 是正確答案。

12-(C) 使用使役動詞的被動語態補語是不定詞 to。

13-(C) expect 的意思是「期待」、「要求」、「認為」。符合句意的是「期待」。be expected to... 表示「被期待做……」，所

以正確答案是(C)。

14-(D) 空格前的 easily 之前有 The lid can be，所以(D) removed 是
正確答案。can be＋過去分詞（可以被……）是有助動詞的
被動語態句型。

15-(C) 從句意應該可以判斷出動詞 identify（確認）當作及物動詞使
用。主詞是 The cause of the problem，所以答案是(C) has
been identified 的被動語態。

16-(B) 空格之前是 were，所以不可以是被動語態的句子。(A) divide
與(C) division 不能接續在 were 之後。(D) divisible（可分割
的）在句意上不符合。

17-(A) 請注意主詞是 Reservations（預約）。預約被「再次確
認」，所以變成被動語態的句子。(A) be reconfirmed 是正確
答案。

18-(D) 「以……聞名」是 be known as...，使用被動語態來表示，所
以(D) 是正確答案。

19-(C) 從句意來看可以判斷空格的部份應該填入「被支付」，是被
動語態的單字。(A) pay 與(B) have paid 不能成為被動語態。
(D) being 是進行式，但是在 paid 之前應該是 be。

**13**

20-(D) 只要了解主詞是 Dogs，應該就能判斷 are no 為被動語態的
句子。正確答案(D) permitted 是過去分詞。

# 練習題的中文翻譯

1. 原文儲存在 8 公分的光碟裡。

2. 這個裝置叫做什麼？

3. 棒球比賽因雨中止。

4. 男子闖入店裡被警衛發現。

5. 山頂上被雪覆蓋。

6. 我們擔心日本是否被視為傲慢的國家。

7. 該項指標是以 2000 為基準來計算。

8. 擴建的費用總額經估算為五百萬美金。

9. 戴維斯小姐被晉升為部門副理。

10. 在市區蓋了一幢新的購物中心。

11. 這棟建築物裡全面禁煙。

12. 秘書被上司要求支付她打給倫敦朋友的電話費。

13. 海鮮產品的消費，從現在到 2020 年為止，可預期將以過去 10 年間的 3 倍速度成長。

14. 這個蓋子只要使用螺絲起子放鬆鉸鏈，便能輕易打開。

15. 這個問題的原因可以被確認以及被修正。

16. 造船工人被分為三個小組，因為只有一個小組的話，無法在交期內建造好七艘油輪。

17. 在 24 小時前，必須打電話給陽光航空，再次確認下列的預約號碼。

18. 下週知名的改革者雷查斯預計取代史湯姆接任 Miraclesoft 公司的軟體設計主任。

19. 邁可‧高密斯－副董事長，資訊最高負責人，將獲支付基本薪資 28 萬美金，如果達到營業目標的話，則有資格獲得不低於基本薪資 45% 的獎金。

20. 公共場所的室內空間不允許狗進入，帶到寢室時請用繩子綁好。

**13**

# Note

# 14th Day 不定詞

To err is human, to forgive divine. ——— 「名詞的用法」
（人非聖賢，孰能無過，恕人之過，善莫大焉。）

I want something to drink. ——— 「形容詞的用法」
（我想喝點東西。）

She went to England to study English. ——— 「副詞的用法」
（她去英國唸英文。）

I didn't hear you come in. ——— 「原形不定詞」
（我沒有聽到你進來。）

To be frank with you, you won't be able to get the job.———
——————————————————————「獨立不定詞」

（坦白地說，你得不到那份工作。）

不定詞、分詞、動名詞是準動詞，本章針對不定詞作說明。

## （1）不定詞的種類

不定詞分為 **to 不定詞**（to＋動詞原形）與**原形不定詞**（動詞的原形）。原形不定詞只限於變成感官動詞，及使役動詞的補語時使用。

I want to **hear** about it.

（我想要聽聽關於那件事。）

I saw Jack **go** into the shop.

（我看到傑克走進店裡。）

## （2）不定詞的用法

不定詞中有**名詞用法**、**形容詞用法**、**副詞用法**等三種用法。

### (a) 名詞的用法

這個時候將做為句子的主詞、受詞、補語。

**To deceive** oneself is very easy. 〔主詞〕

（欺騙自己非常容易。）

It is hard **to please** him. 〔it 是虛主詞、不定詞是真主詞〕

（很難取悅他。）

They began **to criticize** each other. 〔受詞〕

（他們開始互相批判。）

I found it difficult **to get** along with her.
〔it 是虛受詞、不定詞是真受詞〕

（我發現很難與她和睦相處。）

Your job is **to input** the data. 〔主詞補語〕

（你的工作是輸入資料。）

I want you **to go** with him. 〔受詞補語〕

（我希望你和他一起去。）

### (b) 形容詞的用法

I have a lot of work **to do**. 〔修飾名詞〕

（我有很多工作必須要做。）

I want something **to eat**. 〔修飾代名詞〕

（我想要吃點東西。）

The clock seems **to be** wrong. 〔主詞補語〕

（那個時鐘似乎壞了。）

I believe it **to be** true. 〔受詞補語〕

（我相信那是真的。）

14

### （c）副詞的用法

這個時候用來修飾動詞、形容詞、副詞及整個句子。

I went to his office to **pick up** the document. 〔修飾動詞〕

（我去他的辦公室拿文件。）

I'm glad **to meet** you. 〔修飾形容詞〕

（我很高興可以見到你。）

Are you old enough **to drink**? 〔修飾副詞〕

（你已經是可以喝酒的年紀了嗎？）

**To tell** the truth, she is not qualified to do the job. 〔修飾整個句子〕

（說實話，她沒有資格做那份工作。）

不定詞的副詞用法表示目的、原因、理由、結果等意思。

I went to the cafeteria **to eat** lunch. 〔目的〕

（我去自助餐館吃午餐。）

I was surprised **to see** her there. 〔原因〕

（我很驚訝看到她在這裡。）

How foolish of me **to do** such a thing! 〔理由〕

（做了那樣的事，我真是愚蠢啊！）

The naughty boy grew up **to be** a great scientist. 〔結果〕

（那個頑皮的男孩長大後變成偉大的科學家。）

This magazine is easy **to read**. 〔限定表示形容詞意思的範圍〕

（這本雜誌容易閱讀。）

### （3）應該注意的不定詞用法

### （a）不定詞的形式主詞

不定詞的形式主詞用「for＋形式主詞＋to 不定詞」、「It is＋形容詞＋of＋形式主詞＋to 不定詞」句型來表示。後者只限用於 kind（親

切的）、foolish（愚蠢的）、wise（有智慧的）等等表示人類個性的形容詞。

It is impossible **for him to attend** the ceremony.

（他不可能出席那個儀式。）

It was stupid **of you to spill** coffee on the keyboard.

（你真是太笨了，居然把咖啡倒在鍵盤上。）

### （b）不定詞的否定

不定詞的否定形態，將 not 或是 never 放在不定詞之前即可。

I told you **not to open** the door.

（我告訴過你不要打開門。）

I promise **never to do** such a thing again.

（我發誓不會再做那樣的事。）

### （c）疑問詞＋to 不定詞

疑問詞＋to 不定詞變成名詞子句

I don't know **what to do**.

（我不知道該怎麼做。）

Will you tell me **how to use** this computer?

（你可以教我怎麼使用這台電腦嗎？）

### （d）不定詞的完成式

不定詞的完成式，為「to have＋過去分詞」的形式，表示比述語動詞更早的時間點。

He seems **to have retired** from his job.

= It seems that he (has) retired from his job.

（他似乎退休了。）

He seemed **to have retired** from his job.

= It seemed that he had retired from his job.

（他似乎已經退休了。）

### （e）獨立不定詞

用逗點將副詞用法的不定詞與句子其它部份分隔，獨立不定詞修飾整個句子。

**To make matters worse**, she talked back to her boss.

（更糟糕的是，她與她的上司頂嘴。）

She can speak Spanish, **not to mention** English.

（她不僅會說英語，也會說西班牙語。）

其它還有 to tell (you) the truth（老實說）、to be frank (with you)（坦白說）、strange to say（說也奇怪）、to begin with（首先）、to be sure（的確）等等。

### （f）原形不定詞的用法

原形不定詞可做為「感官動詞」與「使役動詞的受格補語」使用。

I heard Mary **say** so.

（我聽到瑪麗那麼說。）

I'll let you **know** when I'm finished.

（當我完成時我會通知你。）

I'll make Oscar **deliver** it to you.

（我會叫奧斯卡寄給你。）

I'll have Mike **take** care of it.

（我會讓邁可來處理。）

### （g）原形不定詞的慣用語法

You **had better get to** work now.

（你現在最好開始工作。）

I **cannot (help) but admire** him.

（我不得不佩服他。）

Judy **does nothing but gossip** all day.

（茱蒂一整天說長道短，其他什麼事都沒做。）

## （4）把不定詞當作受詞的動詞

He would not **agree to subscribe** to cable **TV**.

（他不打算同意申裝有線電視。）

Don't **hesitate to call** me if you need help.

（如果你需要協助，不要猶豫，請打電話給我。）

其它還有 aim（瞄準）、arrange（安排）、choose（選擇）、decide（決定）、expect（期待）、fear（害怕）、hope（希望）、manage（設法做到）、mean（打算）、offer（提供）、plan（計劃）、pretend（假裝）、promise（承諾）、refuse（拒絕）、seek（追求）、want（想要）、wish（但願）等等。

14

## 練習題

時間限制7分鐘

請在以下各題目的(A),(B),(C),(D)之中選出最適合的答案填入空格之中。

**1. Do you have anything _____?**
    (A) declare         (B) to declare
    (C) declaring       (D) declared

**2. I think I'd better _____ now.**
    (A) going           (B) to go
    (C) go             (D) than go

**3. He refused _____ responsibility.**
    (A) take          (B) to take
    (C) taking        (D) having taken

**4. I heard someone _____ the door.**
    (A) open         (B) to open
    (C) opened      (D) to have opened

**5. It may be better _____ avoid wearing white outfits on rainy days.**
    (A) of you to     (B) of you
    (C) for you      (D) for you to

**6. Most young workers in our company have no wish _____ promoted.**
    (A) to be        (B) be
    (C) to have      (D) being

**7. The lawmaker called on Japan _____ its barriers to U.S. products.**
    (A) remove      (B) to remove
    (C) for removal   (D) removing

14

8. How come you decided _____ to the concert?

    (A) to not go        (B) go not to

    (C) go to not        (D) not to go

9. I have to work overtime _____ this assignment.

    (A) finishing        (B) finished

    (C) to finish        (D) finish

10. His lawyer advised him _____ not guilty.

    (A) plead        (B) pleaded

    (C) plea        (D) to plead

11. The guide is full of suggestions on interesting places _____ for sightseeing, shopping, and entertainment.

    (A) go        (B) to go

    (C) going        (D) gone

12. The chief engineer tried to figure out how _____ with the problem on his own.

    (A) dealing        (B) deal

    (C) to deal        (D) to have dealt

13. Many people want _____ working after retiring to help fund their later years.

    (A) to keep        (B) keeping

    (C) to be kept        (D) to have kept

14

14. The aim of these activities is _____ communication and conflict management skills.

    (A) to improvement        (B) improve

    (C) to be improve        (D) to improve

15. With the invention of the microwave oven, it became possible _____ prepare meals in a very short time.

    (A) at housewives to        (B) for housewives to

    (C) housewives to        (D) for housewives

16. The police continued to search for four men who were believed _____ the counterfeit cash.

    (A) passing
    (B) to pass
    (C) to be passed
    (D) to have passed

17. It has become difficult _____ what is real health food by just reading the labels.

    (A) tell
    (B) told
    (C) to tell
    (D) to be told

18. The studies strongly suggest that advertising causes children _____ addicted to cigarettes.

    (A) become
    (B) becoming
    (C) to become
    (D) to have become

19. The minister emphasized his strong intention _____ domestic tourism along with inbound tourism.

    (A) to promote
    (B) promotion
    (C) promoted
    (D) to promotion

20. Small and medium-sized businesses plan _____ their workforce next year.

    (A) increase
    (B) increased
    (C) to increase
    (D) increasing

14

## 正確解答

1-(B) 題目的意思是「你有任何事要宣佈嗎？」to declare 是用不定詞 to 來修飾 anything。

2-(C) 表示「最好……」的 had better 之後，接續原形不定詞。

3-(B) refuse 把不定詞當作受詞。題目的意思是「他拒絕承擔那項責任」。

4-(A) heard 是感官動詞，所以接續原形不定詞。

5-(D) 不定詞形式主詞通常用「for...不定詞 to」來表示。「of...不定詞 to」只限用於表示形容人類個性的形容詞。avoid doing 的意思是「避免做……」。

6-(A) to be promoted 是被動語態的不定詞。promote 是及物動詞，請注意本句中須變成過去分詞形態 promoted。

7-(B) 片語 call on 的意思是「要求」，以不定詞當作受詞。題目的意思是「議員要求日本取消對美國產品的貿易障礙。」

8-(D) 不定詞的否定形態為不定詞之前加上 not 或是 never。

9-(C) work overtime 的意思是「加班」。assignment 的意思是「分配（工作）」。to finish（為了完成）是不定詞的副詞用法。

10-(D) 「advise＋人＋不定詞」是正確用法。但是，請注意不能變成 advise＋不定詞。如果要用 advise，則變成advise＋動名詞。plead not guilty 的意思是「不承認有罪」。

11-(B) 請注意 interesting places 與應該填入空格的單字的關係。有興趣去的地方，也就是「有興趣去觀光的地方」，所以選擇形容詞用法 to go 是正確答案。

12-(C) 請注意空格之前的 how，應該就能判斷出這是疑問詞之後接續不定詞的句子。how to deal with... 的意思是「如何應付……」。

14

13-(A) want 用不定詞當作受詞，所以(A) to keep 是正確答案。

14-(D) 在空格之前有 is，所以在空格中可以判斷應該填入
「做……」之意的英文。to 不定詞可以當作「做……」的名
詞用法。to improve 的意思是「提升」。

15-(B) 句中的 it 是虛主詞。後面應該會接續真主詞的不定詞。不定
詞的形式主詞，以「for＋形式主詞＋不定詞 to」來表示。請
記住「of...不定詞 to」只限用於表示人類個性的形容詞。

16-(D) 不定詞完成式的題目。不定詞完成式用「to have＋過去分
詞」來表示，表示比述語動詞更早的時間點。本題目的重點
是關係代名詞 who 之後的時式，were believed 是過去式。在
空格中填入選項(D) 的 to have passed。

17-(C) it 是虛主詞，真主詞用不定詞（to tell）來表示。選項(D) 的
to be told 在句意上不適合。

18-(C) 動詞 cause（引起……）使用「cause＋受詞＋to不定詞」的
句型。(D) 不定詞完成式 to have become 與 causes 的現在
式時態不符。

19-(A) 在空格之前有名詞（intention），所以應該可以判斷出這並不
是不定詞的形容詞用法。從意思上可以判斷(A) 的 to promote
是正確答案。

20(C) plan 是使用不定詞當作受詞的動詞，(C) to increase 是正確解
答。

**14**

# 練習題的中文翻譯

1. 你有任何事情要宣布嗎？
2. 我想我應該要走了。
3. 他拒絕承擔責任。
4. 我聽到有人開門。
5. 在下雨天或許最好避免穿白色的衣服。
6. 我們公司的年輕員工幾乎沒有人抱著升官的希望。
7. 那位議員要求日本取消針對美國產品的貿易障礙。
8. 為什麼你決定不去演唱會？
9. 為了完成這項工作，我必須加班。
10. 律師幫他以無罪辯護。
11. 那本旅遊書記載著滿滿的關於觀光、購物、娛樂等有趣的地點。
12. 那位主任技師打算自己思考處理的方法。
13. 為了晚年的養老金，許多人想要在退休後繼續工作。
14. 這些活動的目的是提高溝通能力與針對人與人之間的摩擦處能力。
15. 微波爐的發明，讓主婦可以在極短時間內準備好飯菜。
16. 警察繼續搜索四名被發現使用偽鈔的男子的行蹤。
17. 只看標籤，要分辨出哪個為真正的健康食品，是非常困難的。
18. 那項調查強烈暗示廣告是造成孩童吸菸成癮的原因。
19. 那位部長強調他想同時促進來自國外的觀光與國內觀光的強烈意圖。
20. 中小規模的企業計劃明年增加勞動力。

14

# 15th Day 分詞與動名詞

Barking dogs seldom bite. ──────────── 「現在分詞」
（會叫的狗不會咬人。）

John has a broken leg. ──────────── 「過去分詞」
（約翰的腳骨折了。）

Speaking at the meeting, he suddenly collapsed. 「分詞構句」
（在會議中發言時他突然倒下。）

Seeing is believing. ──────────── 「動名詞」
（百聞不如一見。）

## （1）分詞的種類

分詞中有**現在分詞**與**過去分詞**。

Let **sleeping** dogs lie. 〔現在分詞〕

（不要吵醒沉睡中的狗。）〔不要沒事惹事、自找麻煩。〕

The **beaten** road is the safest. 〔過去分詞〕

（常有人行走的路最安全。）

## （2）分詞的用法

分詞中有**形容詞性的用法**與**副詞性的用法**。

Pour **boiling** water into the teapot. 〔形容詞的用法〕

（把熱水倒進茶壺裡。）

He speaks **broken** English. 〔形容詞的用法〕

（他英語說得零零落落。）

**Made** of iron, this pot is very heavy. 〔副詞性的用法〕

（這個水壺是用鐵製成的，所以非常重。）

## （3）限定用法

形容詞用法的分詞，**直接修飾名詞**，這稱為「**限定用法**」。分詞只有一個字時，放在名詞之前；分詞伴隨其它語句時，放在名詞之後。此外，現在分詞具有主動的意思，表示「正在～、做～」，及物動詞的過去分詞具有被動的意思，表示「被～、被～了」。

Let's take a picture of that **sleeping** cat.

（來幫那隻沉睡的貓拍照吧。）

Let's take a picture of the cat **sleeping** on the step.

（來幫那隻在樓梯上沉睡的貓拍照吧。）

He bought a **used** car.

（他買了一輛中古車。）

He bought a car **used** by a famous singer.

（他買了一輛過去是一個著名歌手用過的車。）

## （4）敘述用法

分詞變成主詞補語或受詞補語。

He sat **reading** the magazine. 〔主詞補語〕

（他坐著看雜誌。）

She kept **waiting** for hours. 〔主詞補語〕

（她等了好幾個小時。）

She felt **insulted**. 〔主詞補語〕

（她覺得受到侮辱。）

He didn't seem **convinced** by the argument. 〔主詞補語〕

（他似乎不能接受那個論點。）

15

I'm sorry to have kept you **waiting**. 〔受格補語〕

（很抱歉讓您久等了。）

I smell something **burning**. 〔受詞補語〕

（我聞到有什麼東西燒焦了。）

I couldn't make myself **understood** in English. 〔受詞補語〕

（我無法用英文與人溝通。）

I left the door **unlocked**. 〔受詞補語〕

（我沒鎖門。）

## （5）副詞的用法

分詞當作修飾整個句子的副詞性修飾語句時，稱為「**分詞構句**」。
分詞構句表示理由、條件、讓步、附帶狀況等等的意思。

**Shopping** at the mall, Nancy ran into her old classmate. 〔時間〕
（在購物中心購物時，南希巧遇老同學。）

**Being** sick, the president could not attend the reception. 〔理由〕
（因為生病，所以總裁無法出席接待會。）

**Turning** right at the next intersection, you will find the subway entrance. 〔條件〕
（在下一個十字路口右轉的話，你可以找到地下鐵的入口。）

**Understanding** what you say, I still think you should apologize to him. 〔讓步〕
（我可以理解你說的事，但即使如此，我還是認為你應該向他道歉。）

The president entered the conference room, **accompanied** by his secretary. 〔附帶狀況〕
（董事長帶著秘書進會議室。）

〔**注意**〕為了讓意思更清楚，有時候會在分詞之前放 when, while, though 等等的連接詞。

**While staying** in New York, I went to many jazz concerts.
（當我待在紐約時，去聽了好幾次爵士樂演奏會。）

### （6）獨立的分詞構句

分詞的形式主詞與主要句子主詞不一樣時，稱為「獨立分詞構句」。

**Weather permitting**, we'll hold the party at the poolside.

（只要天氣許可，我們會在游泳池邊舉辦派對。）

**That being** the case, we are not recruiting any female workers this year.

（正因為如此，今年不錄取女性員工。）

### （7）非人稱獨立分詞

分詞的形式主詞是 we, you, they 等等「一般」主詞時，可以將主詞省略，請當作慣用句記住它吧！

**Generally speaking**, Americans are informal and frank.

（一般來說，美國人是不拘小節以及直率的。）

**According to** the poll, Americans regard Japanese as competitive and hardworking.

（根據那項調查，美國人認為日本人有強烈的競爭心以及工作很勤奮。）

其它還有 judging from（由……判斷）、talking of（說到……）、considering（考慮到……）、strictly speaking（嚴格來說）、taking everything into consideration（考慮到所有的事情）、granted that（假定……）。

15

### （8）動名詞的用法

動名詞與現在分詞是同樣的形態，一方面保有動詞的性質，一方面當作名詞使用。

**Finding** a job is not easy in this town. 〔主詞〕

（在這座城鎮找工作並不容易。）

He admitted **having stolen** the money. 〔受詞〕

（他承認偷走了那些錢。）

The mother was accused of **abusing** her child. 〔介系詞的受詞〕

（那位母親被控告虐待自己的小孩。）

My hobby is **collecting** keychains. 〔主詞補語〕

（我的興趣是收集鑰匙圈。）

動名詞有時候當作修飾名詞的形容詞，這個時候表示用途、目的。

Don't jump into the **swimming** pool.

（請不要跳進游泳池裡。）

Please smoke in the **smoking** area

（請在吸煙區抽菸。）

## （9）動名詞的完成式

完成式的動名詞，表示比述語動詞的時間點更早。

He regretted **having sold** the land.

（他後悔賣掉土地。）

## （10）使用動名詞的慣用語法

### （a）feel like doing（想要……）

I don't **feel like eating** fish tonight.

（今晚我不想吃魚。）

### （b）It is no use doing（即使……也沒用）

It is no use advising him.

（即使給他忠告也沒用。）

**（c）cannot help doing（不得不、忍不住……）**

When I saw him in a tailcoat, **I could not help laughing**.

（當我看到穿著燕尾服的他，我忍不住一直笑。）

**（d）worth doing（值得去做……）**

The art exhibition is **worth visiting**.

（那場美術展值得一看。）

**（e）on doing（一……馬上）**

**On arriving** at his office, he called up the client.

（他一到辦公室，便馬上打電話給客戶。）

其它還有 There is no doing（無法……）、cannot [never]... without doing（如果……一定……）、of one's own doing（自己做……）、What [How] about doing（去做……如何？）

## （11）只使用動名詞當作受詞的動詞

MP3 135

She tried to **avoid answering** the question.

（她試著逃避回答那個問題。）

I **advise taking** a few days off.

（我建議休幾天假。）

I **enjoy playing** tennis.

（我喜歡打網球。）

其它只使用動名詞當作受詞的動詞還有 admit（承認）、appreciate（感謝）、consider（考慮）、deny（否定）、escape（逃跑）、finish（結束）、mind（介意）、postpone（延期）、practice（實行）、quit（停止）、resist（抵抗）、approve of（贊成）、give up（放棄）、go on（繼續下去）、leave off（停止）、put off（延期）等等。

15

## 練習題

請在以下各題目的(A),(B),(C),(D)之中選出最適合的答案填入空格之中。

**1. I've been looking forward _____ you.**

    (A) see            (B) to see

    (C) to have seen       (D) to seeing

**2. This is a difficult question, but it is worth _____.**

    (A) to ask           (B) asking

    (C) of asking        (D) asked

**3. The _____ abolition of the system would therefore be a welcome move.**

    (A) proposed        (B) proposal

    (C) proposing       (D) propose

**4. Although she could not speak Swahili, she could make herself _____ with gestures.**

    (A) understand      (B) understanding

    (C) to understand     (D) understood

**5. I can't stand _____ children dying of hunger.**

    (A) seeing         (B) see

    (C) seen          (D) to be seen

**6. _____ her accent, I would say she is from Boston.**

    (A) Judge from      (B) Judged

    (C) Judging from     (D) Having judge

**7. I think we need to postpone _____ a decision.**

    (A) being made      (B) to make

    (C) to be made      (D) making

8. There is a _____ demand for a high-quality American cigarette.

    (A) grow           (B) grew

    (C) growing      (D) grown

9. Japan needs to strengthen its relations with _____ countries.

    (A) oil-produce      (B) oil-producing

    (C) oil-production    (D) oil-productive

10. The number of Japanese cars _____ to that country was about 1. 7 million last year.

    (A) export        (B) exportation

    (C) exported      (D) exporting

11. If you are a retailer _____ in contacting Mega Toys, you can contact them on 800-212-3344, or fax 212-333-4455.

    (A) interest       (B) interesting

    (C) interested     (D) has interest

12. More than eight out of ten consumers _____ believe food safety is a very important issue.

    (A) surveyed      (B) surveying

    (C) survey        (D) have surveyed

13. We pride ourselves on _____ a relaxed and friendly atmosphere with special attention to the smallest detail.

    (A) to create      (B) creativity

    (C) created       (D) creating

14. Japan faces a labor shortage time bomb _____ by falling birthrates and an aging population.

    (A) cause        (B) caused

    (C) to cause      (D) causing

15

15. The talks dealt with topics _____ from general issues on trade and investment barriers to specific areas of bilateral trade such as automobiles and parts.

(A) range
(B) ranging
(C) they range
(D) ranged

16. _____ this situation, I cannot but agree that these transplants should be permitted.

(A) See
(B) Saw
(C) Seeing
(D) Seen

17. Buyers should avoid _____ used cars from sellers that do not provide a permanent address.

(A) buying
(B) bought
(C) buy
(D) to buy

18. _____ by 20 sponsor companies, the Solar Max team has made many improvements for this solar car race.

(A) Back
(B) Backing
(C) Backed
(D) Having been back

19. _____ cholesterol intake lowers the risk for heart disease.

(A) Reduction
(B) Reduce
(C) To reducing
(D) Reducing

20. _____ the overall employment situation in our country, the employment opportunities will be certainly decreased.

(A) Considered
(B) Consideration
(C) Considering
(D) Consider

15

# 正確解答

1-(D) look forward to doing 的意思是「期待……」，to 之後接動名詞。

2-(B) worth doing 的意思是「值得……」，worth 之後接動名詞。

3-(A) 首先思考 propose（提案）與 abolition of the system（那項系統的廢止）的關係。廢止的並不是「提案」，而是「被提案」的東西，所以空格填入具有被動語態意義的分詞，也就是過去分詞。

4-(D) 片語 make oneself understood 的意思是「讓某人了解……」。

5-(A) stand（忍受）可以使用動名詞或是不定詞，不過選項中的 to，不是不定詞。題目是「不忍看到餓死的小孩」。

6-(C) 分詞構句 Judging from... 的意思是「從……來判斷」。

7-(D) postpone 只能用動名詞來當作受詞。

8-(C) 思考 demand（要求）與 grow（變大）的關係。要求「變大」，所以用表示主動意思之現在分詞來修飾。

9-(B) 「石油出產國」是 oil-producing countries，使用包含現在分詞來的複合形容詞來修飾。題目的意思是「日本必須強化與石油出產國之間的關係」。

10-(C) 車輛是被出口，所以使用 exported car 表示被動語態意思的過去分詞來修飾。

11-(C) 「對……有興趣」是 be interested in...，所以正確答案是過去分詞的(C)。

12-(A) 意思是「被調查的消費者」，所以用表示被動語態意思的過去分詞 surveyed。

13-(D) 請注意空格之前有 on。介系詞之後接續名詞或代名詞，或者是可以取代名詞或代名詞的詞句，所以選擇是動名詞的(D)

**15**

creating。(B) creativity 也是名詞，但是在意思上或文法上不能接續 a relaxed and friendly atmosphere（輕鬆又親切的氣氛）。pride oneself on 之後不可以接續不定詞 to，所以(A) 是錯誤答案。

14-(B) 從句意來看，可以知道題目的意思是「因為……造成的人手不足」，選擇表示被動意思的過去分詞 caused。

15-(B) 「涉及 A 至 B 範圍的議題〔話題〕」，用 topics ranging from A to B 表示主動意思。正確解答是現在分詞的 ranging(B)。

16-(C) 空格在句首或是從句意來看，可以知道這是一個分詞構句。空格之後接續 this situation（這個狀況），所以可以理解為「一看到這個狀況」，所以選擇(C) Seeing。

17-(A) avoid 是使用動名詞當作受詞的動詞，所以(A) buying 是正確答案。

18-(C) 只要注意到空格之後的 by，就知道應該選擇 Backed 表示被動的過去分詞。

19-(D) 題目的述語動詞是 lowers，所以空格應該填入主詞，也就是必須填入名詞或是可以當作名詞的詞句。動名詞(D) Reducing（減低）是正確答案。(A) Reduction 必須接續 of cholesterol intake 才可以。

20-(C) 在句中有逗號，所以這是分詞構句。「考慮到……」Considering 是正確答案。

# 練習題的中文翻譯

1. 期待可以與您見面。
2. 雖然這是很難的問題，但是值得詢問。
3. 制度廢止的提案因此變得相當受歡迎。
4. 雖然她不會說斯華西里語，但是她可以透過動作手勢了解對方的意思。
5. 我無法看到孩子們餓死。
6. 從口音判斷，我猜她來自波士頓。
7. 我認為我們有必要晚一點做決定。
8. 品質良好的美國香菸之需求增加。
9. 日本必須強化與產油國之間的關係。
10. 出口至該國的日本車數量，去年大約為１７０萬台。
11. 有興趣連絡 Mega Toys 公司的零售業者，可用以下方式連絡他們，電話號碼是８００－２１２－３３４４、傳真號碼是２１２－３３３－４４５５。
12. 十個消費者中，有超過八個消費者認為食品安全是非常重要的議題。
13. 我們很自豪，因為特別注意到最細節的部份，而能創造一個輕鬆又親切的氣氛。
14. 日本因為出生率降低以及人口高齡化的問題，正面對勞動力不足這個定時炸彈。
15. 在那場會議當中，從貿易、投資障礙相關的一般性問題，到汽車與零件等二國之間貿易的特定領域，都成為了討論話題。
16. 看到這個狀況，不得不同意許可這些臟器移植。
17. 購買中古車的人，應該避免從不提供固定居住地址的賣家購買中古車。
18. Solar Max 團隊有２０家公司贊助，已經針對 Solar Car Race 進行許多改善。
19. 只要減少膽固醇的攝取，就能降低罹患心臟病的危險性。
20. 就我國的總體就業狀況而論，就業機會的確減少了。

15

# 16th Day 假設語氣

I propose that Mr. Brown lead the project. 「**現在式假設語氣**」
（我提議布朗先生領導那項專案。）

If you won 100 million dollars in the lottery, what would you
do with the money? ——————— 「**過去式假設語氣**」
（如果中了一億元樂透，你會怎麼運用這筆錢？）

I wish I were rich like him. ——————— 「**過去式假設語氣**」
（我真希望我可以像他那麼富有。）

If we had not bought this house, we would not have had this
much trouble. ——————— 「**過去完成式假設語氣**」
（如果我們沒買這間房子，我們就不會有這麼多麻煩。）

## （1）何謂假設語氣？

所謂假設語氣，是指說話者不將某件事情當作事實敘述，而是當作
假設、想像、願望等等來敘述的動詞形態。假設語氣有**現在式假設
語氣、未來式假設語氣、過去式假設語氣、過去完成式假設語氣**四
種類型。

## （2）現在式假設語氣

現在式假設語氣表示現在或是未來的想像、假設、願望、讓步等等
的意思。動詞與人稱及數量無關，全都用動詞原形。

If it **rain** tomorrow, **I'll stay** at home. 〔想像、假設〕

（明天如果下雨的話，我會待在家裡。）

Whatever excuses she **make**, her boss **won't forgive** her. 〔讓步〕

（不管她有任何理由，她的上司都不會原諒她。）

但是，在現代英語中使用現在式的直述語氣（將事件當作事實敘述時）。

If it **rains** tomorrow, **I'll stay** at home.

Whatever excuses she **may make**, her boss **won't forgive** her.

如上述的現在式直述語氣為一般用法。

現在式假設語氣在美式英語中，特別用於接續在表示提案、主張、要求、命令等動詞之後的 that 子句，以及接續在表示提案、主張、要求、命令的名詞及形容詞之後的 that 子句之中。

He **proposed** that the annual convention **be held** in Chicago.

（他提議在芝加哥舉辦年會。）

They **insisted** that Mr. Williams **resign** from his post.

（他們主張威廉斯先生應該辭去現在的職務。）

The members **requested** that he **reconsider** his decision.

（會員要求他重新考慮那項決定。）

The court **ordered** that the company **pay** to the plaintiff $100,000.

（法院命令那間公司支付原告十萬美金。）

It is **essential** that Mr. Spencer **join** our project.

（史賓賽先生絕對有必要參加我們的專案。）

It is **desirable** that every worker **attend** the meeting.

（希望全體員工都能參加會議。）

It was his ardent **desire** that his son **take over** his business.

（兒子繼承公司是他殷切的渴望。）

其它還有 suggest, command, urge, demand 等等的動詞，necessary, advisable, preferable（希望）、imperative（必須的）、anxious（掛念的）等等的形容詞，使用現在式假設語氣。此外，在英式英語中，在 that 子句中使用 should。

He **proposed** that the annual convention **should be held** in Chicago.

16

223

## （3）未來式假設語氣

「萬一……的話」，表示比現在式假設語氣更遠的「不確定現在」以及「未來」的假設。

$$If＋主詞＋should＋原形……，主詞＋\begin{Bmatrix} should\ [shall] \\ would\ [will] \\ could\ [can] \\ might\ [may] \end{Bmatrix}＋原形$$

If our company **should go** bankrupt, what **will** you **do**?

（萬一我們公司破產的話，你會怎麼做？）

If you **should be ordered** to transfer to New York, what **will** you **answer**?

（萬一你被調任到紐約的話，你會怎麼辦？）

## （4）過去式假設語氣

與現在事實相反的假設，表示現在不可能實現的願望。動詞使用過去式，但是使用 be動詞時，不管主詞的人稱及數量為何，皆統一使用 were。

$$If＋主詞＋過去式……，主詞＋\begin{Bmatrix} would \\ should \\ could \\ might \end{Bmatrix}＋原形$$

If it **were** not rainy today, I **would go** for a walk.

（如果今天沒下雨的話，我就會去散步。）

If I **were** a billionaire, I **would buy** a private jet plane.

（如果我是億萬富翁的話，我就會買一架私人噴射機。）

If she **could speak** English and German, I **would employ** her.

（如果她會說英語及德語的話，我就會雇用她。）

〔注意〕在口語中使用第一人稱以及第三人稱時，有時候用 was。

If I **was** a billionaire, I **would buy** a private jet plane.

### （5）過去完成式假設語氣

與過去事實相反的假設，表示在過去不可能實現的願望，動詞使用過去完成式。

$$If＋主詞＋過去完成式……，主詞＋\begin{Bmatrix} should \\ would \\ could \\ might \end{Bmatrix}＋have＋過去分詞$$

If I **had had** my credit card with me yesterday, I **could have bought** the diamond ring.

（如果昨天我有帶信用卡的話，我就會買那只鑽石戒指。）

If he **had gone** to work by train yesterday, he **would not have been** in the accident.

（如果昨天他坐電車去公司的話，就不會遇上意外。）

### （6）各種假設語氣的表現

### （a）I wish＋主詞＋過去形（真希望……）

＜無法實現的現在願望＞

**I wish＋主詞＋had＋過去分詞（真希望當時……）**

**I wish I had** more time.

（真希望我有更多時間。）

**I wish you had never said** that to him.

（我真希望你從來沒有跟他說過那件事。）

### （b）If only＋主詞＋過去式（要是……就好了）

**If only I could speak** to him!

（要是可以跟他說話就好了！）

**If only I hadn't signed** the contract!

（要是我沒在合約書上簽名就好了！）

**16**

（c）**It is time＋主詞＋過去式**（已經該是……的時候）

**It's time you went** to see him.

（該是你去見他的時候了。）

（d）**as if [as though]＋主詞＋過去式**（彷彿……）

**as if [as though]＋主詞＋had＋過去分詞**（〔當時〕彷彿……）

He talks **as if he knew** everything about the United States.

（他說得彷彿他對美國瞭若指掌。）

She talks **as if she had been** to France.

（她說得彷彿她去過法國似的。）

（e）**If it were not for...**（如果沒有……）

**If it had not been for...**（如果當時沒有……）

**If it were not for** your financial assistance, he could not start his own business.

（如果沒有得到你的財務援助的話，他無法開始他自己的事業。）

**If it had not been for** your encouragement, she would not have applied for the managerial position.

（如果當時沒有得到你的鼓勵，她不會去應徵管理職位吧。）

（f）**If＋主詞＋were to＋原形**（如果……）

**If I were to be laid off**, I would go back to my hometown and become a farmer.

（如果我被解雇的話，我會回去故鄉當個農夫。）

16

## （7）不使用 if 的條件句

### （a）倒裝

**Had I known** you were coming, I would have prepared a better meal.

（如果早知道你要來，我就會準備更好的菜色了。）

### （b）介系詞句

**But for** his help, she could not bring up her two children.

（如果沒有他的援助，她無法養育兩名孩子。）

**Without** the telephone, life would be very inconvenient.

（如果沒有電話，生活將會變得非常不方便。）

### （c）主詞表示條件

**A Japanese** would apologize in such a case.

（假如是日本人的話，會在那種情況下道歉。）

16

## 練習題

請在以下各題目的(A),(B),(C),(D) 之中選出最適合的答案填入空格之中。

**1. I wish there _____ more time.**

    (A) are                 (B) can be

    (C) be                 (D) were

**2. I wouldn't say it if it _____ true.**

    (A) isn't               (B) aren't

    (C) weren't         (D) has not been

**3. Even if you _____, I wouldn't let him resign from his post.**

    (A) object           (B) objected

    (C) to object       (D) had objected

**4. I wish I _____ forget all about it.**

    (A) be able to      (B) to be able to

    (C) can be         (D) could

**5. I would not sign the contract yet if I _____ you.**

    (A) am               (B) are

    (C) were            (D) have been

**6. It is desirable that it _____ done at once.**

    (A) be               (B) were

    (C) being          (D) will be

**7. What would you say if I _____ yes?**

    (A) said            (B) will say

    (C) had said       (D) am going to say

**8. You wouldn't be working here if it _____ for me.**

    (A) isn't            (B) weren't

    (C) has not been    (D) had been

16

9. If you _____ me about the letter, I might have thrown it away.
   (A) will not tell        (B) have not told
   (C) did not tell        (D) had not told

10. _____ for oxygen, fires couldn't start.
   (A) Only           (B) Just
   (C) Even          (D) But

11. He suggested that more information _____ made available to protect investors.
   (A) be            (B) will
   (C) should have     (D) to be

12. "If I _____ my life to live over again, I would take more chances," stated retiring Chief Executive Jerry Hamilton.
   (A) have          (B) had
   (C) have had       (D) have been

13. Mr. Smith insisted that the construction of the condominium _____ immediately suspended.
   (A) be           (B) is
   (C) are          (D) were

14. If I _____ to be sexually harassed on the job, I would bring the case to court without hesitation.
   (A) were         (B) have
   (C) am          (D) have been

15. _____ not been for your advice, I might have sold the stock.
   (A) It have       (B) It had
   (C) Have it       (D) Had it

16

16. The minister proposed that the discount rate _____ cut as one of five measures to boost the nation's economy.

    (A) should                 (B) is

    (C) be                    (D) is to

17. I wouldn't dream of intruding if this _____ extremely important.

    (A) isn't                 (B) weren't

    (C) haven't been       (D) wouldn't have been

18. He treated her as if she _____ his longtime business partner.

    (A) is                   (B) are

    (C) has been          (D) had been

19. If you _____ jeans to the party, you might have gotten in trouble.

    (A) wear               (B) worn

    (C) have worn         (D) had worn

20. I wish I _____ come up with an idea to make such a large amount of money.

    (A) can                 (B) am able to

    (C) could             (D) should

16

# 正確解答

1-(D) 題目的意思是「如果有更多時間就好了」，這是表示現在無法實現的願望，所以使用過去式假設語氣。

2-(C) 主要子句的助動詞 would 是過去式，所以可以判斷這是過去式假設語氣。在選項中是過去式的只有(C)。

3-(B) Even if... 的意思是「即使……」。助動詞 wouldn't 是過去式，所以可以明白這不是過去式假設語氣。題目的意思是「即使你反對，我也不會讓他辭職」。

4-(D) wish 表示無法實現的現在或是過去的願望，所以條件子句的動詞應該是過去式，或是 had＋過去分詞。

5-(C) 請注意主要子句的助動詞 would。因為是過去式，所以條件子句用過去式假設語氣。

6-(A) 句型為接續在表示提案、主張、要求、命令等等的動詞、形容詞、名詞之後的 that 子句中的現在式假設語氣，所以使用原形 be動詞。

7-(A) 題目的意思是「如果我說 Yes，那麼你會怎麼說呢？」

8-(B) 請注意主要子句 wouldn't 的部份，與條件子句的 if it...for 部份。假設語氣的句型中有 if it were not for...（如果沒有……）以及 if it had not been for...（如果當時沒有……）。

9-(D) 主要子句的述語動詞部份是 might have thrown 與「might＋have＋過去分詞」，所以可以明白這是過去完成式假設語氣的句子。過去完成式的選項是(D)。

10-(D) 表示「如果沒有」的假設語氣句型，可以用 but for... 來表示。

11-(A) 接續在表示提案 suggest 之後的 that 子句，使用現在式假設語氣，所以正確答案是(A) 的 be。

12-(B) 從主要子句的 would 應該就能明白這是過去式假設語氣的句

**16**

子。

13-(A) insist 是表示主張的動詞，所以接續其後的 that 子句中，必須使用現在式假設語氣。

14-(A) 首先從主要子句的 would 可以知道，這是過去式假設語氣的句子。只要能想起在表示「如果……」的假設語氣句型中，有「if＋主詞＋were to＋原形」這個句型，便能順利選出正確答案。

15-(D) 從主要子句的 might have sold 可以知道，這是過去式假設語氣的句子。不用 if 句型，可以利用倒裝來表示條件，所以(D)的 Had it 是正確答案。

16-(C) 接續在表示提案意思的 propose 之後的 that 子句，使用現在式假設法，所以(C) 的 be 是正確答案。

17-(B) 從主要子句的 wouldn't 應該就能明白題目是過去式假設語氣的句子。在選項中過去式只有(B) 的 weren't。

18-(D) 主要子句是過去式 treated，所以從屬子句不可以是現在式或是現在完成式。選擇過去完成式的 had been 為正確答案。

19-(D) 從主要子句的 might have gotten 應該就能明白，這是過去完成式假設語氣的句子，所以選擇(D) 的 had worn 是正確答案。

20-(C) wish 之後接續從屬子句的述語動詞是過去式、或是 had＋過去分詞。前者是無法實現的現在願望，後者是在過去無法實現的願望。

16

# 練習題的中文翻譯

1. 如果有更多時間就好了。
2. 如果不是真的，我不會說這件事。
3. 即使你反對，我也不會讓他辭職。
4. 真希望我可以忘了所有的事。
5. 如果我是你，我還不會簽那份合約。
6. 希望它能馬上被完成。
7. 如果我贊成的話，你會怎麼說？
8. 如果沒有我的話，你不會在這裡工作。
9. 如果你沒有告訴我有關那封信，或許我已經丟掉它了。
10. 如果沒有氧氣，就不會起火。
11. 他建議為了保護投資者應該取得更多資訊。
12. 「如果人生重來一次，我會更加冒險」，這是退休的董事長－傑瑞・漢米敦所說的話。
13. 史密斯先生主張立即中止那間公寓的建設。
14. 如果我在工作上受到性騷擾，我會毫不猶豫地提出告訴。
15. 如果沒有你的建議，或許我已經賣掉股票。
16. 那位閣員提議降低稅率，作為活絡國家經濟的五個對策之一。
17. 如果這不是非常重要的事情，我不會夢見自己介入這件事。
18. 他對待她的態度，彷彿她是他的長久生意伙伴。
19. 如果你穿那條褲子去派對的話，可能會遇到麻煩的事情。
20. 我真希望可以想出像那樣賺大錢的點子。

16

# 17th Day 時態的一致與引述

I think she doesn't drink.
（我想她不喝酒。）
I thought she didn't drink.
（我以為她不喝酒。）
He said to me, "I'll buy you a drink."
（他對我說：「我請你喝一杯。」）
He told me that he would buy me a drink.
（他那時告訴我，他會請我喝一杯。）

## （1）時態的一致

在複合句中，**主要子句的動詞是過去式時，從屬子句的動詞受主要子句的動詞影響，變成過去式或過去完成式**，這被稱為「**時態一致**」。

### （a）時態一致的原則

| 主要子句的時態 | 從屬子句的時態 | |
|---|---|---|
| 現在→過去 | 現在式→過去式<br>未來式→過去式的助動詞<br>現在完成式<br>過去式<br>過去完成式 | 現在進行式→過去進行式<br>現在完成進行式<br>過去進行式 ┐<br>過去完成進行式 ┘ →過去完成進行 |

I **think** that he **is** an honest person.

（我想他是一個正直的人。）

I **thought** that he **was** an honest person.

（我以為他是一個正直的人。）

I'm sure that she **will come** to the party.

（我確定她會來參加派對。）

I **was** sure that she **would come** to the party.

（我那時確信她會來參加派對。）

I **don't understand** why he is **working** so hard.

（我不明白為什麼他那麼努力工作。）

I **didn't understand** why he **was working** so hard.

（我那時不明白為什麼他那麼努力工作。）

I **wonder** why he **hasn't come** yet.

（我想知道他為什麼還不來。）

I **wondered** why he **hadn't come** yet.

（我那時想知道他為什麼還不來。）

It **seems** that he **forgot** to lock the door.

（他似乎是忘了鎖門了。）

It **seemed** that he **had forgotten** to lock the door.

（他那時似乎是忘了鎖門了。）

I **think** I **must talk** with her.

（我想我必須與她談談。）

I **thought** I **must talk** with her.

（我那時想我必須與她談談。）

### （b）不符合一般原則的情況

①一般的真理

The teacher **taught** the students that light **travels** about 300,000 kilometers per second.

（老師教導學生，光能夠以每秒３０萬公里的速度前進。）

**17**

②現在的事實與習慣

He **didn't know** that our head office is in Miami.

（他不知道我們總公司位於邁阿密。）

She **said** that she **jogs** around the lake every morning.

（她說她每個早晨都繞著湖邊慢跑。）

③歷史的事實

We **learned** that the Renaissance **lasted** from about 1300 to about 1600.

（我們學習到文藝復興大約從西元１３００年持續到西元１６００年。）

④假設語氣的句子

He **said** that if he **won** 100 million dollars in the lottery, he **would** buy a house.

（她說如果中了一億元彩券，他會買一間房子。）

### （2）引述

### （a）直接引述與間接引述

將人說過以及想過的事情，傳達給其它人的方法稱為「引述」。引述句中，**有將人說過的話原原本本傳達的「直接引述」，以及將人說過的話，以說話者的立場，用自己的語言傳達的「間接引述」**這二種。

He said, "I have a high fever." 〔直接引述〕

（他說：「我發高燒。」）

He said that he had a high fever. 〔間接引述〕

（他說他發高燒。）

如同上述例子的 said，傳達人說過的話的動詞稱為「傳達動詞」，"I have a high fever." 以及 that he had a high fever 等被傳達的部份，稱為「被傳達的部份」。

## （b）引述的轉換

將直接引述變成間接引述時，必須注意以下幾點：

①傳達動詞之後的逗號與引用符號。

②被傳達部份中的人稱代名詞，必須從傳達者的立場變更為適當的人稱代名詞。

③傳達動詞是過去式時，被傳達部份中的動詞時態要一致。

He said, "**I'm going** to see a doctor."

（他說：「我要去看醫生。」）

He said that **he was going** to see a doctor.

（他說他要去看醫生。）

④傳達動詞是過去式時，被傳達部份中的詞句如下變化：

this → that

these → those

here → there

now → then

(three years) ago → (three years) before

today → that day

tomorrow → the next day [the following day]

yesterday → the day before [the previous day]

next (week) → the following (week)

last (year) → the previous (year)

Linda said to me, "I received **this** parcel **yesterday**."

（琳達對我說：「我昨天收到這個包裹。」）

Linda told me that she had received **that** parcel **the day before**.

（琳達告訴我她前天收到那個包裹。）

但是，被傳達的地點及時間點很清楚時，以此為基準來決定詞句。

John said to me yesterday, "I'll meet you **here** at two o'clock **tomorrow**."

（約翰昨天說：「明天兩點在這裡見面。」）

John told me yesterday that he would meet me **here** at two o'clock today.

（約翰昨天告訴我今天兩點在這裡見面。）

＜傳達者在見面的日子裡，也出現在該地點。＞

### （c）平述句的傳達

只有 said 時，直接用 said，如果是 said to (me) 時，則變成 told
(me)。將平述句接續在連接詞 that 之後。一般可以省略掉 that。

Jack **said**, "I'm going to buy a new printer."

（傑克說：「我要去買一台新的印表機。」）

Jack **said** that he was going to buy a new printer.

（傑克說他要去買一台新的印表機。）

Jim **said to** her, "I'll give you a ride."

（吉姆告訴她：「我送妳一程。」）

Jim **told** her that he would give her a ride.

（吉姆告訴她，他會送她一程。）

### （d）疑問句的情況

said to (me) 變成 asked (me)。有疑問詞時，使用「疑問詞＋主詞＋
動詞」的句型，沒有疑問詞時，使用「if [whether]＋主詞＋動詞」的
句型並去除問號。

He **said to** me, "**Where can I smoke**?"

（他問我：「我可以在哪裡抽菸？」）

He **asked** me **where he could smoke**.

（他問我他可以在哪裡抽菸。）

He **said to** me, "**Do you want** to lose your job?"

（他問我：「你想丟掉你的工作嗎？」）

He **asked** me **if I wanted** to lose my job.

（他問我是不是想丟掉自己的工作。）

17

## （e）命令句的情況

將傳達動詞變成 tell（命令）、order（命令）、request（要求）、ask（請求）、advise（忠告），被傳達的部份變成不定詞。

I **said** to him, **"Turn down** the TV."

（我告訴他：「請把電視的聲音轉小。」）

I **told** him **to turn down** the TV.

（我告訴他把電視的聲音轉小。）

I **said to** her, **"Please don't open** the window."

（我告訴她：「請不要開窗。」）

I **asked** her not to open the window.

（我要求她不要開窗。）

The doctor **said to** me, **"Stay** home for a couple of days."

（醫生告訴我：「在家休息兩三天。」）

The doctor **advised** me **to stay** home for a couple of days.

（醫生建議我在家休息兩三天。）

She **said**, **"Let's take** a break."

（她說：「讓我們休息一下吧。」）

She **suggested** that we **(should) take** a break.

（她建議我們休息一下。）

## （f）感嘆句的情況

將傳達動詞變成 cry (out), shout, exclaim（呼叫）、sigh（嘆息）等等並去除驚嘆號。

He **said**, "What a beautiful lady she is!"

（他說：「她是多麼美的女人啊！」）

He **exclaimed** what a beautiful lady she was.

（他驚呼她是多麼美的女人啊。）

17

**239**

# 練習題

請在以下各題目的(A),(B),(C),(D)之中選出最適合的答案填入空格之中。

**1. He told me that he _____ really anxious to talk to me.**

    (A) being                (B) was

    (C) have been          (D) was being

**2. I was sure I _____ get a speeding ticket.**

    (A) am going to        (B) will

    (C) was going to       (D) will have

**3. Most of them didn't know Ottawa _____ the capital of Canada.**

    (A) is                  (B) was

    (C) had been           (D) will be

**4. She asked me _____ find him.**

    (A) where could she   (B) where she can

    (C) where              (D) where she could

**5. We learned that sound _____ at 331 meters per second through the air at 32 degrees Fahrenheit.**

    (A) travel           (B) travels

    (C) traveled         (D) has traveled

**6. He asked me if my loan _____.**

    (A) approve         (B) is approved

    (C) has approved     (D) had been approved

**7. I was wondering if I _____ something wrong.**

    (A) am doing         (B) do

    (C) was doing        (D) doing

17

8. It meant that the stock _____ on its way to a quick rebound.

    (A) is               (B) was

    (C) have been      (D) will be

9. She told me that she _____ a chance to call Mr. Thomas yet.

    (A) haven't had     (B) don't have

    (C) won't have      (D) hadn't had

10. The teacher told his students that John F. Kennedy _____ by a hidden gunman in November, 1963.

    (A) is assassination    (B) was assassinated

    (C) had been assassinated  (D) was an assassin

11. There was just one little thing that _____ sense.

    (A) is made        (B) making

    (C) hasn't make     (D) didn't make

12. Her voice was so low that I could scarcely hear what she _____ saying.

    (A) be           (B) is

    (C) was          (D) has been

13. My new secretary shredded the entire report that I _____ on.

    (A) will be working   (B) was worked

    (C) have worked     (D) had been working

14. According to the police, the assailants apparently thought he _____ Korean.

    (A) was          (B) being

    (C) has been      (D) is

17

15. The chief operating officer said that he _____ in order to take responsibility for the securities scandal.
    (A) resign           (B) resigns
    (C) was resigning    (D) has resigned

16. The majority of those responding to the poll stated that they _____ their Christmas purchases this year.
    (A) curtail           (B) curtails
    (C) would curtail    (D) are curtailed

17. Sixty percent of those polled said that they _____ a lower standard of living in exchange for safeguarding the environment.
    (A) accepting      (B) acceptance
    (C) being accepted  (D) could accept

18. The policeman said he feared the death toll _____ rise further, since about 70 of the 700 injured were in serious condition with chest and head wounds.
    (A) could          (B) is able to
    (C) can           (D) must

19. The minister said that there _____ 210,000 illegal foreign workers in Japan as of last November.
    (A) are           (B) were
    (C) have been     (D) had been

20. Curator Mike Spencer said that he _____ deeply disappointed by the city's decision to close the museum.
    (A) be           (B) has
    (C) was          (D) will have been

17

# 正確解答

1-(B) 請注意，傳達動詞是過去式 told。題目的意思是「他真的很想和我說話」。

2-(C) 主要子句的動詞是過去式 was，所以從屬子句的動詞也變成過去式。speeding ticket 是「超速罰單」。

3-(A) 「渥太華為加拿大的首都」一事是現在的事實，因此時態不需一致。

4-(D) 這是將有疑問詞的句子改為間接引述的情況，被傳達的部份使用「疑問詞＋主詞＋動詞」的句型。

5-(B) 音速被視為普遍的真理，時態不需一致。

6-(D) 請注意傳達動詞是過去式的 asked。題目的意思是「他問我，我的貸款是否核準了」。

7-(C) 請注意主要子句是過去進行式。這個時候，從屬子句的動詞也要變成過去進行式。

8-(B) 主要子句的動詞是過去式的 meant。題目的意思是「這表示股票的價格馬上就會回升」。

9-(D) 請注意傳達動詞是過去式的 told。被傳達的部份是 hasn't had a chance，就像 hadn't had a chance 一樣時態一致。

10-(B) 「甘迺迪總統遭暗殺」是歷史上的事實，時態不需一致。assassinate 是「暗殺」。

11-(D) 主要子句的動詞是過去式的 was，所以從屬子句選擇過去式的助動詞 didn't。

17

12-(C) 請注意從屬子句的 could scarcely hear（幾乎沒聽到）。本句是過去式，所以 what she [ ] saying（她說過的事）的空格填入過去式。

13-(D) 首先掌握住 that 是關係代名詞，I [ ] on（我致力於）修飾 the entire report。題目的述語動詞是過去式的 shredded（用

碎紙機撕毀），在時間點上報告完成的時間點是更早之前，因此必須使用過去完成式。

14-(A) 主要子句的述語動詞是過去式（thought），所以從屬子句的動詞時態必須一致，變成過去式，選擇(A) 的 was 是正確答案。

15-(C) 傳達動詞是過去式，被傳達的部份時態必須一致，變成過去進行式。在本句的進行式是表示「確定的預定」。

16-(C) 傳達動詞是過去式（stated），所以被傳達的部份時態必須一致，助動詞必須變成過去式 would curtail（縮減）。

17-(D) 傳達動詞是過去式（said），所以被傳達的部份時態必須一致，空格必須填入過去式（could accept）。

18-(A) 請注意題目句子的 he feared（他擔心……）。此外，在 feared 之後可以發現連接詞的 that 被省略掉。that 子句承繼時態變成過去式。選擇(A) 的 could 是正確答案。

19-(B) 傳達動詞是過去式（said），此外 as of last November 清楚表示被傳達部份的時間點，所以空格填入過去式。(D) 的 had been 是過去完成式，不可與表示過去的用語 last November 一起使用。

20-(C) 傳達動詞是過去式，所以被傳達的部份必須時態一致，空格必須填入過去式（was）。

17

# 練習題的中文翻譯

1. 他對我說他真的很想與我談話。

2. 我確定我會收到超速罰單。

3. 他們大部份皆不知道渥太華是加拿大的首都。

4. 她問我在哪裡可以找到他。

5. 我們學習到，聲音在華氏３２度的空氣中，速度為每秒３３１公尺。

6. 他問我貸款是否核準了。

7. 我懷疑自己是否做了一些錯事。

8. 這表示股票的價格馬上就會回升。

9. 她告訴我，她還沒有機會打電話給湯瑪斯先生。

10. 老師告訴他的學生－約翰・F・甘迺迪在１９６３年被神秘的狙擊手暗殺了。

11. 只有一件小事不合理。

12. 她的聲音非常小，所以幾乎聽不到她說什麼。

13. 新秘書把我正在製作的報告書，全部用碎紙機撕毀了。

14. 根據警察的報告，攻擊者似乎認為他是韓國人。

15. 董事長說他為了負起股票醜聞的責任而決定辭職。

16. 超過半數以上的民意調查回覆者表示：今年會縮減聖誕節購物。

17. 接受民意調查的人之中有６０％的人表示：為了環保，願意接受降低生活水準。

18. 警察說他擔心死者的數量可能會增加，因為７００名傷者之中有７０名的胸部及頭部受了重傷。

19. 那位部長說，從去年１１月開始，在日本有２１萬名非法外籍勞工。

20. 館長邁可・史賓塞說，他非常失望市政府決定關閉這間博物館。

**17**

# 18th Day 連接詞

MP3 146

Jack and Nancy are getting married. ——— 「對等連接詞」
（傑克與南希結婚。）

I'll see if he is in the office. ——— 「從屬連接詞」
（我去看看他是否在辦公室。）

There were two calls for you while you were out. ———
——————————————————————— 「從屬連接詞」

（你外出時，有兩通找你的電話。）

As far as I know, he is dependable. ——— 「片語連接詞」
（就我所知，他是可靠的。）

Either you or Tom must attend the meeting. 「相關連接詞」
（不是你就是湯姆，必須出席那場會議。）

## （1）連接詞的種類

連接詞是用來連結句中的單字與單字、片語與片語、子句與子句，從功用來分，可區分為「**對等連接詞**」與「**從屬連接詞**」。此外，從形態來分，可以分為「**單純連接詞**」、「**片語連接詞**」與「**相關連接詞**」三種。

## （2）對等連接詞

MP3 147

對等連接詞是將有對等關係的單字與單字、片語與片語、子句與子句結合的詞，有 and , but, or, so, for, nor 等等。

### （a）and「～和～」

I went to London **and** Rome on business last summer.
〔單字與單字〕

（我去年夏天去倫敦與羅馬工作。）

18

I went there by train **and** by bus. 〔片語與片語〕

（我搭電車及巴士去那裡。）

He studied very hard, **and** he passed the examination.
〔子句與子句〕

（他很努力學習，於是他通過考試。）

Work hard **and** you will get promoted. 〔命令句＋and〕

（請努力工作，那麼你就能升職。）

I'll go **and** get John. 〔不定詞 to 的替用〕
= I'll go to get John.

（我會去接約翰。）

### （b）but「但是」

He is smart **but** selfish. 〔單字與單字〕

（他頭腦聰明，但是很自私。）

I turned on the engine, **but** it didn't start. 〔子句與子句〕

（我打開引擎，但是無法發動。）

I like her, **not** because she is beautiful, **but** because she is
considerate. 〔not A but B（是 B 不是 A）〕

（我喜歡她並不是因為她漂亮，而是因為她很體貼。）

### （c）or「～或～」

Which would you like, tea **or** coffee? 〔單字與單字＜選擇＞〕

（紅茶或咖啡，你想要哪一種？）

Work seriously, **or** you will be fired. 〔命令句＋or〕

（請努力工作，否則你會被解雇。）

This is a hagoita, **or** a battledore. 〔換句話說、說明〕

（這是 hagoita，也就是打毽板。）

18

### (d) nor「即不是……也不是」

I have never driven a car, **nor** do I intend to learn.

（我沒開過車，也沒想過要去學開車。）

### (e) so「所以」

My bicycle was stolen, **so** I bought a new one.

（我的腳踏車被偷了，所以我買了一輛新的。）

### (f) for「因為」

She is not happy, **for** her husband is seldom at home.

（她不快樂，因為她的丈夫幾乎不在家。）

for 是書面用法，在口語中使用 because, since, as。此外，for 不可以放在句首。

## （3）引導名詞子句的從屬連接詞

**MP3 148**

引導名詞子句的從屬連接詞有 that, if, whether。

It is true **that** I embarrassed him. 〔真主詞〕

（我令他尷尬是事實。）

I don't think **that** we can trust him. 〔受詞〕

（我不認為他值得信任。）

I'll see **if** he's ready. 〔受詞〕

（我會去看看他是否已經準備好了。）

I don't know **whether** she will be able to come. 〔受詞〕

（我不知道她是否可以來。）

The trouble is **that** he gets carsick easily. 〔補語〕

（問題是他容易暈車。）

The fact is **that** she has never driven a car. 〔補語〕

（事實上她從來沒有開過車子。）

The fact **that** he has a villa has nothing to do with it. 〔同格〕

（他擁有別墅的事實與那件事完全沒有關係。）

I heard a rumor **that** he divorced his wife. 〔同格〕

（我聽到傳言，他已經和老婆離婚了。）

## （4）引導副詞子句的從屬連接詞

### （a）表示時間的從屬連接詞

表示時間的從屬連接詞有 when, while, as, after, before, since, until, till。

I'll call you **when** I get back.

（我回來會打電話給你。）

How can I reach you **while** you are in New York?

（你在紐約期間，我應該如何與你連絡？）

He stared straight ahead **as** the judge imposed the sentence.

（法官宣判時，他目不轉睛地看著法官。）

She wants to keep working **after** she has the baby.

（即使有了小孩，她希望繼續工作。）

I have to finish this **before** he comes.

（在他來之前我必須完成這件事。）

It's been 20 years **since** I graduated from college.

（自從我大學畢業之後，已經過２０年了。）

Let's wait **until** he calls.

（讓我們等到他打電話過來為止。）

Go straight **till** you come to a traffic light.

（請直走到紅綠燈。）

18

### (b) 表示理由的從屬連接詞

表示理由的從屬連接詞有 because, since, as, now (that)。

He is under a lot of strain **because** his business is not going well.

（因為他的工作不順利，所以他有很大的壓力。）

**Since** she can't type, we'd better ask someone else to do the job.

（因為她不會打字，所以那份工作最好請其他人做。）

**As** he didn't have any change, he could not make the call.

（因為他沒有零錢，所以他沒辦法打電話。）

**Now that** the project is completed, I can take my vacation.

（既然這個專案結束了，我可以休個假了。）

### (c) 表示條件的從屬連接詞

表示條件的從屬連接詞有 if, unless。

You can call me **if** there's a problem.

（如果有任何問題，你可以打電話給我。）

I can't announce the result **unless** he approves.

（在他同意之前，我不能公佈結果。）

### (d) 表示讓步的從屬連接詞

表示讓步的從屬連接詞有 though, although。

**Though** this computer is old, it still serves my purpose.

（這台電腦雖然舊，但是仍然有用。）

**Although** it's a small company, it made a lot of profit last year.

（那間公司雖然小，但是去年賺了很多錢。）

18

### (e) 表示樣態的從屬連接詞

表示樣態的連接詞有 as。

Do **as** I say.

（照我說的去做。）

將兩個以上的單字集合為一個片語與連接詞，而同樣具有連接詞作用的片語有 as soon as（一……就……）、even if（即使）、as if（猶如）、as though（猶如）、as [so] long as（只要……）、as far as（盡可能……）、in case（假使）等等。

He went back to his office **as soon as** the negotiations were over.

（談判一結束，他馬上就回公司。）

**Even if** you're wrong, you should not admit it.

（即使你錯了，你也不應該承認。）

He treats me **as if** I were a child.

（他對待我的方法，彷彿我是個小孩似的。）

She spoke **as though** she knew everything about it.

（她說得好像她對那件事瞭若指掌。）

You can come with me **as long as** you promise to behave yourself.

（如果你可以保證你會表現得有禮貌，那麼你可以跟我一起來。）

**As far as** I know, he is coming back on Wednesday.

（就我所知，他預計在星期三回來。）

Take something to eat, **in case** you have to wait there a long time.

（帶一些東西過去吃吧，以防你必須在那裡等那麼長的時間。）

連接詞與其它的單字相互使用，例如，both...and...（也……也）、either...or...（不是……就是……）、neither...nor...（既不是……也不是……）、not only... but (also)...（不僅……而且……）、so...that...（非常……所以……）、such...that...（非常……所

以……）、so that...can [will, may]...（為了讓……）等等。

We have branches in **both** San Francisco **and** Los Angeles.

（我們在舊金山以及洛杉磯都有分公司。）

**Either** he **or** she must be telling a lie.

（他或她之中一定有一個人說謊。）

He **neither** drinks **nor** smokes.

（他既不喝酒也不抽菸。）

Computer games are popular **not only** in Japan, **but also** in America.

（電腦遊戲不僅在日本流行，也在美國流行。）

Acquiring the land was so difficult **that** they gave up the plan.

（收購那塊土地非常困難，所以他們放棄那項計畫。）

It was **such** a good deal **that** I could not resist signing the contract on the spot.

（那是非常好的交易，所以我忍不住當場簽約。）

I drew a map to the place **so that** he **could** go there by himself.

（為了讓他自己可以去到那裡，我畫了一張地圖給他。）

# 練習題

請在以下各題目的(A),(B),(C),(D)之中選出最適合的答案填入空格之中。

**1. Put your mind to it _____ you will succeed.**
    (A) while                 (B) and
    (C) or                   (D) when

**2. Why don't you have a seat over there _____ you wait?**
    (A) during            (B) then
    (C) for                 (D) while

**3. The idea _____ men are superior to women is laughable.**
    (A) when             (B) if
    (C) what            (D) that

**4. See _____ you can speed things up a little.**
    (A) if                  (B) for
    (C) and              (D) since

**5. By the American definition, a recession occurs _____ the economy contracts.**
    (A) then             (B) for
    (C) when           (D) during

**6. Tobacco smokers are not only hurting themselves, _____ also the people around them.**
    (A) and             (B) or
    (C) nor            (D) but

**7. The president is neither optimistic _____ pessimistic about the present situation.**
    (A) or                (B) nor
    (C) but             (D) as

18

8. Thirty-seven years have passed _____ Japan's overseas aid program was initiated.

    (A) before           (B) for

    (C) ago             (D) since

9. The election will be meaningless _____ an in-depth policy debate is conducted.

    (A) that           (B) whether

    (C) unless        (D) nor

10. In the eyes of the general public, it appeared as _____ the prime minister was being "manipulated" by the faction.

    (A) if             (B) of

    (C) like          (D) because

11. Each candidate had only 15 minutes to speak, either at the joint press conference _____ the speech meeting.

    (A) and           (B) for

    (C) or             (D) nor

12. The committee members were unable to agree on _____ the school lunch program should be abolished.

    (A) that           (B) until

    (C) because     (D) whether

13. _____ her children grew older, Nancy enrolled in a local university and began taking accounting classes.

    (A) As            (B) For

    (C) If             (D) then

14. It is too early to determine _____ the domestic market has recovered, because February sales were slower than last year's.

    (A) since         (B) while

    (C) and           (D) if

18

15. From the beginning, we have been operating in China as _____ we were in our own country, not in a foreign country.

    (A) while         (B) if

    (C) of            (D) that

16. IT skills shortages will women _____ companies take action.

    (A) then         (B) whether

    (C) since        (D) unless

17. There is one vending machine for every 22 people in Japan, compared to one for every 41 people in the U. S. , 43 in Germany, _____ 81 in Britain.

    (A) or           (B) while

    (C) and         (D) when

18. Cheap oil prices are welcome now _____ the world economy has become stagnant.

    (A) that         (B) so

    (C) for          (D) then

19. _____ she liked the lifestyle of the profession, she specialized in anesthesiology.

    (A) Unless       (B) So

    (C) For         (D) Because

20. _____ it was more costly, we decided to take a full-day cruising.

    (A) Like         (B) Although

    (C) During      (D) Until

18

# 正確解答

1-(B) 命令句＋and 構句。put one's mind to 的意思是「將……的注意力放在……」。

2-(D) while you wait 的意思是「當你在等待的期間」。during 是介系詞。不能用 during you wait。

3-(D) the idea 與 men are superior to women 是同格。題目的意思是「男性比女性優秀的想法顯得很愚蠢」。

4-(A) See if... 的意思是「請調查是否……」。題目的意思是「請查看看是否可以用更快一點的速度進行」。things 是指加快的對象。

5-(C) 從句意來看可以發現，空格應該填入表示時間的連接詞。題目的意思是「根據美國的定義當經濟緊縮時會引起景氣衰退。」

6-(D) 本題是考 not only...but also...（不僅……還會……）的相關連接詞知識。

7-(B) neither...nor... 的相關連接詞問題。題目的意思是「董事長對於現在的狀況感到既不樂觀也不悲觀」。

8-(D) 因為是現在完成式，所以很容易判斷出空格應該填入 since。initiate 是「開始」。

9-(C) 仔細思考 The election will be meaningless 與 an in-depth policy debate is conducted 的關係。題目的意思是「如果沒有深入的政策辯論，那麼選舉就變得沒有意義」。

10-(A) as if 與 as though 是片語連接詞，意思是「猶如」。題目的意思是「在一般民眾眼裡，總理大臣看起來似乎被那個派系所操縱。」

11-(C) 在題目中有 either，所以這是考 either A or B（或 A 或 B）的相關連接詞知識。

12-(D) 請注意句中的 agree on（對……取得共識），從句意來看，
空格應該填入表示「是否……」的連接詞。(D) 的 whether
是正確答案。

13-(A) 從句意來看應該可以知道，前半句是表示理由。連接詞的 as
表示理由、原因時，通常被放置在句首。(B) 的 for，雖然也
是表示理由的連接詞，但是不可以放在句首。

14-(D) 請注意空格之前的 determine。這個單字的意思是「決
定」，所以空格應該填入表示「是否……」的連接詞。

15-(B) 請注意空格之前的 as。as if...（猶如）是假設語氣或是連接
詞的標準題目。從句子的後半部應該就能判斷出空格應該填
入表示「猶如」的單字。

16-(D) 明白前半句與後半句的意思，然後思考彼此的關係。連接
「IT 技術不足的情況更加惡化」與「公司採取行動」的連接
詞，為表示「如果不……」的 unless。

17-(C) 「A 與 B 與 C」是用 A, B, and C 的句型表示。

18-(A) 請注意在空格之前有 now。只要知道 now that 的意思是「既
然……」，從前半句與後半句的關係應該就能判斷出(A) 為正
確解答。

19-(D) 從前半句與後半句的關係就能判斷出空格應該填入表示「因
為」的連接詞。 雖然 for 也可以表示「理由」，但是不可以
放在句首。

20-(B) 從句意來看空格應該填入表示「雖然」的連接詞 although。

18

# 練習題的中文翻譯

1. 請將你的注意力集中在那件事。如此一來你就能成功。

2. 在等待期間,為什麼你不坐在那裡等呢?

3. 男性比女性更優秀的想法,顯得十分愚蠢。

4. 請你看看是否可以加快一點。

5. 根據美國的定義,當經濟狀況緊縮時,會引起景氣衰退。

6. 吸菸者不僅傷害自己,也會危害周圍人士的健康。

7. 董事長對於現在的狀況感到既不樂觀也不悲觀。

8. 日本海外援助專案從開始到現在已經37年了。

9. 如果沒有深入的政策辯論,那麼選舉就變得沒有意義。

10. 在一般民眾眼裡,總理大臣看起來似乎被那個派系操縱著。

11. 每位候選人不管是在共同記者會還是討論會,都只有15分鐘的演講時間。

12. 委員會的成員針對是否應該廢除學校供給飲食制度一事,無法達成一致意見。

13. 因為她的孩子長大了,所以南希開始進入當地的大學選修會計學。

14. 在這個時間點判斷國內市場景氣是否恢復仍然太早,因為2月份的銷售額比去年同期更遲緩。

15. 從一開始,我們在中國經營公司,就像在自己國家一樣,並不是在外國。

16. IT技術不足的情況將會更加惡化,除非企業採取行動。

17. 相較於美國每41人有一台,德國每43人有一台,英國每81人有一台,在日本每22人都就一台自動販賣機。

18. 既然世界經濟已經不景氣,便宜的油價仍是受到歡迎的。

19. 因為喜歡這份職業的生活方式,所以她專攻麻醉學。

20. 雖然費用更高,但我們決定選擇整天搭機的行程。

18

# Note

# 19th | Day 介系詞

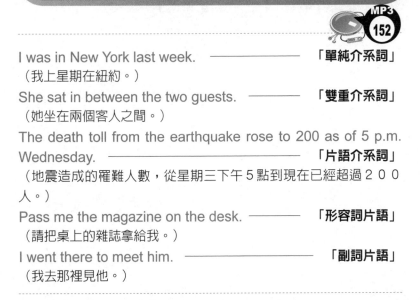

I was in New York last week. ——————— 「單純介系詞」
（我上星期在紐約。）

She sat in between the two guests. ——— 「雙重介系詞」
（她坐在兩個客人之間。）

The death toll from the earthquake rose to 200 as of 5 p.m.
Wednesday. ————————————— 「片語介系詞」
（地震造成的罹難人數，從星期三下午５點到現在已經超過２００
人。）

Pass me the magazine on the desk. ——— 「形容詞片語」
（請把桌上的雜誌拿給我。）

I went there to meet him. ——————— 「副詞片語」
（我去那裡見他。）

## （1）介系詞的種類

介系詞被放置在名詞及代名詞或是與其相當的詞句之前，表示與其
它詞之間的關係。從形態分類可以分為以下三類：

### （a）單純介系詞

單純介系詞只有一個單字，包括 in, at, on, of, from, to 等等。

### （b）雙重介系詞

兩個介系詞並列當作一個介系詞使用，包括 from behind（從……的
後面）、up to（……一直到）、in between（在……的中間）、till
after（直到……之後）等等。

### （c）片語介系詞

集合兩個以上的單字當作一個介系詞使用，包括 in front of（在……

之前）、instead of（代替……）、because of（為了……）、on behalf of（代表……）等等。

## （2）介系詞的用法

介系詞與被放置其後的單字結合成介系詞片語，變成副詞片語或是形容詞片語。被放置在介系詞之後的單字是介系詞的受詞。

### （a）變成副詞片語

He went **to the stadium by car**. 〔修飾動詞〕
（他開車去體育場。）
He was short **of cash**. 〔修飾形容詞〕
（他現金不足。）

### （b）變成形容詞片語

Use some of the floppy disks **in the blue box**. 〔限定用法〕
（請用幾張在藍色箱子中的軟碟。）
This little knife is **of great use**. 〔敘述用法〕
（這隻小刀非常有用。）

## （3）介系詞的受詞

介系詞的受詞，主要以名詞與代名詞為主，其它還有動名詞、子句、形容詞、副詞、不定詞等等也能成為受詞。

Take a look **at** this **picture**. 〔名詞〕
（請看這張照片。）

I spoke **with him**. 〔代名詞〕
（我和他說話。）

She left **without saying** anything. 〔動名詞〕
（她什麼都沒說就離開了。）

I was surprised **at what he said**. 〔子句〕
（我非常驚訝於他說的事情。）

19

Living conditions went **from bad to worse**. 〔形容詞〕

（生活狀況每下愈況。）

It wasn't very popular **until recently**. 〔副詞〕

（直到最近，那個東西才受歡迎。）

I was **about to call** you. 〔不定詞〕

（我正好要打電話給你。）

## （4）介系詞的位置

介系詞原則上放在受詞之前，但是如下情況有時介系詞會與受詞分開。

**What** are you talking **about**?

（你在說什麼？）

Is this **the child** whom Mrs. Jones is taking care **of**?

（這個孩子是瓊斯太太在照顧的小孩嗎？）

Give me **something** to write **with**.

（請給我可以用來寫字的東西。）

## （5）表示時間的介系詞

### （a）at, on, in

at 表示時間與年齡等時間的某一點；in 表示月份與年代等比較長的時間；on 表示特定的日子與時間。

The bank closes **at** three o'clock.

（銀行在三點關門。）

The meeting will be held **on** Wednesday.

（那項會議將在星期三召開。）

The meeting will be held **on** Wednesday morning.

（那項會議將在星期三上午召開。）

Her wedding is **in** June.

（她的結婚典禮是在六月份。）

### （b）by, till [until]

by 表示動詞及狀態的完成期限。till [until] 表示動作與狀態的持續期限。

I can finish this **by** four o'clock.

（我可以在四點前完成這個。）

I'll wait here **till** nine o'clock.

（我會在這裡等到 9 點。）

### （c）since, from

since 表示從過去某個時間點到現在為止的持續時間；from 表示單純的時間起始點。

I haven't talked to her **since** last month.

（我從上個月就沒有和她說話。）

The clinic is open **from** nine to six.

（診所的營業時間是從早上九點到下午六點為止。）

### （d）in, within, after

in 通常表示把現在當作起點的時間過程；within 表示一定的期間之內；after 表示把過去及未來當作起點的時間過程。

I'll call you back **in** a few minutes.

（我在幾分鐘之後打電話給你。）

We'll get there **within** an hour.

（我們將在一個小時內到達那裡。）

You can't go out **after** ten o'clock.

（十點以後，你不可以外出。）

19

### （e）for, during, through

for 表示一般的期間。during 表示特定的期間。through 表示從某個期間開始到結果的持續期間。

I'll stay in New York **for** a week.

（我會在紐約停留一週。）

We received 200 calls **during** the week.

（那一週我們接到超過２００通的電話。）

She sat **through** the entire concert, although she didn't enjoy it at all.

（雖然音樂會很無聊，她仍然坐著聽完整場。）

### （f）about, around

about 與 around 都是表示大約的時間以及期間。

We've been discussing this for **about** three hours.

（我們已經討論這件事討論了大約三個小時。）

I'll stop by **around** three o'clock.

（我大概在三點左右到。）

## （6）表示場所的介系詞

### （a）at, in

at 表示比較狹小的場所；in 表示比較大的場所。

What time does his plane arrive **at** the airport?

（他的班機幾點到達機場？）

What time does his plane arrive **in** Chicago?

（他的班機幾點到達芝加哥？）

### （b）in, into, out of

in 表示在場所內的位置與動作；into 表示向內的動作；out of 表示外面的位置以及向外的動作。

I left the bag **in** the car.

（我把包包忘在車裡。）

They got **into** the car.

（他們坐進車子。）

He came **out of** his office.

（他從辦公室出來。）

（c）**on, above, over, up, under, below, down**

on 表示接觸「在⋯⋯之上」、above 表示有距離的「在⋯⋯上方」；over 表示在距離的「在正上方」；up 表示動作「往⋯⋯的上方」；under 表示接觸或是有距離的「在⋯⋯之下、在正下方」。below 表示有距離的「在⋯⋯的下方」；down 表示動作「向⋯⋯的下方」。

The key is **on** the desk.

（鑰匙在桌子上。）

He hid the key **under** the mat.

（他把鑰匙藏在踏墊下。）

Hang this picture **above** the sideboard.

（把這幅畫掛在餐具櫃之上。）

The epicenter was about 90 km **below** Tokyo Bay.

（震央在東京灣地下約９０公里處。）

We need to hang a lamp **over** the table.

（我們必須把燈吊在桌子上方。）

He went **up** the stairs.

（他走上樓梯。）

He ran **down** the stairs.

（他跑下樓梯。）

19

### (d) by, beside

by 與 beside 都表示較近的位置（～的旁邊。）

Put it **by** the door.

（請放在門旁邊。）

I sat **beside** him.

（我坐在他旁邊。）

### (e) between, among

between 表示在兩個東西「之間」，但是有時候會用來表示在三個東西之間；among 表示三個東西以上的「之間」。

What happened **between** you and Jack?

（你與傑克之間發生了什麼事？）

It is popular **among** young people.

（這在年輕人之間很流行。）

### (f) to, for, toward(s)

to 表示「到達點」；for 表示「方向、目的地」；toward(s) 表示「方向」。

How long will it take to get **to** the place?

（還有多久才能到達那裡？）

She left **for** New York yesterday.

（她昨天離開紐約。）

Walk **toward(s)** the door.

（請往門的方向移動。）

### (g) along, across, through

along 的意思是「沿著……」；across 的意思是「橫越……」；through 的意思是「穿過……」，表示位置與動作。

**19**

Walk **along** this street for three blocks.

（請沿著這條路走三個路口。）

They ran **across** the road. （他們橫越這條路。）

He came **through** the window. （他從窗戶進來。）

### （h）around, round

around 表示「靜止的位置」；round 表示「動作」。但是這兩個字並沒有很嚴格地區分。

Let's sit **around** the table.

（讓我們坐在桌邊。）

She looked **round** the room.

（她瀏覽房間。）

## （7）其它的介系詞

### （a）表示原因、理由的 at, of, from

I was surprised **at** his behavior.

（我對他的行為感到非常驚訝。）

He died **of** a heart attack.

（他死於心臟麻痺〔直接性的原因〕。）

He died **from** a blow on the head.

（他因為頭部受到重擊而死亡〔間接性的原因〕。）

### （b）表示材料的 of, from

This cup is made **of** plastic.

（這個杯子是塑膠製的〔材料沒有變化〕。）

Sake is made **from** rice.

（酒是由米製造的〔材料有變化〕。）

19

### （c）表示手段的 with, by

He opened the door **with** a screwdriver.

（他用螺絲起子打開門。）

I went there **by** bicycle.

（我騎腳踏車去那裡。）

### （d）表示程度、刻度的 by, at

They overcharged me **by** 20 dollars.

（他們多收我２０美金。）

I was driving **at** 80 kilometers per hour.

（我以每小時８０公里的速度駕駛車子。）

### （e）表示穿（衣）的 in

Can I go there **in** jeans?

（我可以穿牛仔褲去那裡嗎？）

### （f）表示交換的 for

I sold my car **for** 5,000 dollars.

（我以五千塊美金賣掉我的車子。）

### （g）表示比例的 for

It is quite warm **for** December.

（以１２月來說，這樣的天氣相當溫暖。）

### （h）表示贊成、反對的 for, against

I'm **for** his proposal.

（我贊成他的提案。）

Are you **for** or **against** the plan?

（你是贊成還是反對那份計劃？）

### （i）表示飲食、從事的 over

Let's talk about it **over** lunch.

（讓我們一邊吃午餐，一邊談那件事）

## （8）雙重介系詞

A child ran out **from behind** the car.

（小孩從車子後面跑出來。）

**Up to** 20 people can take this trip.

（只要達到２０人，這個旅行就能成行。）

The meeting continued **till after** 11 o'clock.

（會議一直持續開著，直到超過１１點。）

## （9）片語介系詞

Let's meet **in front of** the restaurant.

（我們在餐廳前面見吧。）

The flight was canceled **because of** the storm.

（那個班機因暴風雨被取消。）

The event was not successful **on account of** the bad weather.

（因為天候不佳，所以那場活動沒有成功。）

You should have taken the subway **instead of** a taxi.

（你當初應該坐地下鐵去，而不是坐計程車。）

**In case of** rain, we'll put off the picnic.

（如果下雨的話，露營就延期。）

**According to** John, it's a lucrative business.

（根據約翰的說法，這是可以賺錢的生意。）

19

# 練習題

請在以下各題目的(A),(B),(C),(D)之中選出最適合的答案填入空格之中。

**1.** I couldn't bear the thought _____ another year in the hospital.

    (A) to                 (B) for

    (C) in                 (D) of

**2.** I didn't really know about it _____ just now.

    (A) by                 (B) till

    (C) on                 (D) towards

**3.** His office is three doors down the hall, _____ your right.

    (A) in                 (B) for

    (C) on                 (D) with

**4.** I was scared _____ death when the plane suddenly hit an air pocket.

    (A) to                 (B) by

    (C) from              (D) with

**5.** We really need someone _____ experience.

    (A) by                 (B) to

    (C) along             (D) with

**6.** What do you want to see Mr. Jackson _____?

    (A) with             (B) about

    (C) at                (D) under

**7.** I've got to get this report done _____ the end of the day.

    (A) in                 (B) during

    (C) by                 (D) till

8. Why don't you explain it to me _____ lunch?
    (A) while
    (B) of
    (C) with
    (D) over

9. Why do you keep saying the exact opposite _____ what I say?
    (A) to
    (B) against
    (C) for
    (D) of

10. I'll always be grateful to you _____ the chance you gave me.
    (A) with
    (B) for
    (C) from
    (D) by

11. About 400,000 people die _____ smoking-related diseases each year.
    (A) at
    (B) on
    (C) with
    (D) from

12. The success of the new product is the result of the marriage _____ high-quality technology and the publishing industry.
    (A) with
    (B) within
    (C) by
    (D) between

13. As _____ 7 p.m. , the typhoon had a central barometric pressure of 985 hectopascals, with winds blowing at up to 108 kph near its center.
    (A) of
    (B) for
    (C) off
    (D) near

14. The Rotary International Annual Convention will be held from June 17th _____ June 20th.
    (A) on
    (B) at
    (C) in
    (D) to

19

15. This is the nation's first lawsuit filed solely _____ the basis of counter sexual harassment.

    (A) on                  (B) in

    (C) from             (D) through

16. The company will lay off 9,000 employees _____ the next 18 months.

    (A) when            (B) during

    (C) while            (D) by

17. On behalf _____ the company, President Richard Best welcomed the new workers.

    (A) for                (B) from

    (C) toward         (D) of

18. The jet made an emergency landing at Narita Airport shortly after its departure _____ San Jose on Monday evening, because of engine trouble.

    (A) into             (B) for

    (C) at               (D) above

19. The marriage guidance agency said the first few weeks after Christmas is their busiest time of the year, with calls up _____ between 30 and 50 percent.

    (A) to                (B) on

    (C) by               (D) against

20. According _____ a survey conducted by an American financial newspaper, the number of those who think business "will worsen" next year exceeded those believing that it "will improve".

    (A) at               (B) toward

    (C) to               (D) about

# 正確解答

1-(D) 請注意，thought 是名詞，表示「想法、思維」。「想到」是 thought of...。題目的意思是「想到要再住院一年我就無法忍受」。

2-(B) 「直到剛才」是 till just now。till 表示動作與狀態的持續期間。

3-(C) 「你的右手」是用 on your right 表示。

4-(A) be scared to death 是慣用句，意思是「嚇得半死、嚇得不知所措」。

5-(D) 「有經驗」是用 with experience 來表示。

6-(B) 請注意介系詞與其受詞分離。介系詞是 about，受詞是 what。

7-(C) 「在今天之內」是用 by the end of the day 來表示。題目是「必須在今天之內完成這份報告」。

8-(D) 表示「一邊……」可以用 over。over lunch 表示「一邊吃午餐」。

9-(D) 請注意題目的 opposite 是名詞。「與……相反（的東西）」是用 opposite of... 來表示。

10-(B) the chance you gave me 是 grateful（感謝）的理由，所以使用 for。grateful to 人 for... 表示「因～而感激某人」。

11-(D) 「因～而死」是用 die of 或 die from 之一表示。

12-(D) 「A 與 B 的結合」是用 marriage between A and B 來表示。在這裡的 marriage 表示「結合」。

13-(A) 請注意在空格之前有 as，在空格之後有表示時間的 7 p.m.。請記住 as of 可以表示「～現在」。

14-(D) 請注意，在空格前後有兩個不同的日子。因為這是表示舉辦

期間，所以空格應該填入表示「……為止」的介系詞 to。to 也可以用來表示時間、期間的終點。

15-(A) 只要知道 on the basis of 的意思是「以……為基礎」的話，就能順利解答本題。

16-(B) 在空格之後接續的是期間 the next 18 months（從現在開始的１８個月），所以表示特定期間的 during 是正確答案。when 與 while 之後接續子句（主詞＋動詞）。此外，表示時間界限的 by（到……為止）之後接續特定日子及時間，而不接續期間。

17-(D) 只要明白 on behalf of 的意思是「代表……、代替……」，就能輕易解答本題。

18-(B) 「往……出發」是用 departure for 來表示。

19-(C) 請注意在空格之前有 up。這裡的 up 表示「增加」，也就是空格之後的 between 30 and 50 percent 是表示增加的程度。by 是表示程度的介系詞，所以(C) 是正確答案。

20-(C) 請注意在空格之前的 According。片語 according to 的意思是「根據」，所以(C) 是正確答案。

19

# 練習題的中文翻譯

1. 我一想到要再住院一年,我就受不了。
2. 我真的是剛剛才知道這件事的。
3. 他的辦公室是過了大廳後,在你右手邊的第三間。
4. 飛機在空中遇上亂流時,我怕得要死。
5. 我們真的需要有經驗的人。
6. 對於傑克森,你想知道什麼?
7. 我必須在今天之內完成這份報告。
8. 針對那件事,你可以一邊吃午餐一邊向我說明嗎?
9. 為什麼你跟我唱反調?
10. 我會永遠感謝你給我這次機會。
11. 每年約４０萬人因為抽菸的關係而病死。
12. 新商品的成功,是高品質的技術與出版產業的結合。
13. 現在是下午７點,台風中心氣壓是９８５百帕斯卡,中心附近最大風速是時速１０８公里。
14. 扶輪社國際年會於６月１７日至２０日舉行。
15. 這是我們第一件基於反性騷擾提出的訴訟。
16. 該公司預計在未來１８個月內裁減九千名員工。
17. 理查・貝斯特董事長代表公司歡迎新進員工。
18. 那架飛機在星期一晚上往聖荷西起飛不久後,因為引擎故障緊急降落成田機場。
19. 根據那間婚姻介紹所的說法,在聖誕節後的幾週,電話數量增加３０～５０%,是一整年之中最忙碌的時期。
20. 根據美國經濟報紙的調查,認為明年景氣「變差」的人超過認為景氣「變好」的人。

# 20th Day 考前總整理

## （1）名詞

### （a）不可數名詞

| 〔錯誤〕 | → | 〔正確〕 |
|---|---|---|
| advices | → | advice |
| knowledges | → | knowledge |
| mails | → | mail |
| funs | → | fun |
| 〔錯誤〕 | → | 〔正確〕 |
| informations | → | information |
| blames | → | blame |
| conducts | → | conduct |
| progresses | → | progress |

### （b）通常當作複數處理的集合名詞

cattles → cattle　　　　　　　the police is → the police are

a clergy → the clergy

### （c）通常當作單數處理的集合名詞

a furniture → a piece of furniture

baggages → pieces of baggage

machineries → pieces of machinery

### （d）複合名詞的複數形態

mother-in-law → mothers-in-law （岳母）

passerby → passersby （行人）

woman writer → women writers （女性作家）

go-between → go-betweens （仲介）

## （e）複數形的可數名詞

| | |
|---|---|
| scissors（剪刀） | pants / trousers（褲子） |
| economics（經濟學） | measles（麻疹） |
| glasses（眼鏡） | mathematics（數學） |
| physics（物理學） | mumps（腮腺炎） |
| savings（存款） | earnings（所得） |
| belongings（財產） | valuables（貴重物品） |

## （f）單複數意思不同的名詞

arm（手腕）– arms（武器）
custom（習慣）– customs（關稅）
good（好）– goods（商品）
manner（方法）–manners（禮貌）

## （2）冠詞

### （a）不定冠詞 a 加在字首以子音發音的單字之前，an 加在字首以母音發音的單字之前。

特別注意以下單字即使有 u，發音仍然是子音。

an university → a university　　an uniform → a uniform
an union → a union　　　　　　an unit → a unit

### （b）不定冠詞 a 的意思是「每～」

How many words can you type **a** minute?

### （c）a 接續專有名詞表示「像～一樣的人」、「名為～的人」

There was a call for you from **a** Mr. Jones.

### （d）定冠詞 the 以「by the＋名詞」表示單位

I'm paid by hour.〔錯誤〕
→ I'm paid by **the** hour.

### （e）以下情況請注意冠詞的位置

● what [such,quite,rather,many,half]＋a[an]＋（形容詞）＋名詞
What sloppy **a** report!〔錯誤〕

20

→ What **a** sloppy report!

This is **a** quite surprise. 〔錯誤〕

→ This is quite **a** surprise.

● **so [too, as]**

That is too **a** big risk to take. 〔錯誤〕

→ That is too big **a** risk to take.

● **all [both, half, double]＋the＋名詞**

She walked **the** all way home. 〔錯誤〕

→ She walked all **the** way home.

（f）表示身分、官職的名詞當作稱號、專有名詞的同格、補語使用時，冠詞被省略

Alex Haley, **author** of Roots, died of a heart attack. 〔同格〕

Mr. Brown is **president** of the company. 〔補語〕

## （3）代名詞

（a）人稱代名詞的格變化

Don't compare **she** with Nancy. 〔錯誤〕

→ Don't compare **her** with Nancy.

I'm proud of **he**. 〔錯誤〕

→ I'm proud of **him**.

（b）所有格代名詞的用法

This is my ticket. Where is **your**? 〔錯誤〕

→ This is my ticket. Where is **yours**?

（c）反身代名詞

Don't blame **you**. 〔錯誤〕

→ Don't blame **yourself**.

（d）指示代名詞

The birthrate in Sweden is lower than **it** in Japan. 〔錯誤〕

→ The birthrate in Sweden is lower than **that** in Japan.

Working conditions in the U.S. are better than **that** in Japan. 〔錯誤〕
→ Working conditions in the U.S. are better than **those** in Japan.

### （e）不定代名詞的 one

Jack bought a nice car. I want to buy it, too. 〔錯誤〕
→ Jack bought a nice car. I want to buy **one**, too.
The black bags are all sold out. We have only brown **them**. 〔錯誤〕
→ The black bags are all sold out. We have only brown **ones**.

### （f）each

**Each** of the workers has their own computer. 〔錯誤〕
→**Each** of the workers has his or her own computer.

### （g）other 與 another

● **one** － **the other**〔（兩個中的）一個 ── 剩下的那個〕
I have two telephones: **one** is an ordinary telephone, and the **other** is a cordless telephone.
● **one** － **another**〔（許多東西中的）一個 ── 剩下的任何一個〕
I don't like this **one**. Will you show me **another**?
● **some** － **the others**〔（許多東西中的）幾個 ── 剩下的全部〕
**Some** of them were for the proposal, but **the others** were against it.

## （4）形容詞

MP3 164

### （a）只能用於限定用法的形容詞

my **elder** [older] brother（哥哥）
the **former** president（前社長）
the **latter** half（後半）
the **upper** class（上流階級）
the **lower** class（下層階級）
a **mere** child（只是個孩子）
the **only** job（唯一的工作）
the **sole** survivor（唯一的生存者）

20

**sheer** nonsense（完全胡說八道）

the **golden** rule（黃金定律）

her **maiden** name（結婚前的姓氏）

a **wooden** table（木頭桌子）

an **earthen** vessel（陶器的器皿）

He is **elder**. 〔錯誤〕

The table is **wooden**. 〔錯誤〕

### （b）只能用於敘述用法的形容詞

afraid（害怕的）　　　　　　ashamed（羞愧的）

aware（知道的　　　　　　　awake（清醒的）

asleep（睡著的）　　　　　　alive（活著的）

alone（單獨的）　　　　　　alike（相似的）

akin（同類的、同族的）　　　worth（有價值的）

well（健康的）　　　　　　　content（滿足的）

This is a **worth** job. 〔錯誤〕　　He is a **well** boy. 〔錯誤〕

### （c）兩個以上的性狀形容詞重複出現時，原則上依下列順序「①大、小＋②形狀＋③性質、狀態＋④顏色＋⑤年齡、新舊＋⑥材料、專有形容詞」。

a small **wooden rectangular** table 〔錯誤〕

→ a small **rectangular wooden** table

### （d）many 與 much 的用法

There are **much** different opinions. 〔錯誤〕

→ There are **many** different opinions.

They didn't pay **many** attention to him. 〔錯誤〕

→ They didn't pay **much** attention to him.

I've been there **much** times. 〔錯誤〕

→ I've been there **many** times.

I don't have **many** time. 〔錯誤〕

→ I don't have **much** time.

## （e）few, a few, little, a little

**Few** people noticed the sign.

I've been there **a few** times.

**Quite a few** people took part in the race.

It will have **little** effect on our lives.

There is still **a little** hope.

## （f）any

any 表示「無論～都可以」、「任何的」時，可以用在肯定句。

**Any** place will do.

I'll take **any** job.

## （g）表示泛指與多數的表現

dozens of...（幾十個）　　　　hundreds of...（幾百個）

thousands of...（幾千個）　　　millions of...（幾百萬個）

## （h）基數詞用連字號接續單數名詞來修飾其它名詞

They started a **three-years** program.　〔錯誤〕

→ They started a **three-year** program.

## （5）副詞

## （a）與形容詞相同形態的副詞

It's **hard** work.　〔形容詞〕

He worked very **hard**.　〔副詞〕

其它還有 early（早的、提早）、fast（快的、快）、late（遲的、遲到）、long（長的、長久地）、daily（每日的、每日）等等。

## （b）同時具有與形容詞相同詞形，以及「形容詞＋-ly」的兩種詞形，但是意思不同的副詞。

He worked very **hardly** to support his family.　〔錯誤〕

→ He worked very **hard** to support his family.

I **hard** spoke to him.　〔錯誤〕

→ I **hardly** spoke to him.

**20**

其它還有 late（遲到）── lately（最近）、high（高）── highly（非常地）、pretty（相當）── prettily（漂亮地）等等。

**（c）not, never, always 等副詞修飾不定詞的位置**

He told her to **not** pick up the phone. 〔錯誤〕
→ He told her **not** to pick up the phone.

**（d）以「動詞＋副詞」片語形式出現的及物動詞，把代名詞當作受詞時的位置**

She **turned on** it. 〔錯誤〕
→ She **turned** it **on**.

**（e）ago 與 before**

He left the office ten minutes **ago**.
I (have) met him **before**.
I met him **ago**. 〔錯誤〕
→ I met him **before**.
＜ago不可以單獨使用＞

**（f）still, yet, already**

She's **still** typing the letter.
Has Jim arrived **yet**?
The call hasn't come **yet**.
This issue is **yet** to be discussed.
The movie has **already** started.
Have you finished your work **already**?

**（g）too 與 either**

I can drive, and Nancy can drive **either**. 〔錯誤〕
→ I can drive, and Nancy can drive **too**.
I can't drive, and Nancy can't drive **too**. 〔錯誤〕
→ I can't drive, and Nancy can't drive **either**.

20

## （h）副詞不可以加上介系詞

I went **to home**. 〔錯誤〕

→ I went **home**.

Send this **to overseas**. 〔錯誤〕

→ Send this **overseas**.

## （6）比較

### （a）不規則的比較變化

good, better, best

bad, worse, worst

well, better, best

ill, worse, worst

many, more, most

little, less, least

much, more, most

### （b）使用原級的句型

●**as＋原級＋as**

California is **as bigger as** Japan. 〔錯誤〕

→ California is **as big as** Japan.

● **...times as＋原級＋as**（～是～的……倍）

The United States is about **twenty-five times as bigger as** Japan.

〔錯誤〕

→ The United States is about **twenty-five times as big as** Japan.

### （c）使用比較級的句型

●**比較級＋than**（比～還～）

Mary can type **fast than** Nancy. 〔錯誤〕

→ Mary can type **faster than** Nancy.

● **superior [inferior, senior, junior] + to**（優於～〔劣於、年長於、年少於〕）

German cars are **superior than** Japanese cars in many ways. 〔錯誤〕

→ German cars are **superior to** Japanese cars in many ways.

20

●比較級＋than any other＋單數名詞（比其它任何一個都～）

Jack is **more diligent than any other workers** in the section.
〔錯誤〕

→ Jack is **more diligent than any other worker** in the section.

●less＋原級＋than（比～還不～）

Going by bus is **little expensive than** going by train. 〔錯誤〕

→ Going by bus is **less expensive than** going by train.

（d）使用最高級的句型

● the＋最高級＋of all [in]...（在～之中是最……）

Mr. Johnson is **the more influential of all** the executives.〔錯誤〕

→ Mr. Johnson is **the most influential of all** the executives.

●the＋序數詞＋最高級（表示第幾名）

This is **the second longest** tunnel in Japan.

●當作「非常地」表示強烈意思的最高級

This is a **most** important matter.

（7）動詞

（a）容易混淆的活用

lie － lay － lain （躺）
lay － laid － laid （放）
lie － lied － lied （說謊）
wind － wound － wound （捲繞）
wound － wounded － wounded （受傷）
find － found － found （發現）
found － founded － founded （創立）
hang － hung － hung （懸掛）
hang － hanged － hanged （絞死）

## （b）容易被誤用為不及物動詞的及物動詞

They **discussed about** the problem. 〔錯誤〕

→ They **discussed** the problem.

Mary **married with** Jack. 〔錯誤〕

→ Mary **married** Jack.

I **attended to** the meeting. 〔錯誤〕

→ I **attended** the meeting.

## （c）容易被誤用為授與動詞的完全及物動詞

Jane **suggested** the group that they (should) visit the museum. 〔錯誤〕

→ Jane **suggested to** the group that they **(should)** visit the museum.

The secretary **admitted** her boss that she had forgotten to mail the letter. 〔錯誤〕

→ The secretary **admitted to** her boss that she had forgotten to mail the letter.

其它還有 explain, introduce, announce, prove 等等。

## （d）動詞片語

take off, turn off, stand for, take place, put up with, make fun of 等等的動詞片語，請盡可能當作慣用句多背一些。

## （e）主詞與動詞的呼應

動詞的詞形變成與主詞的人稱及單複數一致。主詞如果是單數則使用單數形的動詞，如果主詞是複數則使用複數形的動詞，這是基本原則，不過必須注意以下情況：

**Mathematics are** my favorite subject. 〔錯誤〕

→ **Mathematics is** my favorite subject.

**Ham and eggs are** Jack's usual breakfast. 〔錯誤〕

→ **Ham and eggs is** Jack's usual breakfast.

20

## （8）時態

### （a）現在式

在表示時間或條件的副詞子句中表示未來

I'll wait till he **will finish** his phone call. 〔錯誤〕

→ I'll wait till he **finishes** his phone call.

### （b）在未來式以外表示未來的表現方法

● **be going to**＋動詞的原形

**I'm going to** stay in Chicago for two weeks.

● 用現在進行式表示不久的未來

He **is arriving** tomorrow.

● **be to**＋動詞的原形

We **are to** have a medical checkup next Wednesday.

● **be about to**＋動詞的原形

He's **about to** leave the office.

### （c）現在完成式

現在完成式的句型是「have [has]＋過去分詞」，表示完成、結果、經驗、繼續等等。

●**完成、結果**

這個情況下大多會接續 just, now, already, yet, recently 等等的副詞。

He **has** just **finished** his work.

●**到目前為止的經驗**

這個情況下大多會接續 ever, never, once, before 等等的副詞。

I **have been** to that castle before.

●**持續到現在為止的狀態**

經常使用 for... , since... 的副詞片語。

I **have worked** here for nearly twenty years.

I **have known** him since he was a little boy.

●**不能使用現在完成式的情況**

現在完成式不可以與 just now, ...ago, last...等清楚表示過去的詞以及 when, what time 等疑問詞一起使用。

He **has left** the office ten minutes ago. 〔錯誤〕

→ He **left** the office ten minutes ago.

When **have** you **started** smoking? 〔錯誤〕

→ When **did** you **start** smoking?

**（9）助動詞**

（a）**can** 有能力「可以……」、許可「可以……」、可能性「可能……」等意思。

How many words **can** you read a minute?

**Can** I leave now?

It **can** happen.

請注意以下慣用的表現

I **couldn't help laugh**. 〔錯誤〕

→ I **couldn't help laughing**.

I **could not but laughing**. 〔錯誤〕

→ I **could not but laugh**.

（b）**may**

may 有許可「可以……」、推測「或許……」等意思。

**May** I speak to you?

He **may** not be in today.

過去的推測以「may have＋過去分詞」的句型表現。

He **may** not **have received** the invitation.

（c）**must**

must 有必要、義務「必須……」、當然的推測「一定……」等意思。

I **must** finish this article by three o'clock.

表示過去的意思時可以用 had to。

I **had to** finish that article by three o'clock.

You **must** be tired after such hard work.

**20**

### （d）ought (to)

ought (to) 有義務「應該……」與當然的推測「應該……」的意思。

You **ought to** apologize to him.

You **ought not to** talk so loud.

He **ought to** know how to deal with it.

### （e）used (to)

used (to) 有過去的習慣行動「過去一向……」，以及過去的狀態「以前是……」的意思。

I **used to** walk two miles every morning.

There **used to** be an elementary school here.

### （f）should 的特別用法

should 有義務、勸告的意思，意思為「應該……」、也可表示當然、推測的意思（一定……吧、應該……），或者形容理所當然的義務、表意外等情緒判斷。

You **should** tell him about it.

You **should have called** her again.

The pictures **should** be ready by now.

It is natural that he **should** get angry with you.

## （10）關係代名詞

### （a）關係代名詞的種類與格變化

| 先行詞 | 主格 | 所有格 | 受格 |
|---|---|---|---|
| 人 | who | whose | whom |
| 物、動物 | which | whose<br>of which | which |
| 人、物、動物 | that | — | that |
| 包含先行詞 | what | — | what |

20

The lady **she** is sitting over there is Miss Smith. 〔錯誤〕

→ The lady **who** is sitting over there is Miss Smith.

That is the man **who** daughter is an actress. 〔錯誤〕

→ That is the man **whose** daughter is an actress.

This is the book **which** pages are missing. 〔錯誤〕

→ This is the book **of which** pages are missing.

This is a special type of goldfish **it** comes from China. 〔錯誤〕

→This is a special type of goldfish **that** comes from China.

（b）先行詞接續最高級與序數詞 the only, the same, the very, every, all 等詞組時，所使用的關係代名詞是 that。

This is the most beautiful scenery **which** I've ever seen. 〔錯誤〕

→This is the most beautiful scenery **that** I've ever seen.

（c）what 本身包含先行詞，表示「～的事物」。

I believed **that** he said. 〔錯誤〕

→I believed **what** he said.

（d）關係代名詞與介系詞

The program includes a Japanese version of Hamlet **which** the same man plays Hamlet and Ophelia. 〔錯誤〕

→The program includes a Japanese version of Hamlet **in which** the same man plays Hamlet and Ophelia.

（e）複合關係代名詞的 whoever, whomever, whichever, whatever

**Who** calls, tell him I'm out. 〔錯誤〕

→ **Whoever** calls, tell him I'm out.

**Which** you buy, you'll find it satisfactory. 〔錯誤〕

→ **Whichever** you buy, you'll find it satisfactory.

**What** you say, he won't get angry. 〔錯誤〕

→ **Whatever** you say, he won't get angry.

20

### （f）關係副詞的where, when, why, how

This is the place **which** the accident happened. 〔錯誤〕

→ This is the place **where** the accident happened.

This is one time **that** we have to be very careful. 〔錯誤〕

→ This is one time **when** we have to be very careful.

At the time **which** I visited her, she was quite well. 〔錯誤〕

→ At the time **when** I visited her, she was quite well.

Tell me **what** you turned down the offer. 〔錯誤〕

→ Tell me **why** you turned down the offer.

That's **which** he made the deal. 〔錯誤〕

→ That's **how** he made the deal.

## （11）語態

### （a）被動語態通常是用「be動詞＋過去分詞」的句型來表示

Mr. Nelson **was election** chairman by the members. 〔錯誤〕

→ Mr. Nelson **was elected** chairman by the members.

This document must **send** to Mr. Davis. 〔錯誤〕

→ This document must **be sent** to Mr. Davis.

### （b）片語動詞的被動語態使用「be動詞＋過去分詞＋介系詞」等等的句型

The conference **was putting off** till next Friday. 〔錯誤〕

→ The conference **was put off** till next Friday.

### （c）感官動詞與使役動詞將動詞原形當作受詞的補語時，原形補語變成不定詞 to。

The boy **was seen steal** the toy. 〔錯誤〕

→ The boy **was seen to steal** the toy.

### （d）行為者用 by 以外的介系詞來表示時

I'm **pleasing with** the results. 〔錯誤〕

→ I'm **pleased with** the results.

The boss **annoyed at** Tom's remarks. 〔錯誤〕

→ The boss **was annoyed at** Tom's remarks.

## （12）不定詞

### （a）to 不定詞（to＋動詞的原形）與原形不定詞

原形不定詞，只限用於感官動詞及使役動詞的補語。

I want **take** a break. 〔錯誤〕

→ I want **to take** a break.

I saw Jack **to go** into the shop. 〔錯誤〕

→ I saw Jack **go** into the shop.

I heard him **said** so. 〔錯誤〕

→ I heard him **say** so.

I'll let you **to know** when I'm ready. 〔錯誤〕

→ I'll let you **know** when I'm ready.

Jack made her **to wait**. 〔錯誤〕

→ Jack made her **wait**.

I'll have Jim **to pick up** the package. 〔錯誤〕

→ I'll have Jim **pick up** the package.

### （b）不定詞的名詞用法、形容詞用法、副詞用法。

They started **argue** with each other. 〔錯誤〕

→ They started **to argue** with each other. 〔名詞用法〕

It is difficult **to understanding** him. 〔錯誤〕

→ It is difficult **to understand** him. 〔it 是虛受詞、不定詞是真受詞〕

I found it difficult **please** him. 〔錯誤〕

→ I found it difficult **to please** him. 〔it 是虛受詞、不定詞是真受詞〕

I have a lot of work **do**. 〔錯誤〕

→ I have a lot of work **to do**. 〔形容詞用法〕

I went there interview him. 〔錯誤〕

→ I went there **to interview** him. 〔副詞的用法〕

**20**

（c）不定詞的形式主詞

It is impossible **of me** to attend the wedding. 〔錯誤〕
→ It is impossible **for me** to attend the wedding.
It was stupid **for me** to say such a thing. 〔錯誤〕
→ It was stupid **of me** to say such a thing.

（d）表示不定詞的否定形態時，將 not 或是 never 放在不定詞之前

He told me **to not use** the computer. 〔錯誤〕
→ He told me **not to use** the computer.

（e）完成式的不定詞變成「to have＋過去分詞」的句型，表示比
述語動詞更早的時間點。

He seemed **to finished** his work. 〔錯誤〕
→ He seemed **to have finished** his work.
= It seemed that he had finished his work.

（f）把不定詞當作受詞的動詞

He agreed **appearing** on the program. 〔錯誤〕
→ He agreed **to appear** on the program.
其它還有 aim（瞄準）、arrange（安排）、choose（選擇）、
decide（決定）、expect（期待）、fear（害怕）、hope（希望）、
manage（設法做到）、mean（打算）、offer（提供）、plan（計
劃）、pretend（假裝）、promise（承諾）、refuse（拒絕）、seek
（追求）、want（想要）、wish（但願）等等。

### （13）分詞與動名詞

MP3
**173**

（a）現在分詞與過去分詞

現在分詞具有主動的意思，過去分詞具有被動的意思
Let **sleep** dogs lie. 〔錯誤〕
→ Let **sleeping** dogs lie. 〔現在分詞〕
John has a **breaking** arm. 〔錯誤〕
→ John has a **broken** arm. 〔過去分詞〕

20

## （b）分詞的形容詞用法與副詞的用法

Pour **boil** water into the teapot. 〔錯誤〕

→ Pour **boiling** water into the teapot. 〔形容詞的用法〕

They repaired the house **damaging** by the typhoon. 〔錯誤〕

→They repaired the house **damaged** by the typhoon. 〔形容詞的用法〕

**Make** of paper, this box is light. 〔錯誤〕

→ **Made** of paper, this box is light. 〔副詞的用法〕

## （c）敘述用法

She was **wait** for hours. 〔錯誤〕

→ She was **waiting** for hours.

She felt insulting. 〔錯誤〕

→ She felt **insulted**.

I smell something **burn**. 〔錯誤〕

→ I smell something **burning**.

I left the door unlock. 〔錯誤〕

→ I left the door **unlocked**.

## （d）分詞構句

**Be** sick, Jack could not attend the meeting. 〔錯誤〕

→ **Being** sick, Jack could not attend the meeting.

**Look** for her pen, she came across a ten-dollar bill. 〔錯誤〕

→ **Looking** for her pen, she came across a ten-dollar bill.

While **stay** in London, I saw many plays. 〔錯誤〕

→ While **staying** in London, I saw many plays.

## （e）獨立分詞構句

That **to be** the case, we are laying off 100 workers this summer. 〔錯誤〕

→ That **being** the case, we are laying off 100 workers this summer.

**20**

### （f）動名詞

**Get** a job is not very easy these days.　〔錯誤〕
→ **Getting** a job is not very easy these days.
The parents were accused of **abuse** their child.　〔錯誤〕
→ The parents were accused of **abusing** their child.

### （g）完成式的動名詞比表示述語動詞的時間點更早

He regretted **have sold** the villa.　〔錯誤〕
→ He regretted **having sold** the villa.

### （h）使用動名詞的慣用語法

I don't **feel like to go** to the show.　〔錯誤〕
→ I don't **feel like going** to the show.
It is **no use scold** him.　〔錯誤〕
→ It is **no use scolding** him.

其它還有 cannot help doing（不得不、忍不住……）、worth doing（值得去做……）、on doing（一……馬上）、There is no doing（無法……）、cannot [never]... without doing（如果……一定……）、of one's own doing（自己做……）、What [How] about doing（去做……如何？）等等。

### （i）只使用動名詞當作受詞的動詞

He tried to **avoid to take** responsibility.　〔錯誤〕
→ He tried to **avoid taking** responsibility.
I **enjoy to play** baseball.　〔錯誤〕
→ I **enjoy playing** baseball.

其它還有 admit（承認）、appreciate（感謝）、consider（考慮）、deny（否定）、escape（逃跑）、finish（結束）、mind（介意）、postpone（延期）、practice（實行）、quit（停止）、resist（抵抗）、approve of（贊同）、give up（放棄）、go on（繼續下去）、leave off（停止）、put off（延期）等等。

## （14）假設語氣

### （a）現在式假設語氣

現在式假設語氣在美式英語中，特別用於接續在表示提案、主張、要求、命令等等動詞之後的 that 子句，以及接續在表示提案、主張、要求、命令的名詞及形容詞之後的 that 子句之中。動詞與人稱及數量無關，全部使用原形動詞。

He **proposed** that a subcommittee **was formed** immediately. 〔錯誤〕

→ He **proposed** that a subcommittee **be formed** immediately.

The members **requested** that Mr. Jones **resigns** from his post.
〔錯誤〕

→ The members **requested** that Mr. Jones **resign** from his post.

It is **essential** that Mr. Young **joins** the project. 〔錯誤〕

→ It is **essential** that Mr. Young **join** the project.

其它還有 insist（主張）、order（命令）、suggest, command, urge, demand 等等的動詞，necessary, advisable, preferable（希望）、imperative（必須的）、anxious（掛念的）等等的形容詞，在接續這些形容詞之後的 that 子句中使用假設語氣。

### （b）未來式假設語氣

If＋主詞＋should＋原形……，主詞＋$\begin{cases} \text{should [shall]} \\ \text{would [will]} \\ \text{could [can]} \\ \text{might [may]} \end{cases}$＋原形

If the company **should go** bankrupt, what **do** you **do**? 〔錯誤〕

→ If the company **should go** bankrupt, what **would** you **do**?

### （c）過去式假設語氣

If＋主詞＋過去式……，主詞＋$\begin{cases} \text{would} \\ \text{should} \\ \text{could} \\ \text{might} \end{cases}$＋原形

20

If I **were** president, I **will hire** you. 〔錯誤〕

→ If I **were** president, I **would hire** you.

### （d）過去完成式假設語氣

If＋主詞＋過去完成式……，主詞＋$\begin{cases} \text{should} \\ \text{would} \\ \text{could} \\ \text{might} \end{cases}$＋have＋過去分詞

If you **had listened** to me, you **could avoid** the problem. 〔錯誤〕

→ If you **had listened** to me, you **could have avoided** the problem.

### （e）各種假設語氣的表現

I **wish I am** a bird. 〔錯誤〕

→ I **wish I were** a bird.

**If only I can speak** to him! 〔錯誤〕

→ **If only I could speak** to him!

**It's time you will go** to see him. 〔錯誤〕

→ **It's time you went** to see him.

She talks **as if she knows** everything about England. 〔錯誤〕

→ She talks **as if she knew** everything about England.

**If it is not for** your help, I could not start my own business. 〔錯誤〕

→ **If it were not for** your help, I could not start my own business.

**If I am to be transferred**, I would quit the job. 〔錯誤〕

→ **If I were to be transferred**, I would quit the job.

### （f）不使用 if 的條件句

**I had known** you were coming, I would have come home early. 〔錯誤〕

→ **Had I known** you were coming, I would have come home early.

20

**But** the financial aid he's getting, he could not go to college. 〔錯誤〕

→ **But for** the financial aid he's getting, he could not go to college.

= **Without** the financial aid he's getting, he could not go to college.

## （15）時態的一致與引述

MP3 175

### （a）時態一致的原則

| 主要子句<br>的時態 | 從屬子句的時態 | |
|---|---|---|
| 現在→過去 | 現在式→過去式<br>未來式→過去式的助動詞<br>現在完成式 ┐<br>過去式　　├過去完成式<br>過去完成式 ┘ | 現在進行式→過去進行式<br>現在完成進行式 ┐<br>過去進行式　　├過去完成進式<br>過去完成進行式 ┘ |

I **think** that he **is** an honest person.

I **thought** that he **was** an honest person.

I **am** sure that she **will** come to the party.

I **was** sure that she would come to the party.

I **wonder** why he **hasn't come** yet.

I **wondered** why he **hadn't come** yet.

### （b）不符合一般原則的情況

The teacher **taught** the students that light **travels** about 300,000 kilometers per second. 〔一般的真理〕

He **didn't know** that Tokyo **is** the capital of Japan.〔現在的事實〕

We **learned** that the Renaissance **lasted** from about 1300 to about 1600. 〔歷史的事實〕

He **said** that if he **won** 100 million dollars in the lottery, he **would** buy a house. 〔假設語氣的句子〕

### （c）直接引述與間接引述

He said, "I have a bad cold." 〔直接引述〕

He said that he had a bad cold. 〔間接引述〕

20

（d）傳達動詞是過去式時，被傳達部份中的詞句產生如下的變化：

this → that
these → those
here → there
now → then
(three years) ago → (three years) before
today → that day
tomorrow → the next day [the following day]
yesterday → the day before [the previous day]
next (week) → the following (week)
last (year) → the previous (year)

Mr. Scott said to me, "I received **this** letter **yesterday**."
Mr. Scott told me that he had received **that** letter **the day before**.

（e）疑問句的情況

He **said to** me, "**Where can I find** Jim?"
He **asked** me **where he could find** Jim.
He **said to** me, "**Do you want** a cup of coffee?"
He **asked** me **if I wanted** a cup of coffee.

（f）命令句的情況

I **said to** him, "**Turn off** the TV."
I **told** him **to turn off** the TV.
She **said**, "**Let's get** to work."
She **suggested** that **we (should)** get to work.

（g）感嘆句的情況

He **said**, "What a nice lady she is!"
He **exclaimed** what a nice lady she was.

## （16）連接詞

### （a）對等連接詞

有 and, but, or, so, for, nor 等等的對等連接詞

Study hard **or** you will pass the examination. 〔錯誤〕

→ Study hard **and** you will pass the examination. 〔命令句＋and〕

I like him, not because he is handsome, **and** because he is considerate. 〔錯誤〕

→I like him, not because he is handsome, **but** because he is considerate.

Work seriously, **and** you might be laid off. 〔錯誤〕

→ Work seriously, **or** you might be laid off. 〔命令句＋or〕

He has never driven a car, **or** does he intend to learn. 〔錯誤〕

→ He has never driven a car, **nor** does he intend to learn.

I lost my watch, **because** I bought a new one. 〔錯誤〕

→ I lost my watch, **so** I bought a new one.

**For** her children seldom study, she is not happy. 〔錯誤〕

→ She is not happy, **for** her children seldom study.

＜for不可以放在句首＞

### （b）引導名詞子句的從屬連接詞

有 that, if, whether 等等的從屬連接詞

It is true **if** I borrowed the money from him. 〔錯誤〕

→ It is true **that** I borrowed the money from him.

I'll see **for** he's finished. 〔錯誤〕

→ I'll see **if** he's finished.

I don't know **while** she can type. 〔錯誤〕

→ I don't know **whether** she can type.

### （c）引導副詞子句的從屬連接詞

●表示時間的從屬連接詞

有 when, while, as, after, before, since, until [till] 等等表示時間的從屬連接詞。

**20**

How can I reach you **during** you are in Miami? 〔錯誤〕

→ How can I reach you **while** you are in Miami?

It's been five years **before** I went to the United States. 〔錯誤〕

→ It's been five years **since** I went to the United States.

I'll wait **before** she calls. 〔錯誤〕

→ I'll wait **until** she calls.

●表示理由的從屬連接詞

有 because, since, as, now (that) 等等，表示理由的從屬連接詞。

**So** he didn't have the key, he could not get into the room. 〔錯誤〕

→**As [Because, Since]** he didn't have the key, he could not get into the room.

●表示條件的從屬連接詞

有 if, unless 等等表示條件的從屬連接詞

You can call him **whether** there's a problem. 〔錯誤〕

→ You can call him **if** there's a problem.

I can't buy the car **despite** my wife agrees. 〔錯誤〕

→ I can't buy the car **unless** my wife agrees.

●表示讓步的從屬連接詞

有 though, although 等等表示讓步的從屬連接詞

**Therefore** it was hard work, he enjoyed it. 〔錯誤〕

→ **Though** it was hard work, he enjoyed it.

（d）片語連接詞

有 as soon as（一……就……）、even if（即使）、as if（猶如）、as though（猶如）、as [so] long as（只要……）、as far as（盡可能……）、in case（假使）等等的片語連接詞。

（e）相關連接詞

both...and...（也……也……）、either...or...（不是……就是……）、neither...nor...（既不是……也不是……）、not only... but (also)...（不僅……而且……）、so...that...（非常……所以……）、such...that...（非常……所以）、so that...can [will, may]...（為了讓……）等等的相關連接詞。

## （17）介系詞

### （a）表示時間的介系詞

The meeting will be held **at** Friday. 〔錯誤〕
→ The meeting will be held **on** Friday.
The meeting will be held **in** Friday morning. 〔錯誤〕
→ The meeting will be held **on** Friday morning.
I'll wait here **to** three o'clock. 〔錯誤〕
→ I'll wait here **till** three o'clock.
I'll call you back **at** a few minutes. 〔錯誤〕
→ I'll call you back **in** a few minutes.
We received 100 calls **while** the week. 〔錯誤〕
→ We received 100 calls **during** the week.

### （b）表示場所的介系詞

What time does his plane arrive **to** the airport? 〔錯誤〕
→ What time does his plane arrive **at** the airport?
I left the key **at** the car. 〔錯誤〕
→ I left the key **in** the car.
She sat **to** him. 〔錯誤〕
→ She sat **beside** [by, next to] him.
What happened **among** you and Mary? 〔錯誤〕
→ What happened **between** you and Mary?
She left to Texas yesterday. 〔錯誤〕
→ She left **for** Texas yesterday.

### （c）其它介系詞

He died **by** a heart attack. 〔錯誤〕
→ He died **of** a heart attack.
He died **of** a blow on the head. 〔錯誤〕
→ He died **from** a blow on the head.
This bag is made **from** genuine leather. 〔錯誤〕
→ This bag is made **of** genuine leather.

20

Wine is made **of** grapes. 〔錯誤〕

→ Wine is made **from** grapes.

This doll is made **with** hand. 〔錯誤〕

→ This doll is made **by** hand.

Let's talk about it **within** lunch. 〔錯誤〕

→ Let's talk about it **over** lunch.

（d）片語介系詞

The concert was canceled **because** the storm. 〔錯誤〕

→ The concert was canceled **because of** the storm.

The expressway was closed **on account for** the heavy snow. 〔錯誤〕

→ The expressway was closed **on account of** the heavy snow.

You should have taken a taxi **instead on** a bus. 〔錯誤〕

→ You should have taken a taxi **instead of** a bus.

**According at** the weather report, it's going to rain tomorrow. 〔錯誤〕

→ **According to** the weather report, it's going to rain tomorrow.

20

搶分高手 002

# New TOEIC 20天文法高分特訓

| | |
|---|---|
| 作　　者 | 白野伊津夫（Itsuo Shirono） |
| 譯　　者 | 曾美玲 |
| 顧　　問 | 曾文旭 |
| 總 編 輯 | 王毓芳 |
| 編輯總監 | 簡文玲 |
| 行銷經理 | 何慧明 |
| 主　　編 | 高致婕 |
| 執行編輯 | 何語蓁 |
| 美術主編 | 阿作 |
| 美術編輯 | 洪政扶 |
| 網頁美術設計 | 鄭嘉佩 |
| 特約編輯 | 許祐瑄 |
| 文字校對 | 許祐瑄 |
| 法律顧問 | 北辰著作權事務所　蕭雄淋律師 |
| 印　　製 | 凱立國際資訊有限公司 |
| 初　　版 | 2009年01月 |
| 出　　版 | 凱信出版事業有限公司 |
| 電　　話 | （02）6636-8398 |
| 傳　　真 | （02）6636-8397 |
| 地　　址 | 106 台北市大安區忠孝東路四段218-7號7樓 |
| 定　　價 | 新台幣360元（附1 MP3）/ 港幣120元（附1 MP3） |
| 總 經 銷 | 聯寶國際文化事業有限公司 |
| 地　　址 | 221 台北縣汐止市康寧街169巷27號8樓 |
| 港澳地區總經銷 | 和平圖書有限公司 |

「新TOEIC®テスト文法特訓プログラム」　白野伊津夫 著
"SHIN TOEIC®TEST BUNPO TOKKUN PROGRAM" by Itsuo Shirono
Copyright © Itsuo Shirono. 2006. All rights reserved.
Original Japanese edition published by ALC Press, Inc.
This edition is published by arrangement with ALC Press, Inc., Tokyo
Through Tuttle-Mori Agency, Inc., Tokyo

國家圖書館出版品預行編目資料

New TOEIC 20天文法高分特訓 / 白野伊津夫著
；曾美玲譯.

-- 初版. – 臺北市：凱信, 2009.01

面；公分. --（搶分高手；2）

ISBN 978-986-6615-06-1（平裝附光碟）

1. 多益測驗 2. 語法

805.1895　　　　　　　　　　　　97022738